AP000,
Best Wishes!
Victoria Wells

When Love Comes Around

Victoria Wells

Xpress Yourself Publishing, LLC
P. O. Box 1615
Upper Marlboro, Maryland 20773

When Love Comes Around is a work of fiction. Names, characters, places and incidents are either products of the authors' imagination or are used fictitously. Any resemblance to actual persons, living or dead, business establishments, events or locales is entirely coincidental.

ISBN-10: 0-9818094-7-2
ISBN-13: 978-0-9818094-7-2

Library of Congress Control Number: 2008942623

Printed in the United States of America

Cover Design and Interior Layout by
The Writer's Assistant
www.TheWritersAssistant.com

Visit Xpress Yourself Publishing online:
www.XpressYourselfPublishing.org

Dedication

To my great niece Michal Mackenzie Ajah Fortt,
sweet baby play on with the angels.

June 30, 2007-August 3, 2007

Other titles by Victoria Wells

A Special Summer

Acknowledgements

Lord, I thank you for your never-ending compassion. You are more than amazing.

Mardi, I love you so much. Thanks sweetie for sacrificing your time traveling up and down the highways supporting my dream.

Mommy & Daddy your love knows no boundaries. You can't even begin to imagine how much of a blessing you are.

A special shout out to my family in Philly, Pottstown, PA, Portsmouth, VA and Milwaukee, WI, thanks for showing me much love! I love you!

To my sister-girl, Esther Wells, without your constant support this would not be possible. Thanks for always giving a shoulder to lean on when I get tired and encouraging me to go on when I get discouraged.

To my Refuge Evangelical Baptist Church and Thomas Jefferson University Hospital families you have been such a blessing. I appreciate you more than you can ever imagine.

Philly African American Book Club and Diva of Discussion Book Club, you ladies gave a newbie a chance when no one else was willing to do so. From the bottom of my heart I thank you for showing me much love. God Bless!

Yasmin Coleman and APOOO Book Club how can I express my gratitude? You were supporting a sister all over the internet without her knowledge! Much love and success to you and APOOO!

Beverly Jenkins and B'land crew – thank you for accepting me into your family. I am so fortunate to have experienced your genuine love and support. Ms. Bev, I want to be just like you when I grow up!

Gwyneth Bolton you are an angel. I don't know if you realize how much you give of yourself. And that's what I love so much about you. Crossing paths with you has definitely enriched my life.

Jessica Tilles, thank you so much for always having an open door and a listening ear. I truly appreciate knowing you're never far away when I need you.

Please if there's anyone I didn't acknowledge please charge it to my head and not my heart.

Peace and Blessings,

When Love Comes Around

Chapter 1

The movement of pedestrians, whizzing and weaving along the busy sidewalk, did not faze Starr as she walked in a daze down Chestnut Street, with no particular destination in mind. The warm spring afternoon, which was her favorite time of the year, no longer held her interest. She kept replaying in her head the conversation she just had with Dr. Neil. "Starr, your ultrasound results revealed you have a mild case of endometriosis." He told her the news nonchalantly as if he said, "The sky is blue."

The diagnosis blew Starr away. She was not prepared to hear any of this. When she mentioned to her doctor at her annual check up two weeks ago that her cycle had become a little heavier with more cramping than usual, she hadn't thought anything of it. She thought it might have been a change in her hormones or something. Every few years since the onset of her menses her body experienced changes. Initially, her cycle was irregular, then for a while, she had severe cramps and a heavy flow. And a few years later, migraine headaches would attack monthly. So when her body seemed to be reverting to how it behaved in her early twenties, it hadn't fazed her. After all, she'd just turned thirty-two and figured she was undergoing another change. But now that her doctor confirmed the change wasn't normal, she was concerned. Really concerned.

It was Starr's nature to think of the worst possible case scenario. This new condition made her take inventory of her life. In her mind, she envisioned herself an old lady, living with a bunch of cats. Even though she wasn't crazy about the four-legged fur balls, it would beat being old and all alone. Just the thought of such a bleak future was enough to send her into a mild depression.

Babies…I won't be able to have any, Starr sadly mused as she mentally kicked herself for not settling down and having children. That was easier said than done. It wasn't like any of the men she'd dealt with were remotely husband, let alone father, material.

There was Marcus, the two-timing snake. It had taken her five years to break away from him. Whoever said you'd always love your first love should be shot dead, brought back to life, and shot again. There was absolutely nothing Starr loved about that idiot. The demon-possessed man had almost single-handedly ruined her life.

Between the lying, cheating, and running up every charge card she had to the limit, destroying her credit and self-esteem, Starr had almost lost her mind. By the time she was twenty-three years old, she was up to her neck drowning in debt and self-doubt. Taking her sister Karen's advice, she gave up her apartment and moved in with her and her family until she could get her finances straighten out. Most importantly, Karen had wanted to get her sister out of Marcus' clutches.

Unbeknownst to her, Marcus had found the one credit card he hadn't maxed out, that she had stashed away for emergencies, while helping her move her things into her sister's home. Three months later, she received a call while at work from the collections department wanting to know when she was going to make a payment on her delinquent bill. Stunned, Starr argued with the representative insisting she hadn't made any purchases. As soon as she got home to her sister's that evening, she went tearing through the shoebox in the back of her closet looking for the credit card she thought was well hidden. Her heart dropped when she found the empty birthday card her mom had given her on her tenth birthday. From the moment she spoke with the woman in the collections department, she knew somehow Marcus had gotten a hold of her credit card, but didn't want to believe it. How could he do such a terrible thing after she had forgiven him time and time again for mistreating her?

Not only had he stolen from her, he had the audacity to have charged hundreds of dollars in lingerie from Victoria's Secret. None of which was housed in her lingerie drawer. This infraction was the proverbial straw that broke the camel's back. From that day on Starr had cleansed Marcus completely from her life. No matter how much he begged and pleaded to be forgiven and promised never to do anything like that again, Starr stood her ground. Marcus was history.

Then there was Stephen the miser. Starr had gone from one extreme to another. No longer was she with a man who carelessly spent money. *Her money*. Now she had hooked up with one so stingy, if he could, he'd squeeze change from a penny.

Initially, his cheap ways hadn't mattered. It hadn't bothered her that he hardly took her out. And when he did take her out, somehow, she'd end up paying for a portion of the date. Nor had it annoyed her when Stephen insisted on celebrating Kwanza instead of Christmas, so they could make gifts instead of buying them.

None of this mattered, because unlike Marcus, Stephen was always preaching about saving money for the future and not acquiring unnecessary debt. Starr could appreciate his logic since she had been working hard to pay down her debt when she met him. Between working several overtime shifts and making payment arrangements with her creditors, Starr had significantly paid down the bills Marcus had charged up in her name.

In all honesty, Stephen's miserly ways were a benefit. He was forever sharing some little tidbit on how she should save money. Like encouraging her to yearly increase her 403B plan and putting away at least fifteen percent of her paycheck each time she got paid. Taking heed to his advice, her checking and savings accounts slowly over time accumulated into the thousands.

So no, it didn't bother her he was the stingiest man alive. Well, that wasn't completely true. She did, for once, wanted to go out on a date and have him splurge for the entire evening. Just once. But then she would think to herself, *at least he's not begging me for money or trying to burn through my credit cards.*

However, everything changed when he had the gall to ask her to split the cost of a box of condoms. "What? You're joking, right?" she asked him incredulously, not believing he could fix his mouth to say such a thing. For crying out loud, the man was employed as a software designer for a major technology company, making some serious cash...Okay. This was insane. *Cheap bastard.*

Shaking his head, not realizing how ridiculous he was being, he dug his heels in. "I think it's only right you help out with the cost of birth control," Stephen mumbled as he lifted his fork to his mouth taking a healthy bite of macaroni and cheese.

Starr stared at him as if *she* had lost *her* mind. *This fool must think I'm crazy. I'm about to show him just how crazy I am.* Storming over to her front door, she flung it open, yelling at the top of her lungs like a lunatic. "Get your stingy, greedy, black behind out of my house!"

Suddenly, Stephen realized he made the terrible mistake of asking her for money as he sat at her table eating the scrumptious dinner she'd prepared. Since dating Starr, he hadn't had to buy groceries as often. At least three times a week he ended up on her sofa watching cable and eating dinner. He tried to back peddle with, "Umm…it's okay…you don't have to give me any money this time."

What? This time! Oh this fool is trippin'! Starr reached for the baseball bat she kept near the front door for protection. "I said get your stingy, greedy, black behind out of my house!"

Raising the baseball bat like she was about to knock him into left field, Stephen jumped up from the table, stammering as he hurried to the front door. "Look, I…I'm sorry. I didn't mean to get you mad. I'll call you tomorrow. Okay?"

"Don't bother!" Slamming the door, she yelled to no one in particular, "Another two years of my life wasted!"

After a few months of being alone, Starr jumped back into the dating scene when she met Leon at a coffee house on Second and South Streets. He was the prettiest man she had ever seen in all her twenty-seven years. Six feet tall, bronze skin, jet-black wavy hair and eyelashes so long any woman would be jealous. She, along with the other women in the coffee house, was literally drooling when he came swaggering through the door. Starr was all too giddy when he strolled over to her table pulling out a chair, smiling at her. "Do you mind if I sit here, pretty lady?"

Starr swooned in her chair from the deep, husky baritone words floating from his thick, kissable lips. "Not at all," she told him, grinning from ear to ear looking like a simpleton.

The relationship with Leon, if you could call it that, was the shortest of them all. Three weeks to be exact. It all came to a screeching halt on their third date. Walking side by side, the couple was engrossed in conversation when the cutest brotha yelled out the window of a sparkling white Acura. "Hey, baby, let me holla at you."

Flattered, feeling extremely sexy, Starr swung her head around in the direction of the white Acura. Her jaw length bob covering one eye, giving her that 'come hither look,' she nearly hit the concrete face first. Fine brotha man was *not* trying to holla at her! This became clearly evident as Leon's rough boy swagger became a switch, as he sashayed his feminine self over to the vehicle. Starr could not believe her eyes as she witnessed Leon lean into the driver's side window and began stroking the side of dude's face like they were lovers.

Dumbfounded, her eyes became round as saucers as Leon had the nerve to sashay back over to her. Her jaw dropped to the ground when he picked back up his rough boy baritone. "I need to make this run with my man. I'll see you later."

How does he do that? Starr wondered in awe as he smoothly transitioned from feminine to masculine.

Hunching her shoulders, feeling like she was in the twilight zone, she said, "Okay." What more could she say? Leon was on the down low...Waaaay down low. There wasn't a woman in Philly who could make that crooked line walk straight. Now, she understood why he ended both of their previous dates with a chase kiss on the cheek. Silly her, she thought he was just being a gentleman. Needless to say, she never heard from Leon. Good riddance.

If anything, she was thankful she had taken a sworn vow of celibacy after dealing with Marcus and Stephen. After her break up with Stephen, she'd promised God the next man she laid down with, invited into her bed, would be her husband. That was five years ago. And up until now, she had been happy with her choice. Being celibate meant no serious dating. Too much temptation was involved. No dating meant no meeting a future husband. No prospects for a future husband, meant no babies.

A wave of sadness shook Starr's very being. Here she was, thirty-two years old, with no man. No babies. No life.

Why couldn't she have the same kind of life as her sister Karen and her friend Summer? She hated to admit it, but she was a wee bit jealous. Not hating, just a smidge jealous of them. Both her sister and friend were blessed to have decent men love them, marry them, and give them beautiful babies. What had she done so wrong, that she hadn't been blessed like them?

Continuing her walk down the busy street, she let out a big sigh. Things weren't as severe as her run away mind was telling her. Dr. Neil assured her at this point infertility wasn't necessarily an immediate danger. However, he did stress she was thirty-two years old, had never been pregnant, and if she did plan on having children, she needed to seriously think about doing so preferably in the very near future. "After you turn thirty-five, you'll be in the 'high risk' pregnancy category which may bring on an entirely different set of potential complications. And keep in mind, the endometriosis may significantly progress by then."

The doctor briefly discussed treatment options. For now, the only option was taking non-steroidal anti-inflammatory drugs, such as Motrin or Advil for the cramping. If the bleeding became progressively worse, he told her hormone therapy could be prescribed to control it.

As far as becoming pregnant in the very near future, that was another issue. Since there were no prospects of a husband in sight, the likelihood of motherhood was dismal. So when Dr. Neil suggested artificial insemination, the only thing Starr could do was seriously consider the suggestion. What other choice did she have?

Somehow, Starr mindlessly wandered her way four blocks down and one block over to Macy's on Market Street. She was supposed to meet her sister for lunch at the Chestnut Hill Grill. After leaving her appointment, she called Karen to reschedule their monthly lunch date. She felt terrible about canceling, but there was too much on her brain and she didn't want to put her problem on her sister. Karen had enough on her own plate to handle, which began four years ago when she became a young widow with two small children.

I won't be good company anyway, she'd told herself. What she needed was some time alone to think. She had a lot to consider and no offense to Karen, but right now, she didn't feel like being around anyone.

For years, she believed she had time to settle down, get married and start a family. She was young and enjoying her freedom. And whenever the maternal crave would gnaw at her, she would get her fix by spending time with Karen's and Summer's children. But now, with ever step she took, she suddenly felt as though she was in a race against time. Was she imagining things or could she hear a clock ticking? *Tick-tock, tick-tock, tick-tock.* With sagging shoulders she wondered, *who's going to win? Me or father time?*

Not only did she have that to worry about, but also what would her family and friends think of her getting pregnant with the aid of artificial insemination? And if she did, what would she tell her child when he or she asked, "Who's my daddy? Where's my daddy?" Starr felt a sharp pain pierce her heart. How many times had she and Karen asked their mother, "Where's daddy?" Would she be able to put a child through the pain of not knowing who, let alone where his or her father was?

"Decisions, decisions. What is a girl to do?" She mumbled under her breath as she steered her way to the shoe department. Buying pretty shoes always made her feel better.

Chapter 2

Holding up a different shoe in each hand, her wrists rotated, giving her a view of both at different angles. "Which one of you do I want?"

"If you ask me, I like the black stilettos," rumbled a deep, sexy familiar voice.

Starr spun around; embarrassed she had been caught talking to herself like a madwoman. Momentarily, irritation pricked at her that some man had invaded her afternoon of solitude. That was until she gazed up into the handsomest face she'd ever seen.

Kevin Dawson. Sexy as sin, Kevin Dawson. Starr had finally met Kevin at NJ's christening four years ago. He along with her and Ava were godparents to both NJ and Autumn.

That particular Sunday morning, Starr had to concentrate double time on what the pastor was saying during the sermon. Kevin was absolutely gorgeous in a chocolate Hugo Boss suit. He had that whole Boris Kodjoe thing going on from the caramel coloring, to his six feet-four, well chiseled hard body. As the minister was preaching, Starr kept imagining her fingertips seductively gliding over his bald, shiny head. Yes, Kevin definitely was a hottie.

If that weren't bad enough, the entire service she had to squeeze her thighs tight together and pray the throbbing between her legs would go away. She thought for sure God would strike her down, right there in the pew. Her death certificate would read: *Cause of Death: Due to lusting in a house of worship.*

The prettiest smile broke across Starr's beautiful, cocoa brown face, showing off a set of deep dimples.

"Hey, Kevin."

"Hey, yourself. What's going on?"

"Nothing much. Just doing some last minute shopping before we head off to Vegas."

Henry Stiles was marrying Joan Williams, Nick's housekeeper. After that Christmas everyone spent together in Upstate New York, they all suspected it would be a matter of time before Henry wooed Joan.

Although she was still employed by the younger Stiles, Joan was viewed as family and not hired help. Even Nita Jackson, Summer's mother, relied on her as family. She had become a second mother to Summer with Nita's blessing. "Joan, please watch over my baby as if she was your own."

Nita had requested this of Joan as she and her husband were planning to return to North Carolina after spending six weeks with Summer. Nita was worried sick. Things were still rocky between her daughter and Nick after the birth of NJ. It killed Nita that she was so many miles away from her child and grandson. Her husband, James, had to remind her, "Nita, Summer's a big girl, and she's a mother now. You have to let her go. It's time she made her own way in life." Everything her husband said was true, but still she worried about her only child. So having Joan as her eyes and ears had been a blessing. It certainly helped her to sleep at night.

The minute Nita met Joan they became fast friends. Mostly because Summer had told her mom how kind the older woman had been to her, taking care of her while she was on bed rest during her last month of pregnancy. How could she not befriend a woman who had taken such good care of her daughter?

Starr and Ava had also taken to the matriarchal figure as well. On several occasions, the elderly woman shared her pearls of wisdom. "I'm just telling you babies this because I don't want you to go through the things I had to coming up. You girls have so many more opportunities then I did when I was your age. Take advantage of *every one* of them. And whatever you do, don't let a good for nothing man stand in your way."

Summer, Ava and Starr cried like babies when Joan bared her soul to them about her past. Each of the young women was heartbroken for Joan as she told her story of the botch abortion that changed her life forever. How she had never gotten over the fact that she would never have her own biological children, grandchildren or great-grandchildren. How her past experience with one man left her so shaken, she could never give her heart to another. Because of this, Starr and her friends were ecstatic Joan had finally found *true* love after so many years of being lonely.

Having met Henry Stiles, it was certain this time around, he would cherish his second wife. Married to Nick's mother he had been a younger man and not cognizant of what it meant to be a *good* husband and father. Years faded away with him taking his first wife and son for granted, all for the sake of his ambitious career goals. His desire to achieve the status of a federal judge had been his main focus in life, which over time, he had accomplished. The shame of it all, when he felt as though he was ready to pay attention to his wife, it was too late. Misery ate at him after losing the wife of his youth to pancreatic cancer. This misery was further compounded when having to contend with a son who despised and wanted nothing to do with him.

This was going to be one joyous, monumental occasion. The elderly couple would be getting a second chance at love. A chance that neither of them expected, nor believed would come around again.

Henry and Joan would be joined in holy matrimony in Las Vegas on Friday, June 15 at the Bellagio, seven o'clock in the evening. The invited guests were close friends and family, which included Nick, Summer, NJ, Autumn, Ava, Starr, Kevin, Nita, and James. After Joan's shameful past so many years ago, she became estranged from her family; not her choice. Her family felt she had embarrassed and disgraced them. The only time she had returned home to the small southern town was to attend her mother's funeral, and then a few years later, her father's. That was well over twenty years ago. So as far as Joan was concerned, *her* family would be in attendance to share in her special day.

That's right; Starr would be there since she and Summer are practically sisters. Too bad. We could've gotten into some things. Kevin was immediately drawn to Starr the first time he saw her at the christening. At five feet-six inches, Starr was a curvaceous size twelve, bombshell. Usually he was attracted to women with longer hair. However, he'd become a fan of short hair the first time he peeped Starr's cropped haircut. Whenever he saw her at different functions, she always sported a fierce precision cut. Today was no different. Her hair was styled similar to Halle's in that James Bond flick, showcased by perfectly arched brows, sparkling ebony eyes, full sensual pouty lips, and a gorgeous set of dimples. If Nick hadn't firmly warned that Sunday afternoon, "Starr and Ava are off limits. Period," he would have pursued her years ago.

Kevin folded his arms across his broad chest as he grinned at Starr. "Now, why does a woman always find a reason to buy shoes?" He teased, mischief gleaming in his eyes.

"What? Man, don't you know a woman needs a new pair of shoes for every occasion?" Starr threw over her shoulder, a saucy smirk playing at her lips, before turning her attention back to the shoe she held. "You should know," she softly mumbled, for his ears only.

Starr suppressed a giggle. She couldn't believe she had just put Kevin on full blast. Thanks to Summer, she was very much aware of all the women he ran through. Shoot, the man had sampled more booty than Starr had shoes. And that was saying a lot. Starr had nothing but some shoes all up in her closet and under the bed.

"Ouch! I see I've been the topic of somebody's conversations." Kevin was certain Summer had told her about the numerous women who accompanied him on several double dates and dinner parties over the years. *Whatever.* It wasn't his fault he loved beautiful women and lots of them.

"No, my brotha, nothing like that," Starr denied, lying through her teeth as she moseyed over to a pair of Coach stilettos

On her heels, he challenged, "You mean Summer hasn't told you how much of a dog I am?"

Starr wasn't quite sure how to read Kevin. He seemed somewhere between joking and serious, she couldn't decipher which it was. Just as she was about to respond to him a sales lady interrupted. "Would you like to see that shoe in your size Miss?"

"Um, yes. A seven and a half please." *They're sure gonna look sooo cute with my dress.* Just because she was down in the dumps, didn't mean she was going off to Vegas looking like it. After this, she was heading over to Ladies Apparel to pick out a couple new outfits for the trip.

Turning her attention back to Kevin as the sales lady walked off, "now, you know my girl better than that. She would never refer to you as a dog. She loves you like the brother she never had."

Tilting his head and absently scratching his chin, *that's true.* Summer and Kevin were tighter than some blood bothers and sisters. Nevertheless, women always stuck together. He didn't want to call her a liar to her face, however, he knew better than to believe he hadn't, at some point, been the topic of conversation. This was one time he felt uneasy about his reputation with women.

"Well, she may not have called me a dog, but she had to say something for you to make that little smart comment."

Starr look surprised, almost offended. "What little smart comment?"

Kevin stared at her holding her gaze before letting out a short chuckle. *This woman is a trip.*

"No, for real. Summer has never called you a dog. She just said...umm...how should I say this?" Starr put a manicured finger to her lips as if in deep thought as she searched for tactful words. It would have been extremely rude of her to tell him her friend had referred to him a womanizer.

When she didn't answer after several seconds, becoming inpatient he said, "Well?"

A bashful grin curved Starr's full lips. "She said you have a lot of lady friends."

"A lot of lady friends, huh?"

"Yup, that what her said," Starr teased, bobbing her head up and down like her seven-year-old niece.

Again, the sales lady intruded on their conversation. "Here you are Miss, a size seven and a half."

"Thank you. Would you please ring them up for me? I don't need to try them on." Starr didn't feel like being hassled with trying the shoes on. If they didn't fit, she'd just bring them back tomorrow. She was having too much fun watching Mr. Sexy squirm.

Kevin followed Starr, hypnotized by the sway of her hips as she went to the register to complete her transaction.

Before she could reach for the bag from the sales associate, Kevin had smoothly taken it, as they headed to another department. Walking side by side, she didn't know what had come over her. Here she was supposedly spending some *alone time* with herself, but somehow ended up *shopping* with a playa. *How did that happen?* Shrugging her shoulders, she didn't give it another thought. She went with the flow as she kept up with his long strides.

After a couple moments of silence, it didn't take long for Kevin to pick up where they'd left off. "So Starr, you're a lady and my friend. Does that make me a bad guy?"

"First of all, Kevin, I never said you were a bad guy. And second, we're not friends."

Feigning hurt, he clutched his chest near his heart. "Ooh, double ouch! Girl, ya killing me!"

Starr giggled, rolling her eyes. "You know what I mean. The only thing we have in common is that our best friends are married and we're godparents to their children.

"So that doesn't make us friends?"

"Uh-uh, not really," she confirmed, wrinkling up her nose, shaking her head.

"Why?" Kevin questioned, raising a thick, dark brow.

"Because it doesn't. We're more like associates, not friends," she clarified.

Kevin frowned. "Associates?"

"Yes. Don't sound so offended."

"I'm not," he lied, his tone indifferent. He'd never had a woman to call him an associate, at least not to his face. The title made him feel so insignificant.

"Good," Starr said, offering up a smile to his handsome gaze. Wanting to change the subject she inquired, "So what brings you to Macy's?"

"My mom."

"Your mom?" Star parroted, bunching up her brows. Could brotha man elaborate just a little bit more?

"Mom's birthday is tomorrow," he sheepishly admitted.

"Shame on you, waiting 'til the last minute to get your momma a gift."

Kevin thought Starr was too cute as she playfully wagged her finger at him as if he were a naughty boy.

Well, he was a naughty boy. She'd probably smack his face, if she could see the vision of herself, in his head sprawled out naked on his head.

"I know, I know. But I'm a busy man," he chuckled, defending himself as he struggled to erase the image.

"That's right. I hear you're starting up your own investment firm."

"Yes. I've been doing a little free lancing here and there." Hunching broad shoulders he said, "I might as well start my own firm."

Curious, she looked up at him and tilted her head. "So what made you want to go out on your own?"

For the last two years, Kevin had assisted others with making investments decisions. Initially, it started small with answering questions for his mother's friends and their children. Before long, they were referring friends and other family members to him for advice. Within a short span of time, a substantial clientele base had been established.

When the firm he worked for got wind of his side hustle, they weren't pleased. "You're taking potential clients from the firm," one of the partners had casually mentioned over a business lunch. Kevin read very well between the lines. His firm wanted him to either convince his clients to come aboard, or to stop providing services to them all together. He wasn't having any of it. Hell would freeze over before he'd charged hard working families outrageous fees to help them invest money for retirement, or their children's education. Sure, the larger company accounts he dealt with were able to afford the fees without batting an eye. This was hardly the case with everyday working folks. He firmly believed everyone, no matter how much money they made, had a right to be given guidance on how to plan financially for the future.

Despite his firm's subtle warnings, he continued to provide his services. It hadn't surprised him one bit when he was called into a meeting by the partners and given an ultimatum. "Devote a hundred percent of your time to the firm or resign." Kevin never batted an eye at the blunt threat. Didn't they know? Kevin Dawson was his own man.

Shrugging broad shoulders, he called their bluff. "Fine, you'll have my resignation first thing in the morning."

Several weeks later the head partner offered Kevin back his old position. "Dawson we need you back on the team." Kevin wanted to laugh in the man's face. The partner hadn't disclosed that a number of Kevin's big corporate accounts were threatening to walk if he was no longer handling their accounts. In fact, every one of them personally contacted him wanting to know where he had set up shop. This is how Dawson Investments was created.

Starr was impressed as he shared with her why and how he decided to branch out on his own. Having had financial troubles in the past, she admired his commitment to bring financial stability to everyday folks. Without thinking, she had placed a delicate hand on his massive bicep. "That's great Kevin. I wish you much success."

Kevin momentarily was thrown off kilter by Starr's soft touch. He hadn't expected to feel the jolt that shuddered throughout his large frame. For some inexplicable reason, he wanted to take her in his arms and hold her. *Where did that come from?*

Slightly stepping back before he did something crazy to embarrass himself, he simply said, "Thanks that means a lot."

Looking at her watch, she decided it was time to get going. She'd spent too much time with Mr. Sexy. Talking to him was becoming *too* comfortable. "Well, it was nice running into you, but I have to get going."

Kevin nodded his head in understanding. Yeah, it was time to go. His thoughts were running places they had no business going. Handing her the bag, he gave her a lopsided grin, his intense gaze caressing her. "It was good seeing you again, Starr."

"You too, Kevin," Starr said as she reached for the outstretched bag, butterflies fluttering in her belly from the warmth of his stare. When their fingers grazed, she nearly dropped the bag from the surge of electricity. The tingling sensation dispersed from her fingertips traveling throughout her body. Turning quickly, hiding her heated, flushed cheeks, she began walking in the opposite direction not quite sure where she was going. One thing for sure, though, she was getting as far away from Kevin Dawson as possible. The man was too virile for his own good.

She wasn't alone in feeling the electrical current. He felt it too. So much so, he wanted to run after her, begging her to stay just a little longer. Instead he called out, "Hey, Starr."

Squeezing her eyes shut, she prayed for strength as she stopped in her tracks at the sound of the deep, sexy rumbling voice behind her. Why did he have to call her name like that? Slowly she looked over her left shoulder. The sexy grin he wore made her knees slightly buckle.

Man, why'd she have to be so fine? And off limits? "Are we friends yet?"

Smiling, her trademark dimples came out to play. "I'll let you know the next time I see you, Mr. Dawson."

And with that, Kevin watched as Starr sashayed away putting a little extra sway in her hips, until he could see her no more.

Chapter 3

"I'm coming, I'm coming," Starr called out to the unidentified caller in a singsong voice as she jingled the keys in the front door of her Manyunk home. Kicking off her shoes, she hurried to the phone, the smile she wore all afternoon remaining in place. Running into Kevin had taken her mind off her troubles for the moment. Dr. Neal had laid some heavy stuff on her. Stuff she didn't want to face let alone deal with. Spending the short amount of time she had with Kevin had lightened her mood.

"Hello?"

"Hey, girl, you ready for Vegas?" The upbeat voice questioned.

"Hey, Summer. Yeah girl, I'm more than ready. I was thinking about staying a few days longer." Starr's voice was flat, lacking energy. Suddenly, her good mood evaporated and her heart became heavy as she thought of her future. Staying a few days longer in Vegas amongst the flashing lights and nightly shows would give her a passage of escapism.

Summer didn't miss the melancholy tone. She'd thought Starr would have sounded a little more excited, since she had decided on staying a few extra days. Something wasn't right. Summer could feel it. Just as she was about to ask her what was up, Starr's other line clicked.

"Hold on a minute, Summer."

"All right."

Starr clicked over to the other line. "Hello?"

"What's up, Chica?"

"Hey, Av."

"What's wrong?"

"Girl..." Starr, swallowed hard as her voice began to quiver. *This is so hard.* Her friends and sister knew her well. Earlier she had been able steer clear of Karen and her probing questions. This time, she wouldn't be so lucky.

"Oh sweetie, you want me to come over?"

Starr smiled sadly as she clutched the cordless phone hearing the concern in her friend's voice. "No, Av. Besides, I have Summer on the other line."

"Oh, Okay. I'll let you get back to her then."

"Hey, why don't you hang up and I'll three-way you in." Now was as good a time as ever to tell them what was bothering her. Eventually, she would have to tell them.

"All right, hurry up, I'll be waiting."

Starr clicked back over to Summer. "Hold on a second while I bring Ava in on three-way. I have something to tell y'all." Summer patiently waited as she connected Ava to the call.

Ava picked up the phone on the first ring. "Starr?"

"Yeah, it's me and Summer on the line."

"Hey, Summer."

"Hey, Av what's going on?"

"Nothing much. Just worried about our girl."

Silence hung in the air as Summer and Ava waited. They were patient as Starr gathered her thoughts. They sensed something was serious, but what? Their friend never had difficulty telling them anything. However, this time she was clearly struggling with her emotions.

Letting out a deep breath, Starr began to speak as she tried to keep her voice from shaking. *Oh God, this is so hard.* "I have endometriosis," she blurted out.

The sharp intake of her friends' breath at her confession pierced the quiet space surrounding her. This quickly prompted her to say, "It's not an advanced case…yet."

"That's good, Starr. Right?" Ava softly commented, not really knowing what to say. Being in the medical profession, they were aware an advanced case could mean infertility, which would devastate Starr.

"Yeah, it's not a *huge* concern just yet." She heard herself saying in an attempt to soothe her own fears. "Dr. Neil said I shouldn't have a problem conceiving at this stage. According to him, I need to start thinking about having a baby soon. Like within the next year or so."

"Oh, Boo. What are you going to do?" Summer inquired, fully realizing Starr's dilemma.

"Don't know. Ain't like I got a man hanging around."

Both Ava and Summer fell silent. The sadness floating through the phone lines was painfully palpable. Neither knew what to say to their hurting friend. What could Summer say to comfort her? She had two beautiful babies? And Ava had been telling them since the day they met that she had no desire to be a mother.

Grasping at anything to make her feel better, Ava said, "Maybe you'll meet someone soon."

"Yeah, that could happen, you never know. People meet, fall in love and marry within a few months all the time," Summer added trying to add hope to the situation.

"Mmm hmm, by the time you're thirty-four and a half, you'll be married with a baby and another one on the way," Ava predicted, trying to lift her spirits.

Starr softly chuckled. In her heart, she knew they meant well. But where in the world was she going to find a man? The only men around were at work. And messing around where you made your dough was a no-no. She learned this lesson the hard way when she casually dated a research assistant for a few weeks. The maniac turned out to be a stalker, showing up at the hospice unit whenever he felt like it, sitting in the back pew at church, or walking his dog in the park around the corner from Starr's house. One evening he went so far as to follow her to Karen's home. Though he called himself trying to be slick, he hadn't counted on Summer showing up to keep her company as she babysat Alicia and Kyle.

"Starr, I think somebody's outside in the bushes," Summer whispered as if the person outside could hear her.

Sucking her teeth, she huffed over to the bay window peeping out into the dark. "I don't see anything, but I think it's that jackass Todd, with his drunk self. Whoever heard of a drunken research assistant?"

"What you gonna do? He's been following you since you told him you just wanted to be friends. I told you not to go out with him. He always gave me the creeps," Summer said as she crunched up her face.

Starr was about to tell Summer to shut up when she let out a high-pitched scream.

"What? What is it?" Summer yelled, startled by Starr's outburst.

"That son of a gun is in my sister's bushes! I just saw him right over there!" she shouted pointing to the window.

"Come on! Let's get that stalking rat bastard!" Summer yelled as she ran to the kitchen grabbing a frying pan, while Starr grabbed a poker from the fireplace.

Before Todd knew what hit him, Starr and Summer were in the bushes raining down blows that were being blocked by long arms and legs. When he finally got his bearings, he pushed Summer to the ground and shoved Starr, sending her toppling over on top of her petite friend.

Jumping up, she pulled Summer to her feet. Taking off they ran down the block like two banshees on his heels shouting and screaming, "You better run…you nasty, low-life nothin'!"

If she hadn't been so depressed with her current situation, she would've been doubled over laughing hysterically, as she allowed her mind to roam down memory land.

"You guys know I don't need a man to have a baby?"

Come again? Ava thought not getting where Starr was going with this. "What are you talking about you don't need a man?"

"Dr. Neil proposed artificial insemination."

Just as she thought, silence greeted her as they processed what she'd just said.

Stunned, Ava incredulously questioned, "What? Is *he* for real? Are *you* for real?"

Immediately, Starr became defensive. "Well, what's wrong with that?"

Oh boy, Summer thought. Ava was about to get Starr hot up under the collar. She figured she'd better say something quick to diffuse the impending argument.

With a tender inflection in her voice, she addressed Starr as if she were talking to one of her patients. "Is this something you have considered? I mean really considered? Having a baby without a father?" No matter what her friend decided, she would support her decision. However, she hoped Starr fully understood how the emotional turmoil of being alone and pregnant might have on her.

Starr let out a deep sigh. "Summer, I've been doing nothing but thinking about this whole situation. I really want to have a baby. With or without a man." *What other choice do I have?*

She wished she could give her girl a big hug. The longing in her voice for a child was so heart wrenching. "Then honey that's what you should do. You know we'll be here to support you one hundred percent."

Ava couldn't hold it in any longer. What were they thinking? A frozen pop? For a daddy? And how dare Summer encourage her to have a baby on her own. She had a freakin' millionaire for a husband for goodness sake! She didn't have to worry about a thing. "Come on y'all, this is so not right."

"What? The fact that I want to have a baby before it's too late for me?" Starr was steaming. Ava could really work her nerves at times.

"No, the fact that you won't know who your child's father is. Not to mention if you fall on hard times financially, who's going to help you take care of that child?"

Coming to Starr's defense, "Ava, that's enough," Summer firmly warned. She could shake Ava. Sometimes her mouth was out of control.

Sucking her teeth, Ava reiterated, "All I'm saying is the father should be in the picture. At least to help financially support the kid." She didn't understand it. What was it they weren't getting? How many times have they all heard single mothers crying about how difficult it is raising kids on their own?

Fighting to hold back the tears, Starr couldn't believe Ava was coming at her like this. She, of all people, knew how much she loved children and wanted to one day be a mom. "Of course I would want to know the father of my child and have him involved in my child's life. But that may not be possible if I want to have a baby within the next two years. I have to face the fact I'm not getting any younger and the longer I wait to get pregnant the more difficult it may be. And, I don't even what to think about this endometriosis situation…"

Neither Ava nor Summer had a clue as what to say as her voice trailed off. Emotions were too raw. Ava hadn't heeded Summer's warning and now Starr was on the verge of tears suddenly unsure of what she was considering. Earlier, she had been so sure, almost resolved she could go through with having a baby by artificial means. But if Ava felt this way, how would her mom and sister feel?

Needing and wanting to be alone, she decided to end the call. "Look y'all, I'm gonna go now."

Concerned, Summer wanted to know, "You gonna be all right?"

Star let out an audible sigh. "I guess so. I just want to be alone. I have a lot to workout right now."

"Listen, Starr I didn't mean to upset you," Ava apologized, suddenly feeling bad for bluntly voicing her opinion. She realized she always pushed further than need be at times. It was a good thing her friends loved her unconditionally.

Hunching her shoulders as if they could see her, "Don't worry about it. You were only being honest with me."

Awkward silence filled the phone lines as Starr's words hung in the air. She sensed her friends were at a loss for words. Wanting to put an end to everyone's discomfort, she finally ended the conversation. "I'll talk to you guys later."

Not waiting for a response, the next sound her friends heard was that of a dial tone.

Chapter 4

Beverly Dawson eagerly waited with gleeful anticipation. Today was her birthday, and she was ready for a celebration. And what a celebration it would be. Beverly had an abundance to be thankful for and to celebrate. God had been good to her for eighty-three years. She was relatively healthy for a woman her age, blessed with two sons who absolutely adored her, and had been fortunate to spend over fifty years with the love of her life, her late husband, Richard Sr.

The day began with the delivery of a beautiful bouquet of gardenias, her favorite flowers from her eldest son, Richard Jr. and his wife, Audrey. Before she could get to the phone to dial their number to thank them, her phone was ringing. Grinning from ear to ear, she gloried in the off-key musical treat of their rendition of happy birthday.

After an hour-long conversation, Beverly ended the call. "I have to get off this phone. I'm going to be late for my date."

The rest of the morning, she busied herself getting ready. She wanted to look her absolute best. When all her priming and primping was completed, she was pleasingly satisfied with how she looked. Dressed fashionably to the nines in a powder blue Chanel pantsuit, a single strand of pearls gracing her elegant neck, matching earrings adorning her lobes, and a white gardenia in her sparkling silver hair, Beverly Dawson was a classic beauty.

Tilting her head to the side and smiling, Beverly admired her reflection. *I look good for an old lady.*

As Beverly gently touched the delicate flower, another smile curved her lips as she remembered the first time she wore one in her hair. Richard Dawson, a young, handsome military man had arrived at her parents' home for their first date. In his hand, he held the prettiest white gardenia she'd ever seen. Beverly fell in love with him that night as he gingerly placed the delicate flower in her shoulder length, dark brown hair.

Caught up in reliving the past, she never heard the unannounced visitor entering through the front door.

Kevin let out a low whistle. Even at her age, he found his mother beautiful. He had often wondered if it was good genes, healthy living, or the fact that his mother didn't smoke or drink, which kept her looking so youthful. Whatever the secret was, Beverly Dawson didn't look anywhere near her eighty-three years. Nor did she act like it.

Kevin chuckled as Beverly put her hands on slender hips and did a little cha-cha move. "Watch out now, you might hurt somebody with your fine self," Kevin teased, winking at his mother.

"Come here boy and give your momma a hug and some sugar." Beverly lovingly held her arms open to her youngest son. Richard Jr. had been the child of her youth, whereas Kevin had been her miracle baby. After Richard Jr. came along, she and her husband unsuccessfully tried to have other children. Their plan was to have a house full of babies and show them the world as they traveled from army base to army base. Coming to terms that Richard Jr. would be an only child, Beverly became content with nurturing her son and being a good military wife.

At the age of forty-two when she missed three consecutive periods she hadn't given it much thought. All the women in her family had gone through the *change* in their early forties. Never in her wildest dreams would she have guessed she might be pregnant. Fifteen years had gone by since she'd last carried a child. An inkling of suspicion toyed with her as she begin to pay closer attention to her body. Suddenly she noticed her breasts were heavier, fuller, and more tender than usual, accompanied by vague waves of nausea that would come at the oddest of times.

The woman nearly fell off the examine table when the doctor informed her she was in family way. To Beverly's delight six months later, a bouncing baby boy, weighing in at nine pounds, three ounces came bursting on the scene.

Obediently, Kevin enveloped his momma in a snug embrace as he leaned down and kissed her on the cheek. Releasing his mother, Kevin pulled out two tickets from the inside pocket of his sport's jacket. After going to a number of department stores and boutiques, he had yet to find the perfect gift. Rounding the corner onto Walnut Street after his search on Jeweler's Row came up empty, he proceeded to walk pass the Walnut Street Theater. That's when it him. Broadway!

His mother hadn't been to Broadway in years. His parents would take weekend getaways to New York City when he became a teenager. Kevin never minded his parents' weekend excursions because he was always left in the care of the Stiles'. During those weekends, he and Nick would find all kinds of devilment to get into.

"Happy birthday, Momma."

Taking the tickets in her hands, she held them to her chest. "Oh, baby… The Color Purple on Broadway. Mmm, the last time I saw a play on Broadway your daddy was living."

Briefly, a sad expression crossed her beautiful features. The last ten years without Richard Sr. at certain times was unbearable. But God is good. Every time she became blue, a ray of sunshine would come shining through in the form of her children, reminding her she still a part of her beloved husband. Although Richard Jr. followed in the footsteps of his father, becoming a three star general and traveling the world, he always made time to call her twice a week. If she didn't know better, she'd swear her boys orchestrated their schedules. When Richard Jr. wasn't calling, Kevin was popping up for impromptu visits.

The sad expression wasn't missed. Concerned, he pressed, "Momma, you all right?"

"Yes, baby. I was just missing your daddy, that's all." Lightly patting Kevin on the chest, she smiled up at her son. "You look so much like him. You know he was a ladies man much like yourself." Winking a bit flirtatiously, Beverly added, "Until I came along and set him straight. Had him hooked the first time he looked into these here dreamy eyes of mine."

Kevin chuckled as his momma batted her lashes. Hooking his arm through hers, he said, "Come on foxy Momma, your chariot awaits you."

Leading Beverly to the waiting limo her words danced around in his head. *"You know he was a ladies man much like yourself… until I came along and set him straight."* Kevin wanted to laugh out loud. *Is there a woman out there who can do that? Set me straight?* Kevin pushed the absurd question from his mind.

Beverly Dawson was one of a kind. Only she could tame a wild, worldly man like Richard Dawson. *I love you Daddy, but I ain't going out like you did. Naw, there ain't a babe out there who can tame me.*

After making such a boastful statement to himself, Kevin frowned. Why was Starr Avery prancing to the forefront of his mind flashing her thousand watt dimpled smile?

Beverly Dawson wore a faint smile as she spied the frown her son wore. He was thinking about what she just said. Richard Jr. had settled down and married twelve years ago. He and his wife Audrey couldn't have children because of a childhood injury she had suffered. Kevin was her last hope of her becoming a grandmother. All he needed to do was stand still long enough to find a *nice* girl.

Lord have mercy! Some gal calling herself *Trina* had showed up knocking on her door looking for her boy. She was a mess! The child's skirt was so short, if she bent over everybody would have seen where the good Lord had spilt her!

Beverly had given Kevin a good tongue-lashing. "You tell that half-naked tail gal to put some clothes on before she come tipping up here at my front door again. Boy, what's wrong with you? Your father and I didn't raise you to chase after everything in a skirt. You need to find yourself a nice, decent girl. And not one that looks like she was walking the streets all night."

Taking her boy's hand, Beverly patted it as they headed for the expressway. Her baby would be all right. She and her late husband had raised him well. *It's only a phase he's going through dating all these women.* Too many for Beverly to remember their names. If his best friend Nick could settle down and start a family, there was hope for Kevin. Yes, he would give her what she wanted. Grandbabies.

Patting his hand again, she prayed, *Lord, just bless me with one grandchild to love before I close my eyes.*

Chapter 5

Her face burned with embarrassment, as she was the center of attention. "Oh my Lawd, my Lawd! Stop that! Stop that right now!" Joan chided the twenty-something male stripper gyrating in front of her to the beat of the music blaring from a boom box. The only thing the muscle bound exotic dancer wore was a silky, red G-string.

Nita Jackson shook her head as she stared narrow-eyed at Ava, Summer, and Starr. Of the three, one of them hired the stripper. *She* hadn't done such an awful thing as to hire the almost naked, hip-thrusting youngster. And since she had planned and given the bridal shower for Joan, it had to be one of them. Nita was going to have whoever did this act of debauchery fast little tail in a sling! But which one had done it? They would never snitch out the culprit. Shaking her head again, *Poor Joan looks like she's 'bout to have a heart attack!*

Everyone erupted into laughter as the barely dressed stripper gyrated in Nita's direction.

"Boy, don't you bring your nasty behind over here! Shaking o'va top of me!"

Rolling his eyes, the buff stripper pulled Karen, who had been sitting next to Nita, to her feet. The younger women in the room hooted and hollered as Karen let her hair down and indulged the stripper.

Three hours later the only guests left in the ballroom at the Hilton on City Line Avenue were Joan, Nita, Summer, Ava, Starr, and Karen. The women chatted as they pulled down decorations and stacked gifts near the entrance.

Joan smiled as she stacked the last gift. No longer would she be lonely. She had found love again after so many years, had a family that cared about her and for the first time in years a best friend.

After being betrayed by Alice and Sam all those years ago, she never trusted anyone, especially women. With Summer coming into her life, came Nita's friendship Though the two lived miles a part they constantly talked on the phone and even made time to visit one another at least three times a year since meeting.

Coming over to Joan, Nita laid her hand on her shoulder. "Did you have a good time?"

Reaching up to hold the hand on her shoulder, she smiled at her friend. "Yes, thank you for throwing me a bridal shower." Chuckling she added, "Never thought I'd have one."

"Oh, honey, you are so welcome. I knew you and Henry were going to get together after last Christmas. The man kept sniffing around you ever ten minutes."

The two women laughed, remembering how Henry shamelessly flirted with Joan.

"Did you have a good time?"

"I sure did." Nita again for the hundredth time threw the trio a scowling gaze. "With the exception of that boy shaking his funky behind all over the place."

Chuckling, Joan said, "Tell me 'bout it. Boy young enough to be my grandchild…but, Lawd knows I sure hope Henry can move like that!"

Nita gasped, the younger women snickered. "That's what I'm talkin' 'bout!" Ava yelled, grinning with mischief as she pulled a plastic trash bag from a box on the table.

"Mmm hmm, that's what I thought." Nita gave Ava a stern motherly look. "Ought to come over there and whoop your little fast behind."

Ava covered her mouth, giggling, she was busted. Summer and Starr tried to tell her weeks ago not to hire a stripper. But of course, Ava being Ava hadn't listened. Blowing a kiss in Nita's direction, "I love you, Mommy."

Nita couldn't resist smiling at Ava. She would never admit it to them, but that young, fine thing gyrating had her eager to get home to James. "I love you too, baby."

Pulling crape paper from the wall, Starr hadn't notice Ava coming over to her holding open a trash bag. "Here, you can put that in here."

Ava let out a soft sigh. Starr hadn't had much to say to her after their disagreement a week ago. Tonight was no different. She barely said much of anything. When Karen asked, "What's up with my sister?" Both Ava and Summer hunched up their shoulders. If Starr hadn't told her sister about her condition, it wasn't their place to do so.

Clearing her throat, Ava whispered, "Starr, I'm sorry about the other night."

Starr just looked at Ava. She loved her dearly; however, Ava needed to work on being a bit more tactful. "Av, you really hurt me."

Dropping her head in shame, she mumbled, "I know I did and I really, really feel bad about it. Do you…think you can forgive me?"

"Of course I can, you're my friend. But what you said still hurts."

Ava pulled her friend into a tight embrace. "I really am sorry. I didn't mean to hurt you."

She returned the embrace. "Don't worry about it, Av. I'll be okay."

"Are you sure?" Ava was no dummy. Although Starr was saying one thing with her lips, her eyes told a different story. She was not okay and Ava didn't know what she could do to make it better.

Feeling like she needed some space, Starr broke the close contact. "I'll be right back; I have to go to the bathroom."

With curious gazes, the other women in the room watched the two friends. Everyone noticed how uncharacteristically quiet Starr had been all evening. Usually she was a social butterfly at events such as this. Seeing her talk with Ava was the most anyone had seen her do all night.

Summer let out a sigh of relief. Hopefully with Ava apologizing things would get back on track. She didn't like it one bit when there was friction between them. All week she listened as Ava went on and on about how she didn't mean any harm. Summer point blank told her, "then you need to think about what you're gonna say, before you say it." Miserably Ava responded, "I know, I know."

With her back to the bathroom stall door, Starr massaged her temples. "What a night. I'm so ready to go home…so I can be alone."

It wasn't that she wasn't happy for Joan, really she was. However, it was so hard to put up a front for everyone. She knew they all were wondering why she wasn't her usual wild and crazy self like she always was at parties. She could see it all in their faces as they asked, "Is everything alright?" Though she tried to get into the spirit of things, especially when the stripper was making Joan blush, her laughter was faked; it was forced. How could she be happy when she felt no hope? Why did it seem everywhere she went she saw pregnant women, or women pushing babies in strollers? A thousand times she wanted to know, "Why can't that be me?'

All night as she looked at Karen and Summer, a twinge of guilt nipped at her. All week she avoided talking to them. How could she tell them that it was too painful overhearing the pitter-patter and angelic chattering of toddlers and school aged children in the background? Would they think she was over reacting? Or worse, just being jealous of their lives? Most likely they wouldn't. After all, both women had had their own heartaches to deal with.

Karen one morning woke up the wife of her high school sweetheart, Gregory Johnston, only to be widowed forty-five minutes after he'd left for work. Not wanting to be bothered with driving downtown, Gregory had taken the Regional Rail Line. Karen nearly came undone when a newsflash interrupted Good Morning America announcing a grave accident. The news announcer reported that the signals had somehow crossed resulting in a head on collision of north and southbound trains. It took everything out of her to hold it together as she completed the task of dressing her two small children, Alicia and Kyle, who were at the time one and three years old.

And though Summer had two beautiful children, she was devastated when she started to have cramping and spotting during the first trimester of her third pregnancy. An ultrasound confirmed the absence of a fetal heartbeat. Starr remembered how frantic Nick had been when he called her and Ava to give them the news. She also would never forget how they had to help Nick take care of NJ and Autumn because Summer had temporarily shut down for days. All her body would allow her to do was cry, sleep, and then cry some more.

Starr let out a groan. *How can I be so selfish? Why am I pushing away the people who love me the most?* Facing the music, she painfully admitted to herself, *Because I want what they have.*

Chapter 6

"Starr, you in here?" The feminine voice asked as she squatted looking under each stall.

"Yeah, Karen. I'm coming out so stop looking under the doors."

Karen gave up a little laugh. Ever since they were little girls, they'd peep under stalls looking for each other, especially at church during Sunday school when one of them tried to get out of having to recite a bible verse. The only safe place to hide had been in the bathroom stall.

Oh boy, I know Karen's gonna grill me to death. I'm so not up for this, Starr thought as she mentally prepared herself to deal with her sister. She knew Karen would not leave her alone until she found out what had been troubling her.

Karen leaned against the wall, her arms crossed over her chest as she patiently waited for Starr to come out. She was finally going to find out why Starr was avoiding her like she had some communicable disease.

Alarm over came her as she looked into her baby sister's red, puffy eyes. Karen's heart rate accelerated as Starr laid her head on her shoulder for comfort. She hadn't been this distraught since her Marcus years.

"Hey, Starry, what's going on?"

Automatically Karen's arms wrapped around her sister and soothingly rubbed her back. She always affectionately called her that when something was troubling her. Karen had an uncanny knack of knowing when her baby sister was hurting. Like the first time she'd caught Marcus cheating, it was Karen who for some inexplicable reason had to drive over to Starr's apartment in the middle of the night to check on her. Or the time their father unexpectedly showed up *again* wanting to play daddy, only to disappear after becoming bored with a wife and two kids. Again, it was Karen who assured her it was their father who had issues and not them or their mother.

Putting all defenses aside, exposing her deepest desire, Starr blurted out, "I want to have a baby."

Confused, still rubbing Starr's back, Karen assured her, "Oh, Starry you can have a baby."

Shaking her head on Karen's shoulder, she cried, "No, no, it may be too late."

Karen was still confused. Starr wasn't making sense. "Huh? I don't understand?"

Freeing herself from the protective embrace, Starr began telling her story. By the time Starr told her everything, starting with her diagnosis of endometriosis, her contemplation of artificial insemination, and her fall out with Ava, Karen felt slighted. Mostly because she felt like she'd been left out of the loop. Her own sister hadn't even come to her for support.

Karen didn't mean to sound disappointed, but she couldn't keep the hurt from her voice when she asked, "Why didn't you come to me with this?"

"Because I thought you would have felt the same way Ava had."

Well, that explained why she was so distant. Karen didn't think now was the time to tell her, but she agreed with Ava. All of their lives they dealt with their father's lack of interest in them. She recalled all the times they had try to be good little girls by keeping their room clean and doing all their chores, hoping that doing so would keep their father home. It never worked; he'd end up leaving anyway.

Gently taking her by the shoulders, she said, "Starry whatever you decide to do I'm behind you one hundred percent." Karen paused. She had to say it. She just hoped it came out in love. "But I really want you to pray on this artificial insemination thing. You know what we went through not having Daddy around. Like I said, whatever you decide I'm here for you, all the way, baby sis."

Starr nodded her head in understanding. "I know you're right, and so is Ava. That's why I'm leaning toward adoption." Lowering her head, she softly admitted, "But I still want my *own* baby. I want to experience carrying my child in my body. Is that so wrong?"

Karen pulled her sister back into her arms. "No Starry, it's not wrong. Not at all."

Oh my God! I look a hot mess! Starr knew her eyes were bloodshot from all of the crying on her sister's shoulder. If she had known Kevin, was coming, she would have stayed in the bathroom until everyone left. But she knew that that wouldn't be fair to Joan. This was her night to celebrate her upcoming nuptials and she didn't want to spoil it. It was bad enough everyone kept asking her if she was okay. Lying through her teeth she pasted on a fake smile, "I'm fine." Taking a deep breath, she pulled herself together and pushed her troubles to the farthest corner of mind. Self-consciously she ran her fingers over the smooth hair lying on her neck.

Joining the group, Starr put on her best smile. "Hey, every body."

"How's my other favorite girl?" James Jackson's voice boomed as he affectionately swept her up in a hug.

Starr was only too happy to return the hug. Every time she hugged this gentle soul, she wished with everything in her that he belonged to her. That he was the daddy her father had never materialized into. Enjoying the warmth of the fatherly embrace for the moment soothed her aching heart. Yes, James Jackson was her daddy, if only for that moment.

"Thanks, Mr. Jackson, I needed that."

Playfully he tweaked her nose as if she were a little girl. "Anytime sweetheart."

"Hey, can another old man get a hug?"

Starr squealed as Henry Stiles squeezed her in a gentle bear hug, released her and then swirled her around as if dancing, into the arms of Nick. Nick continued the playful choreography as he twirled her round and round.

Lighthearted giggles bubbled from Starr. They had no idea of the balm they were so lovingly applying to soothe her weary soul.

Standing back watching the other men having a good time with Starr, Kevin noticed how the sullen expression she wore when she entered the room had dissipated. He couldn't explain it, but seeing her so sad had bothered him.

Kevin was slightly caught off guard when a laughing and squealing Starr was hurled into his arms. Quickly recovering, without hesitation he drew the soft feminine body close.

"Nick! I'm gonna kill you!" Starr continued to laugh breathlessly. Attempting to maintain her balance, dainty fingers curled around bulging biceps as her breasts firmly pressed against a set of rock hard pecs.

Starr's breath caught and held as she felt large hands being planted on her hips holding her in place. Everything and everyone stood still in time. The only thing she was aware of was the loud beating of her heart in her ears and the warmth of a very male body.

Closing her eyes, Starr thought this might be a dream. It had been so long since a man had held her like this. The feel of him, the smell of him, was making her come apart. A soft moan escaped her lips. She could stay in his arms forever.

Kevin enjoyed the feel of her softness. Heat coursed throughout his loins as he felt the rapid pulsation of her heart beating against his chest. The close contact also afforded him the pleasure of feeling every deep breath she took that made her full breast rise and fall.

A smile curved the corners of his full lips. "Are we friends yet?" The question came out in a low, husky whisper against her ear.

The hot, seducing whisper snapped her out of her trance. As she attempted to break the intimate contact, Kevin held her tight. He needed to hold her just a second longer.

"Huh?" Her voice came out in a breathy whisper.

Before Kevin could respond, a tight voiced Nick clipped out, "Starr."

When he playfully flung her into Kevin's arms, he hadn't

expected him to practically make love to her standing up in front of everyone! Good grief! Although there wasn't any music playing the two were sensually fused together in a Tango hold. Spinning on her heels, wide eyed, she gawked at Nick. "Yes?"

Nick jerked his head to the other side of the room. "Summer wants you."

Summer had also spied the pair in a heated embrace. Making eye contact with her husband, she motioned for him to "break it up!" As much as she loved Kevin, she thought the last thing her friend needed right now was to get tangled up with a man like him.

"Oh, okay." She dared not turn around when she heard Nick hiss through clenched teeth, "Man, what the hell is your problem?"

Not hearing Kevin's response didn't matter. All that mattered was that Kevin Dawson had made her feel good. He made her feel gorgeous and desirable. Something she hadn't felt in a very, very long time.

Chapter 7

"Come on man. You still trippin' over that?" Kevin asked annoyed as he sat in the casino lounge drinking a beer.

"Dude, I peeped you looking at her during the entire ceremony," Nick coolly stated. He couldn't understand Kevin's sudden interest in his wife's best friend. The man watched the woman all night like a fox outside a chicken coop.

He wasn't about to deny it. He couldn't take his eyes off of her. When Starr walked into the chapel, Kevin had to remind himself to breathe. She was absolutely, breathtakingly gorgeous in the strapless dress, the color of bubbling champagne. Her smooth cocoa brown skin shimmered with sparkling dusting powder from her delicate shoulders, down to her French pedicure feet covered in strappy high-heel sandals perfectly matching her dress. "Man, even you have to admit Starr looked hot tonight."

His friend nodded his head in agreement. "True dat. But I'm warning you my brotha to… leave… that… alone."

A smirk on his lips, he shot back, "Who said I was trying to mess with that."

Nick chuckled, "Kev, man, it's me you're talking to."

Feigning offense, he questioned, "What's that supposed to mean?"

"Man, I know you're not that dense. It means you'll hit it as long as you can, and then when you get bored you'll be out."

No longer in a jesting mood, Kevin's face became tight. Nick was beginning to piss him off. He was acting as if he wasn't a playa until Summer came along. They both knew if he wasn't married and didn't love his wife and kids he would probably be somewhere right now between some woman legs *hittin' it*.

"Like you used to do?" Kevin threw back in a clipped tone.

Shrugging broad shoulders, what could he say? He mastered the art of hittin' it. "All I'm saying is Starr is good people. She's a sweet girl. I don't want to see her get hurt."

"First of all man, she's a grown woman, not a girl. And you're making this out to be deeper than it needs to be." Taking a swig of beer, he set the bottle down. "I don't plan on hurting anybody."

Nodding his head, he gazed directly into the other man's eyes. "Cool. That's all I want to hear." The last thing he wanted or needed was a hysterical Summer ranting and raving when the crap hit the fan if Starr and Kevin were to get involved and things didn't work out.

"Are we done Daddy Nick?" Kevin asked as he grinned. Just as quickly as his irritation had come, it vanished. He could never stay upset long with his best friend, his brother.

Nick chuckled, "Yeah son. Come on let's go shoot some pool. I haven't spanked you in a long time."

In good nature, Kevin slapped Nick on the back as they left the lounge. "Whatever you say old man."

Tiptoeing back into the living room area of the suite in the luxury hotel, Summer plopped down on the soft, plush sofa next to Ava. "Whew, I'm tired. I thought those little rug rats of mine would never go to sleep." She commented stifling a yawn. It had been a chore getting NJ and Autumn to bed. The tots were still keyed up from the day's events. Both were still excited about being part of their grandparents' nuptials.

Everyone in attendance cheered as NJ, just as handsome he could be, carried the rings down the aisle on the satin ivory pillow. Autumn was just adorable, receiving her fair share of cheers as she dropped one rose petal at a time on the white runner. Because of all of the attention, NJ and Autumn were wearing Summer out with, "We want Mom-Mom and Pop-Pop to get married so we can be in the wedding." When she tried to explain to them that Mom-Mom and Pop-Pop were already married, Autumn, wide-eyed and innocent, suggested, "They can get married again like Grandma Joan and Grandpa Henry."

Ava smiled. "I know you are. I thought my godchildren would never go to sleep."

"Girl, tell me about it." Starr took a small sip of her white wine spritzer, and then set it down on the coffee table. Now that the children were asleep, she could freely talk. "Do you think Starr is ever going to come out of her funk?"

Ava shrugged a shoulder. "Don't know." Pausing for a second, she let out a small groan, "I think she's still mad at me."

"Av, you know Starr isn't one to hold a grudge. I just think she's going through a tough time now and needs her space."

"I know, but she has never distance herself like this from us before."

Summer put a comforting arm around Ava's shoulder. "Don't take it so personal, honey. Maybe it's hard for her to be around us. She's not only avoiding us, she hasn't been calling Karen as often either."

Ava screwed up her face as if to say, *What?* It was no secret the two sisters were tighter than tight. If she was avoiding her own sister then she must be hurting in a bad way. This made Ava feel even more horrible for the words she had so carelessly spoken to her friend. *Stupid, stupid, stupid me. I didn't make matters any better by spouting off at the mouth.*

"Yup, Karen and I talked a few nights ago. Starr finally told her everything the night of the shower. She confided in Karen that it's hard to be around us because we have kids."

This made Ava feel a smidge better. At least it wasn't just her feeling left out in the cold. "Oh, I'm sorry," Ava said grabbing Summer's hand and gently squeezing it.

Summer returned the squeeze. "It's okay. I understand. As much as she loves Autumn and NJ, they are painful reminders of what she wants, just as Alicia and Kyle are."

Silence fell over them. A crucial element of the group wasn't there. It was like a missing arm or leg. As the festivities of Henry and Joan's nuptials drew to a close, the lovebirds were eager to be alone. Bidding everyone farewell, the honeymooners skipped out to their love nest.

Everyone else had paired off into their perspective groups. Nita and James made a beeline to the casino. Nita wanted to hit the slots and James the blackjack table. Nick and Kevin wasted no time heading to the nearest bar for a beer. It was naturally assumed that the trio would hang out, laughing, and catching up on the latest like always. However, Starr turned down their offer to "kick back and chill." Her excuse had been, "I'm tired. I want to get some sleep so I can be ready for our big day of shopping tomorrow."

As much as it bothered Ava and Summer, neither wanted to challenge her. It was barely ten o'clock in the evening. So to keep the peace they each gave her a hug and wished her a good night's sleep.

"Well, at least she didn't cancel on us for tomorrow," Summer offered with a weak smile. Honestly, she wasn't so sure Starr would show up. She had stood her up for dinner twice last week.

"Yeah, I suppose you're right."

Bringing an end to the silence, not feeling much like company, Ava let out a deep breath. "Summer, I think I'm gonna head back to my room." Replaying the evening in her mind, she began to feel some kind of way. Was it her imagination, or was Starr talking to everyone else but her? She knew she had overstepped her boundaries with the whole artificial insemination thing. How many times could she apologize for being an insensitive jerkette?

Sensing Ava's mood, Summer coaxed, "Come on sweetie, and stay just a little longer. There's no use in you being alone, too. Stop worrying, you're gonna make yourself sick. Besides, you're taking this way too personal. "

Ava let out a deep sigh. Was she taking this too personal? She didn't think so. Although she and Starr had numerous disagreements over the years, they had never put a strain on the friendship like this one had. She just prayed that they would be able to get over this little snag in their relationship.

"If it makes you fell any better, we only talk because I call her. It's not like she's calling me. And when I do call half the time, she let the call roll over to her voicemail. I know that heifer is home when I call."

A small smile touched Ava lips. Maybe she was taking things a little too personal. "Yeah?"

Summer lightly slapped Ava on the thigh. "Mmm hmm, now stop all this mopping. One sad friend is enough!" Getting up, she went over to the wet bar and filled two glasses with white wine and club soda. Picking up the wine glasses Summer made her way back over to the sofa.

The cool liquid splattered over the rim of the glass as Summer handed it to Ava. "Oops. Girl, take this before I spill it all over you."

Ava giggled. "What you trying to do? Get me drunk?

"Nope I'm trying to get me drunk! Those little monsters wore me out! I need to sleep real good tonight."

"Stop calling my babies names! They ain't gonna be too many more rug rats and little monsters."

Laughing, Summer caught the pillow in mid-air before it could wallop her upside the head. "Fine, godmother of the year, you take them back to your room tonight so they can wake you up at o-dark zero thirty."

"I don't think so. You know I need my beauty sleep."

Playfully, nudging her friend, she told her, "Yeah, that's what I thought."

The heavy, oppressive gloom that threatened to cast a heavy shadow was replaced by an air of giddiness as the young women continued to indulge themselves and watch an old Eddie Murphy comedy.

Somewhere around midnight, lightheaded and tipsy, Ava staggered to her room. The last thought she had before passing out was *I miss my buddy Starr.*

Chapter 8

"Oooh, my head hurts," Starr moaned from the unrelenting pounding. *Had too much to drink.*

Pulling the covers over her head, Starr never wanted to get out of bed. The pouring rain made her want to stay right where she was. In bed all day long.

Lazily she stretched, rolled over and inhaled deeply, followed by a slow release of air from her mouth. *Mmm, that's strange,* sniffing the air, *I smell a man's cologne... A man's cologne!*

Bolting up into a sitting position, throwing the covers off of her body, she shrieked, "Oh my God! Where are my clothes?"

To her horror, Starr was booty butt naked as the day she was born.

"Where are my clothes? Where are my clothes?" She nervously chanted as she leaped from the bed. Spotting her bra, panties, and denim dress haphazardly scattered in various areas on the floor, she nearly twisted her ankle as dizziness overtook her as she stumbled retrieving each discarded item.

Starr's body froze as her eyes widen in shock. The pouring rain came to an abrupt end. Not wasting another second, she hurriedly pulled her dress over her head and jetted out the door.

She ran as fast as her wobbly legs would carry her. There was a man her bathroom!

♥♥♥

Bang! Bang! Bang! ... Bang! Bang! Bang!

Untangling himself from the warmth of his wife's petite body, Nick hissed, "Who in the hell is banging on the door like that?

"I don't know," Summer sleepily purred as she rolled over, pulling a pillow over her head.

Yanking a pair of jeans from a nearby ottoman and pulling them on, he grumbled, "It's six-thirty in the damn morning. Whoever it is better not wake up those kids."

Taking long strides, he'd already made up in his mind whoever was at the door was about to get a good cussing out. As much as he adored his children, they were quite cranky and evil when sleep deprived. A trait they'd inherited from him.

Not bothering with looking through the peephole, snatching the door open, Nick growled, "What the—" His annoyance was cut short by the sight before him.

Hair sticking straight up in the air, smeared makeup, wrinkled dress, panties in one hand, bra in the other, and barefooted, stood Starr Avery. He had never seen such a beautiful woman look so unsightly. Starr was torn up from the floor up! She looked a hot mess!

Taken aback, Nick just stood there like an idiot staring at her wondering what in the world had happened to her.

Starr was the first to break the uncomfortable silence. Shifting from barefoot to barefoot, she stammered, "Um, Nick…is Summer here?"

He wanted to ask her where else would she be at six-thirty in the morning. Instead, he held his tongue. Stepping aside allowing her entry, he had to jump back as the unkempt blur darted pass him nearly trampling his bare toes. She didn't even give him a chance to respond to her question.

Leaping on the bed, she cried, "Summer…Summer, wake up. I need to talk to you."

Summer moaned, "Give me five more minutes." After a night of drinking white wine spritzers and then later happily indulging her husband, she was beyond exhausted. The man had the stamina of twenty year old.

Starr pulled the pillow from Summer's head and shook her more vigorously. "Come on, wake up. There's a man in my room and I don't know how he got there."

Starr nearly jumped out of her skin. And Summer was like the dead coming back to life at the sound of the deep, baritone roar coming from the doorway. "What the hell do you mean there's a man in your room and you don't know how he got there?"

Neither woman had been aware Nick was standing behind them overhearing Starr's tearful confession.

Starr covered her face with her hands and wept from pure embarrassment. Never in her adult life had anything like this happened to her. The last thing she remembered…*Oh, no, no, nooo.*

Wrapping her arms around her friend who was in apparent distress, Summer soothed, "It's okay, honey. Everything's going to be all right."

Shaking her head, sobbing even louder, "No, Summer, I think…I think…I did something stupid."

Becoming further irritated, Nick demanded, "I'm still waiting for an answer."

How in hell does she not know who's in her room? I know she has more sense than to have picked up some man off the street

Shooting her husband an evil glare, Summer snapped, "Why don't you go down there and see Nicholas!"

Nick clenched his jaw. Summer only called him by his full name when she was mad at him. How had his morning gotten off to such a terrible start? If they hadn't been interrupted, he probably would have eased himself between the warmth of her legs again, and rode her one last time before the kids woke up. *That's not going to happen...* That last thought made him throw his hands up in the air and bark, "maybe I will!"

"Well good! Go then!" His once timid wife barked back, rolling her eyes at him.

Crossing the room, huffing, he snatched his shirt from off the same ottoman his jeans earlier occupied. Throwing on the shirt and shoving his feet into a pair of casual loafers he threw over his shoulder as he left the room, "I'll be back."

Hearing the door slam, Starr apologized. "I'm so sorry. I got you and Nick fighting over me."

"Girl, don't pay him any mind. He'll get over it. Now tell me what happened."

Feeling embarrassed all over again, she admitted, "That's just it. I don't know. I can't remember everything."

"Well, tell me what you do remember. Maybe it'll come back to you."

"Okay."

Starr started with everything she could remember from the time they'd left each other the evening before.

After going back to her room, she had taken a shower and dressed for bed. Not really being all that tired she decided to watch some television. Everything on cable she had already seen. Instead of going up to Summer's room to hangout with her and Ava, she'd decided to go to the lounge for a drink. As of lately she just wasn't in the mood to be around anyone. It wasn't that she no longer cared for her friends. She just didn't want to bring them down. Nor was she in the mood to have them try and cheer her up. Nothing could cheer her up.

Sipping on Malibu and pineapple juice, her sadness became even deeper. Before she knew it, an hour had turned into two, that's when a friendly male voice asked if he could sit with her.

Everything after that became fuzzy and hazy. Things came in and out, in snapshots. Starr vaguely remembered going to a chapel watching a couple get married, then going to a lounge in another hotel, and then waking up booty butt naked in her bed.

At the end of her story, Summer's mouth hung wide open in disbelieve. Starr had always been the most leveled headed one. *Lord have mercy what in God's name did Starr do?*

"Don't look at me like that," Starr tearfully pleaded, attempting to keep the tears from falling again.

"I'm sorry, honey. I'm just a little shocked."

"I know. I shocked myself. I can't believe I did something like this."

Summer gently asked, "Did you sleep with him?" Just because she woke up naked in bed with a man in her bathroom didn't mean she had slept with him…right? She prayed that her friend hadn't. With all of her past failed relationships, Starr was determined to be celibate until she meant the man of her dreams, her future husband. It would be a crying shame to see years of being celibate go to waste if she'd slept with a man she picked up from God knows where, and in Vegas of all places.

She didn't even want to bring up getting tested for sexually transmitted diseases if she had slept with mystery man. It would have to wait until later, once Starr had gotten herself fully together.

Hunching her shoulders, she whispered, "I think so." This was so humiliating admitting to her best friend that over night she'd become a whore, a slut, a tramp. What would people think once this all got out. It was bad enough that her best friend and her husband knew.

"You think you did?" *Oh no, please no.*

With shame, Starr hung her head. "Yes. I'm a little sore," lifting her gaze to meet Summer's, she pointed, "down there."

Dropping her face into her hands, she shook her head from side to side. "What am I going to do?" She muffled out to her friend between her fingers.

This was heavy. One of the people she loved most in this world was hurting so bad she had acted out of character and irresponsible. And as a result, she may have to suffer some very harsh consequences. At a loss for eloquent words, she told Starr the plain truth. "I don't know. But we'll figure it out."

Chapter 9

He was wearing the carpet out, pacing back and forth, forth and back. Finally, he said, "Let me get this straight, because I'm not understanding something." He couldn't believe he was having this conversation. "You picked Starr up last night."

"Uh-huh."

"And she'd been drinking...so you brought her back to her room and banged her brains out," he gritted out between clenched teeth.

Kevin winced from Nick's accusing words and being pinned down by his menacing stare. It wasn't exactly like that. He was making it sound as if Kevin had taken advantage of her. As if he'd dragged her by the hair caveman style back to her hotel room.

"Come on Nick, man, that's not how it went down. I mean she wasn't that drunk. Hell, she knew what she was doing. She invited me here!" Kevin shouted in his defense. As a matter of fact, she was the one who had seduced him! But he wasn't about to tell Nick that. It wasn't any of his business.

Lifting a dark brow, "How in the hell do you explain her showing up at my front door reeking like a damn distillery? I almost got drunk just by standing within five feet of her."

Kevin chuckled. When he stumbled upon her, she had been teetering on that fine line between being tipsy and smashed. The more she drank the frisker she became. By the time they reached her room, she was tearing at his shirt and then his pants. Again defending himself, "Man, Starr wasn't drunk, just tipsy when I saw her down at the bar."

Losing his patience again, Nick snapped, "Tipsy, drunk, whatever! Dude, all I know is my wife is pissed at me and it's your fault!"

"My fault? How?" Kevin shouted, an incredulous scowl masking his handsome features.

"Yes! All your damn fault!" It wasn't even seven thirty in the morning yet and Nick had a headache. "Starr's up there crying, talkin' 'bout there's a man in her room. Summer's yelling at me, to come down her to check things out because her friend did something stupid like bringing a man back to her room. I ought to punch you dead square in the face! I told you stay away from her!"

Although Nick was pissed off, relief rushed through him when Kevin opened the door at his persistent pounding. At least Starr hadn't ended up with some skuzzy stranger she'd been rolling around with all night,

Kevin's jaw clenched. He didn't care that Nick had just threaten to physically harm him. He could hold his own if they'd ended up scraping. What had him incensed was that Nick had no right to pass judgment on Starr. "Man, don't call her stupid."

The flash of anger and snarling tone took Nick by surprise. He had never seen Kevin so protective over a woman. Maybe, just maybe his friend was interested. And not for just a one night stand.

"Whoa, dude, didn't mean to offend you." Nick said as he held up his hands up in surrender.

"Yeah…well, you did." Kevin mumbled under his breath, rolling his eyes.

Staring at his buddy it became difficult to maintain a straight face. *Oh snap! My man is sprung after one night! Daaayum!*

With that thought, Nick threw his head back as rumbling laughter began bubbling up from his gut escaping from his lips.

Releasing his clenched jaw, Kevin roared, "What's so damn funny?"

Still laughing, Nick teased, "You man! I mean, you spend one night with the girl and you're sprung like a mug! Man oh man! That must've been some good lovin'. I've never seen a woman have your nose so wide open."

Nick was so preoccupied with ribbing his buddy he hadn't paid attention to him stalking over to the dresser snatching a piece of paper from off the top of it. Nick's laughter came to a halt as the paper was shoved in his face.

Centimeters from his nose, Nick yanked the paper and glanced over it, his dark complexion ashen as he looked from the paper to Kevin. "What the hell have you gotten yourself into?"

Sitting on the foot of the bed, Kevin hung his head and rubbed his hands over the smooth baldness. Finally, after a few seconds he looked up at Nick. Not knowing how to say it any other way, he just calming stated the truth. "Me and Starr got married."

"But how…why…I don't understand," Nick all but sputtered out confused.

Shaking his head, Kevin admitted, "I don't know. I'm still trying to figure it out. We both were pretty lit by the time we stumbled into that little wedding chapel."

"You actually don't remember getting married?" Nick inquired, still perplexed by the whole situation.

"Man, I remember us coming back here. We started going at it hot and heavy. Next thing I know she was out cold. So I went to sleep." Taking a deep breath he continued, "When I woke this morning I thought I had dreamed everything until I found Starr curled up next to me sleeping. I didn't just want to get up and roll out on her. So I took a shower to try and clear my head. You know, figure out what the hell was going on. When I came out of the bathroom, she was gone and that thing in your hand was on the floor.

Shaking his head, Nick said, "That's some deep stuff, Dawson."

"Yeah, tell me about it." Kevin agreed as he stared emotionless at the piece of paper. *A wife…this can't be happening to me.*

Chapter 10

Philadelphia, Pennsylvania
Two Weeks Later

I...I...can do this. Yes, I can. Starr counseled herself as she picked up the phone and then put it down again for the fifth time.

She had been home for two weeks and was practically in hiding since leaving Vegas. What happens in Vegas stays in Vegas. Yeah right! As If! More like, what's done in the dark, will come to light! Starr had a husband to prove it!

Letting out a deep breath, she plopped down on her bed tucking her left foot beneath her. Staring at the cordless phone in her hand, she dialed the number again. She had no idea what she would say to him when he answered. She had been avoiding his calls all week long.

When Kevin showed up at Summer and Nick's suite that dreadful morning, she nearly dropped dead. She started hyperventilating when he produced a marriage certificate. "I don't want that!" she yelled shoving the document back into his hands. No one was surprised when she stormed out the door mumbling incoherently something about, "A seducing womanizing creep."

Embarrassment seeped from her at the memory of how she'd behaved. As angry as she was with him, he wasn't solely to be blamed. She realized she had to take and accept accountability for the role she played in this mess of a marriage. If she hadn't gone off by herself to the bar drinking like a lush, none of this would be taking place.

Every time she thought about how it could've been another man, one that got his kicks out of torturing women, and not Kevin she had wandered off with, her blood ran cold. As the old folks say, "God watches over babies and fools." That night she was a fool. By God's grace she wasn't laying in some morgue tagged a Jane Doe.

The sexy male voice on the answering machine startled Starr from her musing. "Can't get to the phone right now so drop me a line and I'll holla at you later." Beeeep.

"Um…Um…Kevin this is Starr."

Before she could continue her shaky message, the call was picked up.

"Hello, Starr?"

"What are you doing? Screening your calls?" Starr questioned, irritation lacing her words. She hated when people let you begin to leave a message and then picked up the phone. Why didn't the idiots just either answer the phone in the first place or just let you leave a message?

"Well, yeah, something like that," he answered truthfully. He'd been waiting for her to return his calls.

"Thought I was one of your little girlfriends?" Starr accused, her voice no longer shaky, but dripping with sarcasm.

Baby if you only knew the half of it. Over the last few months, a dozen or more past bed buddies were blowing up his home and cell phones. Some claimed to be calling only to say, "Hey, haven't heard from you in awhile." While others boldly inquired, "When can we hook up again?"

None of the calls interested him. His mind was preoccupied with other things. Between putting in long hours at Dawson Investments and getting Starr to talk to him for half a minute, he had no desire to reconnect with any of his former lady friends.

Every previous bed buddy graciously accepted the brush off with the exception of Trina. The girl had the tenacity of a bulldog. He tried giving her the brush off several weeks ago with the excuse of working long hours. Being the gentleman he was, he didn't want to hurt her feelings by telling her there was no hope of them ever hooking back up again. He'd thought if he ignored her, she would go away. That wasn't the case. The calls kept coming.

Each call Kevin deleted before she could get into her seductive purring. If he had succumbed and picked up the call, she would've start talking dirty working her voodoo. Before he could bat an eye, they'd be in bed rolling around, limbs tangled, and going at it like rabbits in heat.

Tempting as she may be, the truth was, Kevin was downright bored with Trina. Their relationship had run its course. Sure, in the beginning everything was cool. They had agreed to a no commitment, no strings, and a no exclusive arrangement. Friends with benefits. This arrangement worked well for the first two years of their on again, off again, three year arrangement. Some time during the third year, Trina began hinting at a *serious* relationship, which Kevin always laughed away. "You know I don't do serious."

Trina lacked ambition. In the three years he'd known her, she remained an entry-level administrative assistant—aka glorified secretary—at a Center City law firm. For the life of him, he could not understand why she refused to take advantage of the firm's tuition assistance program. On numerous occasions, her supervisor encouraged her to take courses towards a paralegal degree. He assured her there would be a position waiting for her once the course work was completed. When she shared this information with Kevin, he asked, "Why don't you take a few classes this coming semester then?"

Instead of taking a golden opportunity, utilizing it, she snapped, "I don't have time for college courses."

Trina's only interests were looking good and spending other men's money. Weekly hair, manicure and pedicure appointments were what she lived for. And whatever man she was dealing with at the time contributed to the "Trina Look Good Fund," including Kevin.

Kevin thought his ties to her were finally severed when she stepped off to date a professional athlete. Was he a basketball or football player? Who cares? All he cared was that she was out of his life, for good. This however, was short lived. Months later, she came crawling back singing the blues about how insufferable and arrogant the ball player had been.

This hadn't been the first time she'd gone off to be with another only to come crawling back. Usually when she did, Kevin would take her back. Not necessarily because he loved her or even deeply cared for her, but rather because she was passive and never *really* pressured him to make the relationship more than what it was. Even when she would start in with her *I want a serious relationship*, all he had to do was give her a look that said *stop tripping*. However, this go around was different.

He had no intentions on recycling her as a lover. His Trina days were done. Finished.

Several seconds ticked by without Kevin uttering a word. "Look, if you're busy I can talk to you later."

Snapping out of his reverie, he assured her, "No, I'm not busy."

"Good. Now are you going to answer my question?"

"What question?"

Sucking her teeth, she snapped, "Did you think I was one of your girlfriends calling?" Starr wasn't sure why, but she needed to know if there was anyone special in his life. After all, she had the right to know. *She* was his wife.

Kevin let out a nervous chuckle. "Naw baby, don't have any."

"Any what?" *That's right I'm playing dumb. I'm gonna make this playa sweat!*

"Girl, what you trying to do to me? Get me to confess to something?" Kevin chuckled. "If you are, then today is not your lucky day because I don't have a girlfriend. Haven't had one in a minute."

He heard the distinct sound of sucking teeth again as she mumbled, "Yeah, right. Probably have three in the closet and another two under the bed."

"What was that? I didn't hear you." Kevin couldn't contain the amusement his voice held. He heard every word she mumbled. *I can't believe she's jealous*. It tickled him that she was jealous of a woman who didn't exist.

"Nothing. Nothing at all." She didn't call him to play word games over the phone. Getting to the point, she asked, "What's up Kevin?"

Laying aside his playful bantering, he's tone became serious. "I think we need to sit down and talk."

Starr fell on her back, rolled over and buried her face into a pillow on her bed. *That voice*! It did strange things to her. Like make the hairs on the back of her neck stand at attention and sent shivers up and down her spine. She liked it better when he wasn't so serious. At least when he was playful she could come back at him with a quick, witty jab. But when he spoke like he was doing right now, soft words caresses every inch of her, her brain turned to mush. She couldn't put her finger on what it was about the man that belonged to the sensuous voice that pulled at something deep in her soul.

Stifling a moan, she unintelligently garbled, "We're talking now."

"Not good enough, Starr."

He was right. They hadn't even scratched the surface as to what needed discussing. From the firmness in his tone, a telephone conversation wouldn't do. He was demanding a face to face.

"Okay. You're right. Do you want to meet somewhere so we can do this thing? *I've made this mess, now I've got to clean it up. No use in avoiding the inevitable,* she chastised herself as she grounded her left eye with the heel of her fist.

"Name the place and time, I'll be there." Not wanting to put any unnecessary pressure on her, he gave her control of the location and when they would meet. He would play by her rules if it meant sorting out their future.

Wanting to make this as painless as possible, she decided upon the most logical place, her home. If anything went down she didn't like or wasn't comfortable with, she could always ask him to leave.

"You could come over here." She whispered holding her breath waiting for his response. Even though he told her she could pick the location, what if he didn't want it to be her home? After all, he might feel like he's at a disadvantage.

"Cool. When?" The last place he thought she would agree to meet would be her home. This, however, pleased him. He would take this opportunity to observe how she was on home turf. He wanted to see her in her element. Most people tend to be their authentic selves in a comfortable environment. With what they were about to deal with they both needed to lay their cards on the table and be completely honest with one another. Kevin was ready to be honest. He wondered if Starr was.

"How about Thursday around seven?"

"Sounds like a plan."

"Great. I'll see you then."

Immediately after ending the call, Starr called an emergency gathering with her posse. What was she thinking? Thursday was the day after tomorrow!

Chapter 11

On cue, the posse fell in one by one like dominos as they entered Starr's townhouse. After exchanging greetings and pleasantries, Karen, Ava, and Summer took a seat at the small table in the kitchen.

"Anybody want some tea?" Starr offered.

"Nope. Come on, sit down and tell us what's going on," Karen urged, only how a big sister could as she nodded to the empty chair at the table.

Taking a seat, she felt three pairs of eyes boring into her with interest. They each looked as if they were waiting to hear some top-secret information.

Nervousness made her giggle. "Y'all stop looking at me like that. I just need to run something by you guys and didn't feel like having to repeat myself three times."

No one mumbled a word. They continued silently gazing waiting for her to get down to the issue at hand. Whatever that might be.

Taking another sweeping glance, their facial expressions screamed, "Come on already and spit it out!" Starr always had a flair for being on the dramatic side.

Reading their body language she rushed out, "I have a date with Kevin on Thursday."

Back on speaking terms, after coming to a mutual understanding that their friendship wasn't worth losing over words spoken out of misunderstanding and frustration, Ava was the first to comment.

"A date?"

"Uh-uh. Well, not really a date," she mumbled, checking under her fingernails for dirt that didn't exist.

"Baby sis, is it a date or not?"

Running her fingers through her freshly trimmed hair, she let out a sigh. "We're getting together to talk about this whole shame of a marriage."

"Do you think he wants to get it annulled?" Summer questioned as she got up going to the sink filling the teakettle with water. This was going to be a long night. Cups of nice steaming tea were in order.

"Hey, I thought you didn't want tea, Miss Thing."

Though Starr had been talking to Summer, it was Karen who teased, "It's Mrs. Thing to you. Stop stalling and answer the question, Mrs. Dawson."

Turning to Ava with a pitiful look, she pleaded, "Don't let these heifers gang up on me."

Ava laughed. "You might as well include me in the number. I'm heifer number three. Now answer the question."

She, too, wondered if that's what Kevin had in mind, an annulment. Why else was he blowing up her phone every day, leaving messages saying they needed to talk? Not realizing how sad she sounded, she truthfully admitted, "I think that's what he wants to talk about. I just don't see him as the marrying type anyway."

Trying to invite some optimism into the atmosphere, Ava suggested, "Maybe that's not it at all. You never know, he just might surprise you."

"Then what else could it be? Y'all know I love Kevin. He's Nick's best friend and godfather to my children. But him, married…I have to agree with you Starr, I don't think so." Sucking her teeth, she went further to say, "Shoot, we all know that man changes women quicker than he changes his drawers."

Karen felt bad for her sister. She didn't miss how she cringed from Summer's blunt, yet truthful assessment of Kevin. But she had never lied to her, and she wasn't about to now, even if it meant hurting her feelings. "I don't know him that well, but from what you guys say about him it doesn't seem like he's ready to settle down. Men like him rarely, if ever, settle down with one woman."

With regret, even Ava had to cosign on what the others were saying. Everything that was said was the cold truth.

Kevin had had a long chain of women he dealt with over the years throughout the tri-state area. Listening to her sister and best friends comment on his womanizing ways, Starr felt like an idiot. She'd become another link in his chain. Another woman he would carelessly discard.

"Starr? Starr?" Karen gently called.

"Huh?"

"You okay, baby sis?"

"I'm all right. I was just thinking about something."

"About?" Ava asked as she got up taking mugs from the cabinet filling them with water from the whistling teakettle.

Joining Ava at the counter, dropping an herbal tea bag in each mug, Starr cried, "Look at my life! It's a mess! On top of already having drama, I had to go add drama on top of drama by getting pissy drunk and marrying the *Mack Daddy* of *Mack Daddies*! And to make matters worse, I wake up booty butt naked not knowing if I'd slept with *Mr. Mack Daddy*! How freakin' pathetic!"

The sympathizing young women tried to contain the giggles that were hopelessly escalating into robust laughter. After dropping the tea bags in the mugs, Starr in her normal dramatic flare imitated a pimp stroll with a bounce each time she spat out *Mack Daddy*. Explosions of laughter filled the confines of the small kitchen as the posse watched her perform.

Fuming she didn't understand what was so funny. Here she was pouring her heart out and they were laughing at her!

"What the heck is so funny?"

"You! That's who! Mack Daddy of all Mack Daddies! That is so played out!"

"Oh shut up, Karen! You get on my nerves!"

"And what's up with that little pimp bounce you got going on?" Ava ribbed, holding her stomach to keep it from bursting wide open from laughing so hard.

Fury curled her hands into tight fist as Summer snapped her fingers and sang, "Mmmm, Mack Daddy, Mack Daddy… mmmm, Mack Daddy, Mack Daddy."

More laughter bounced off the walls as Summer's petite body did the old school dance, the Whop, as she sang.

Oh, okay. I'll fix these little immature heifers. I'm trying to have a serious heart to heart about my sorry, pitiful life, and they got jokes.

Casually walking over to the sink, Starr turned on the cold water. Lifting the spray nozzle, she aimed her weapon… and fired! They never saw it coming. All clowning came to a screeching halt as laughter turned into screams and squeals.

The stampede of running feet in the direction of the narrow doorway, sounded like a heard of wild buffaloes. Starr sniggered at the comical sight of the women pushing, shoving, elbowing, and squeezing there way out of the space. Her kitchen would be a wet mess, but she didn't care. It felt good playing the childish prank on them.

Starr's face held a smug, satisfied smirk. *That'll teach them to mess with a Queen Bee in her own hive!*

Twenty minutes and three frizzy, wet heads later, Starr pleaded with the disgruntled young women. "Come on, y'all suppose to be my girls. Don't do me like this. I was only playing."

"Playing my foot! You got us looking like a bunch of wet rats!" Karen snapped, throwing her an evil glare as she touched her damp hair.

"Look, I said I was sorry."

"Okay, okay, we forgive you."

Summer rolled her eyes at Ava mumbling, "Speak for yourself, suck up. I just got my hair done today."

Ava roughly nudged Summer in her side with her elbow.

"Ow! Girl! Your boney elbow hurts!" Summer hissed.

"Whateva." Ignoring Summer, Ava shifted her hips to face Starr. She was given another chance to be there for her friend. This time around, she wouldn't mess up by saying something that was insensitive. If anything, she learned from her recent ordeal with Starr that ill spoken words hurt, and had the potential to kill a friendship. Getting back to the purpose of their meeting, she asked, "So what is it you really want?"

Hunching her shoulders, Starr didn't know what to tell them. Should she be completely honest and tell them she's been attracted to Kevin since NJ's christening? Should she tell them how he made her feel attractive, sexy and desirable? Something a man hadn't done in years. Or how being in his presence for that short period of time made her forget all about her worries, simply because he was there?

In spite of his womanizing ways, Starr was honest about her feelings for Kevin. If they didn't like it, that was their problem. She was grown and any decisions she made she ultimately had to live with them. "I really want to get to know him."

Taking a few deep breaths and counting to ten, Karen was trying to get her thoughts together. No way was Starr serious. Getting involved with Kevin was asking for trouble...big time. She had seen her sister go through enough heartache behind a man. "Starr, are you sure about this? What if—"

"What if what?" Starr interrupted a little on the unnerved side. She wasn't about to let Karen pull her big sister act on her.

Quickly wanting to diffuse the tension before it had a chance to build, Ava gently rested her hand on Starr's thigh. "Honey, please don't get upset. Your sister is only concerned for you, just as we are." She pleaded, shifting her gaze to Summer, who nodded her head in agreement.

"I appreciate your concern, really I do. But none of you know or understand what I'm going through." Turning an unshed tearful gaze to Karen and Summer, she pointedly accused, "Both of you have children." She let out a pent up of breath of frustration. "And Ava, you're always talking about you don't care one way or another if you ever have any."

Before she could go on, her sister challenged, "You're right. I don't understand how getting to know Kevin has anything to do with having a baby." Yes, her sister was grown and had a right to make her own decisions. But she could not, and would not, see her go back to that place after Marcus walked all over her, ruining her emotionally and financially.

Not able to hold the tears back that were stinging her eyes, Starr spoke straight from her heart. "Because Karen, when I'm with him he makes me forget just how messed up my life is. He makes me feel beautiful every time he looks at me like I'm the only woman in the room. He makes me laugh; something a man hasn't done in a longtime. And yes, he may be a womanizer, but if staying married to him and possibly getting my heart broken may be my only chance of becoming a mother, then I'm willing to take that risk." At least this time around, she'd have something of value from a broken heart. This time she wouldn't walk away empty and alone.

Each woman in the room felt the raw pain that seeped from Starr's soul. Circling her in an embrace, cocooned in love, each vowed their devoted and unwavering support. Each also prayed the journey would be one of healing and not desolation.

Chapter 12

Standing back, she studied her handiwork. Wanting to make a good impression, she dressed the table with a fleshly starched white linen tablecloth. White bone china trimmed in silver, polished silverware, crystal wine goblets, and long stemmed white candles held in sterling holders, beautifully adorned the table.

A small smile played at the corner of Starr's lips as she appreciated how elegant her table looked. If she didn't know any better, she'd swear she was standing in one of those posh five star restaurants in Center City.

"I ain't neva, I mean neva go through all this trouble for a man. Shoot, I got it lookin' like the Four Seasons up in here." She openly praised herself, proud of her domestic skills.

Earlier in the day, Starr had called her dinner date, *husband*, for suggestions on dinner. Rattling off a list of foods he enjoyed, which was everything, she was pleased he wasn't a finicky eater. When he mentioned seafood, she had the perfect meal in mind.

Buzz…Buzz

Hurrying from the dining room, Starr briefly stopped at the mirror hanging on the wall in the cozy vestibule. Checking her reflection, everything looked good, not a hair was out of place and what little makeup she had on was flawless.

Opening the door, she stared up at the gorgeous man towering over her. *Whew! Lord! Talk about weak in the knees! This man is too fine for his own good!*

Kevin was leisurely dressed in a navy short sleeve polo shirt, well-worn jeans, that weren't too baggy or too tight, and dark brown leather casual loafers. Her eyes lazily traveled the length of him. She appreciated how his broad shoulders and chest tapered into a slim waist that flowed into a pair of muscular, sturdy legs.

What have I gotten myself into again? Starr mused as she literally salivated.

"I brought this for dinner…Can I come in now?" Kevin requested as the corners of his mouth twitched halfway between a smirk and a smile. The unmistakable attraction that jumped off every time they were near each other was magnetizing. How could he not feel it? Starr was mouth watering in a soft pink, just above the knee sundress, hugging every luscious curve. As usual, the hair was fierce. He wondered what it would feel like between his fingers as he made love to her.

The extended muscular arm snapped Starr out of her momentary stupor. Reaching for the bottle of wine, she apologized. "Oh, I'm so sorry Kevin. I don't know where my manners are." Waving her free hand, beckoning him, she stepped aside to allow him entry. "Come on in."

The tight cozy confines of the vestibule made her head dizzy. The heat from his solid body and woodsy sent of his aftershave caused Starr to swoon as their bodies, breasts to chest almost made intimate contact as he walked past her the short distance into the living room.

Nice. Kevin surveyed his new surroundings. The walls throughout were painted soft beige, with the baseboards and crown molding painted in an off white. Each window was adorned with wood shutters the same off white color giving the space an exquisite, airy appearance.

The overstuffed pastel blue sofa and loveseat, decorated with cream and royal blue throw pillows, begged to be lounged in. Hardwood floors so highly polished, one could actually see their reflection. In front of the sofa was an antique cedar chest with a hand blown glass vase holding dry flowers as its centerpiece served as a coffee table.

Pointing with his eyes to Starr's fresh pedicure in the color of mauve, he asked, "Should I take off my shoes, too?" Some folks were funny about their flooring. He didn't want to offend her by walking on her beautiful hardwood floors with his shoes on.

Looking down, wiggling her toes, Starr giggled. "No, you don't have to. I just like walking barefoot whenever I can. Know what I mean?"

Kevin chuckled. "A woman after my own heart. I hate wearing shoes, too." Following suit he stepped out of his loafers explaining, "My momma said when I was a baby I used to take off my diaper and shoes every chance I got."

"Is that so?" She smiled lifting an arched brow as she moved towards the front door. "You can take off your shoes, but under no circumstance are you to remove your diaper."

"You-who! Starr! Starr!" Mrs. Virginia yelled waving her hands capturing her attention before she could close the door.

Sucking her teeth, *here we go.* Putting on a plastered smile, Starr waved. "Hi Mrs. Virginia, how are you?" Because the older woman was her elder, she was bound by duty to respect her. However, at times the elderly woman grated on Starr's last nerve.

"I'm good. I see you have company."

See what I mean?

Mrs. Virginia winked at Starr, making a poor attempt to whisper. The woman was so loud the entire block probably heard her raspy voice from all the years of smoking Winston's. "It's been a long time since you've had male company."

Mrs. Virginia was one nosy old biddy. Every time someone came to visit she had her head hanging out the screen door peeping. If it was someone she didn't recognize, she had the annoying habit of making some inappropriate, unsolicited remark… like she was doing right now.

An impish childishness came over Starr. Leaning out the front door, she loudly whispered imitating Mrs. Virginia's raspy voice. "He's not company. He's my husband."

The deer in the headlights gaze was priceless. Starr closed the door not giving the older woman time to recover. Once back on her square, the elderly woman would want to know when the marriage had taken place.

Kevin chuckled as Starr turned to face him. "Now why you shock that poor old woman like that?"

"What? I only told her the truth." Unconsciously, she demurely lowered her eyelids and softly whispered, "You are my husband. Aren't you?"

The sweetness of her voice along with the meaning of her words made Kevin want to take her right there, up against the wall. She was staking her claim. And for some reason the very thought of her sexy subtle possession didn't bother him a bit.

Starr's stomach did flip-flops as Kevin closed the distance and ever so gently lifted her chin with his forefinger. Leaning down, softly kissing her lips he huskily whispered, "That's what I've been told."

♥♥♥

Leaning back in his chair, content from a very full belly, Kevin easily mused, *I can get used to this.*

"Girl, I didn't know you could cook. You got a brotha wanting to come to dinner every night!"

He knew he was a little on the excited side, but dayum, not only was the girl super fine, she could cook her butt off. That was a major plus. Kevin was a connoisseur when it came to a good meal. The fresh Caesar salad, grilled lemon peppered mahi-mahi, sautéed asparagus, and penne pasta literally melted in his mouth. He could tell all the ingredients used were fresh, not frozen nor from a can or a jar. He was out done when she pulled his favorite dessert, a homemade banana pudding from the fridge. He was further amazed when she retrieved a pint of heavy cream from the fridge, confectionary sugar from the cupboard and commenced to whipping up a batch of fresh whipped cream.

Since meeting Starr, he had always liked her. What was not to like? She was beautiful, classy, and intelligent. She had moved up another notch in his book. The woman could not only cook, but could eat! He hated when women nibbled on lettuce and carrots during dinner, as their hungry stomachs protested by shouting angry growls. The fact she was comfortable eating in front of him was definitely a turn on.

Again, for the second time that evening she lowered her eyes from his penetrating gaze as she blushed from his compliment. "Thanks, I'm glad you enjoyed your dinner."

A sensation of pleasure flowed through her entire body. It had been such a long time since she truly enjoyed the company of a man, a *very* handsome man at that. Kevin was easy going, a great conversationalist, and comical in his own quirky way. With him, she was free and didn't feel the need to put on airs while in his presence, especially when it came to eating. Usually she was self-conscious while eating on a date. She always felt as if her dinner partner was counting every calorie she'd put in her mouth. As if they could see the pounds piling up on her hips and thighs. But not with Kevin, he didn't even flinch when she dug in for seconds. So what she wasn't a size two? She loved every curvy feminine inch of her well toned, size twelve sexy body. Thank you very much.

"Enjoyed it! Girl, I already told you I'm trying to be fed like this every night."

Giggling, Starr stood up and headed into the kitchen. "Come on fool and help me clear the table."

"Clear the table? Woman, I'm ready to kick back and chill. You know watch some cable while the wifey, that would be you, clean up," he leisurely teased as he folded his hands behind his head and crossed his feet at the ankles.

Like a flash of lightening, Starr was standing directly in front of the sexiest man she'd ever laid eyes on. Hands on her hips, head cocked to the side, "Say what?"

Looking up into her mocked scolding features, he further taunted, "You heard me little woman. The only thing missing are my six sons ripping and running all up in here."

"Six sons! How about six daughters climbing all over you putting ribbons and barrettes in your hair!" Quickly, she covered her mouth, holding back laughter. "Oops, my bad. I forgot you're just as bald as Mr. Clean!"

Without warning, Starr felt herself being pulled onto his lap. Strong muscular arms wrapped around her in an affectionate, crushing embrace as she felt the rumbling vibration from Kevin's chest as he laughed. "I see you got jokes."

Closing her eyes for a split second, she allowed herself to be absorbed in his embrace. In his arms, she felt as though the heavy weight she'd been carrying for weeks was no longer a burden. If she could stay right here forever, all would be well.

Starr let out a small sigh. As wonderful as this felt, she couldn't get her hopes up. Extracting herself, she stood, taking a step back. Playfully swatting him with the dishtowel, she ordered, "Yup, now come on and get to steppin' if you every plan on me cooking you another meal."

"A'ight lovely, I hear ya, I hear ya." Kevin chortled as he gathered the rest of the dishes and followed the hip swaying, sassy woman into the kitchen.

By Kevin's standards, this evening was getting better by the minute. From the moment he entered her home, Starr had been at ease with him. From the gentle kiss he gave her, to the easy flowing conversation, and now their playful bantering was only making his decision about their future that much easier. He knew what direction he wanted to take the relationship. But was Starr willing to follow along?

Chapter 13

The moment of truth was demanding to be heard. All night long, the couple tipped toed, danced around and skirted the issue at hand. Nervously Starr sat on the loveseat, her bottom lip tucked between her teeth as she stared at her hands neatly folded in her lap. Earlier in the day she'd hyped herself up to believe she was ready to handle Kevin, now she wasn't so sure. What if he didn't take what she was willing to give?

"What's the matter, Starr?"

The deep, sexy hypnotic drawl of his voice made her shiver. "Just a little on the nervous side that's all," she honestly admitted as she nibbled at her lip between her teeth.

"You want me to get you another glass of wine?"

Vigorously shaking her head, she declined. "Uh-uh, no thanks, I'm fine." *Last time I had drinks with you I ended up butt naked. Or did you forget?*

Kevin chuckled. All during the meal, she nursed one glass of wine. It was apparent she was being extremely careful with her alcohol consumption. "It might help you relax."

"No, I just want to get this talk over and done with."

Squeezing her eyes shut, she wanted to kick herself. She didn't mean to come off like that, didn't mean to sound as if this whole situation was trivial or insignificant. When she opened her eyes and saw the muscle in his jaw tighten, immediately she went into damage control mode.

"I mean…I'm just as anxious to see what your thoughts are since we haven't had a chance to discuss everything until now."

For a minute, he thought he would have to set her straight. He had been more than patient letting her set the pace. He had no intentions on being dismissed by her. The irritation that began to creep up his neck settling in his jaw quickly dissipated as she began to back pedal, explaining her curt response.

"Well then let's stop beating around the bush and get to why—"

Starr wanted to scream, "Darn it!" *Why was his cell phone ringing? Let it roll over to voicemail!*

Pulling the phone off his hip, he gave a quick glance at the display. "I'm sorry, I need to get this."

I don't believe this crap! Starr silently fumed as she listened to the one sided conversation.

"Hey, yourself," he said as his face lit it up like morning sunshine. There was a silent pause before he said, "Uh-uh, uh-uh, I'll take care of that first thing tomorrow." He became silent again as he intently listened to the caller on the other end.

Crossing her arms over her chest, she wondered whom in the world he could be talking to. His focus was totally on whoever the caller was. An emotion as old as time snaked its way around her as she sat rooted in place on the loveseat. Not wanting to believe what she was feeling, she pushed the emotion as far away as possible as she continued to intently listen to him talk.

"I understand, yes." Another brief pause followed and he mouthed the words, "I'm sorry" to Starr as she locked her gaze on him. Nodding his head as if the caller on the other end could see him he said, "Okay, I'll be over sometime tomorrow afternoon." A small curved his lips before saying, "Back at you. See you tomorrow."

Ending the call, Kevin turned the phone off before placing it back on his hip. "Now where were we?"

You should have done that the first time. "If you need to leave we can do this some other time."

Kevin didn't miss the coolness of her tone. Nor was he unaware of her change in body language as she pointedly stared at him as he talked on the cell phone. He was certain she'd believed it was another woman, probably an ex or worse a current lover. "No, it's okay. It's getting pretty late. Momma should be going to bed soon."

Her mouth formed into a perfect circle as she said, "Oh" barely above a whisper. Inwardly she groaned, *His momma. I feel like a fool.*

He choked back the laugh that wanted to free itself deep from within his chest. He had been correct in assuming she believed he was talking to another woman. "No, we're going to do this now. We've put this off long enough. Don't you think?"

She nodded her head in agreement. She was letting her insecurities get the best of her. Having been involved with a man like Marcus had left a sour taste in her mouth. Never again would she allow another man to mistreat her. Young, naïve, and in love she fell for every lie he had told her to conceal his philandering ways. But now she was older, wiser. Just because she was willing to take a chance to get what she wanted, didn't mean she would tolerate being mistreated again. *There's always the sperm bank.*

"Hey?" No longer did he feel the urge to laugh as he witnessed sadness weave its way around her shoulders causing them to slump as she securely wrap her arms around her body.

"Hmm?" She answered softly, too embarrassed to say anything that might put her foot in her mouth again. Kevin had been nothing but kind to her and patient with her. He was not Marcus. So why was she treating him like it?

"Come over here," he commanded in a deep sexy whisper making her heart thump in her chest as he motioned for her to sit next to him. Slowly she stood, crossing the short distance taking small steps in his direction.

Kevin's dark eyes followed her every movement. She was simply gorgeous. He wanted nothing more than to touch every sexy, curvy inch of her. He dreamt about it every night.

When she sat on the farthest corner of the sofa, he reached over and grabbed her soft, delicate hand. "Baby, come closer."

From the moment their hands touched, she felt flames of sensual heat begin a slow kindling in the pit of her stomach. The smooth, sultry timber of his deep voice drew her without hesitation as she sat next to him, their bodies so close they appeared to be conjoined. Just when Starr thought their contact couldn't get any more intimate, Kevin intertwined his fingers with her then gently laid them on her lap.

"So Mrs. Dawson, where do we go from here?"

Straight to the bedroom! How did he expect her to think, let alone string together a coherent sentence? Especially when he was so close, she could feel heat radiating from every pore in his body. All she could think was *How would those big hands feel touching me all over? How would his lips feel kissing me all over?*

Nervously she licked her bottom lip. All last night she rehearsed in her mind what she would say when this moment came. She had pumped herself up thinking, *Girl, just tell him what you want. What do you have to lose?*

It all seemed so easy last night when she was alone. But now that this hunk of a man was so close, his full attention captivated, she was punking out like a sissy. *I can't do this. He's going to think I'm crazy.* Panic pricked at her as she suddenly felt as if she had everything to lose.

Gently she disengaged her fingers from his as she slid a few inches away. She didn't want to be holding his hand when he laughed in her face. What made her think she could get a man like Kevin Dawson to stop his skirt chasing and father a couple of babies?

Maybe he had been a little too aggressive when he suggested she sit next to him. When she pulled away, his immediate reaction had been to pull her back. However, he did not want to push her, she would come to him when she was ready. He wouldn't take her any other way.

"Are you going to talk to me?"

Letting out a deep breath, she confessed, "I was hoping we could get to know each other better. You know become friends."

A smile curved the ends of Kevin's sexy full lips. "So now you want to be my friend?"

Starr couldn't help but to laugh. The second the words left her lips, she immediately remembered their conversation that day in Macy's.

"Yes, I want us to be friends." She confirmed as her lips twitched from the smile taking shape.

"Not just associates?" he teased lifting a thick brow.

Taking one of the decorative throw pillows Starr swatted Kevin across the chest. "Stop making fun of me. I'm serious."

Kevin gave an exaggerated groan as if he was hurt. "Come on baby, you have to admit you walked dead smack into that one."

Dropping her face into her hands, she moaned, "I know, I know."

Rubbing her back in a soothing circular motion, "I'm just messing with you. If that's what you want we can be friends." *For now that is. I plan on being much more than your friend.*

Setting herself upright, she turned until she was fully facing Kevin. He was beautiful. Other men she dated were good looking, but Kevin was a Greek god, a Black Adonis. She always thought he was handsome from afar. However, being invited into his personal space was something entirely different. It was as if she was seeing him for the first time, seeing his gentleness, his kindness. And she liked what she was seeing. And *wanted* what she was seeing.

Kevin had always been attracted to her, but never acted on it. He'd told himself he never pursued her because of Nick's repeated warnings. However, as he sat close to her he knew that was just a lame excuse. He was his own man and didn't have to answer to anyone. Now he could admit the reason was because Starr wasn't like his other flings. Every man put women into two categories. The ones you bed and the ones you wed. She was definitely the latter.

In all his years of dating, he never went into a relationship with the consideration of marriage. Now here he was married to a woman with whom he never had a relationship. Talk about putting the cart before the horse.

"Now that we're friends what are we going to do about our marital status?"

His handsome face was unreadable as she gazed at him. Should she tell him everything? Tell him that he may be her last hope for happiness? Would she scare him off if she were completely honest with him? The last thing she wanted was to deceive him in any way. The good Lord in heaven knows she did not want to go through the same hell Summer had gone through with Nick because he'd thought she had purposely gotten pregnant. Although she felt this in her heart, she wasn't ready to confess why he possibly held the key to her happiness.

"Honestly, I want to know if there is a reason why we've ended up where we are. I know the circumstance under which we were married is crazy." Starr gave a nervous giggle as she admitted, "I've never done anything so ridiculous in my life... then again I've never been that drunk before."

Listening to Starr Kevin's mind ran a million miles per second. Was she saying what he thought? If he was interpreting her correctly, she wanted what he wanted.

"Are you saying you don't want an annulment?"

Lowering her eyes from his penetrating gaze, she did not want to have to look him in the face when he rejected her. When she spoke, her voice came out in a soft quiver. "Yes, that's what I'm saying, unless you want one. If you do then I'll agree to it. I'll understand."

Kevin did not expect the overwhelming feeling to comfort her to rush in and overtake him. Something in her quivering voice squeezed at his heart. The heavy sadness resurfaced, claiming a hold of her again. An invisible cord drew him to her. It was as if she needed him as a lifeline. She was sinking, drowning, but he didn't know why. Nor did he know what he could do to save her right at that moment. In his heart, he pledged *Baby, I'm gonna save you. I won't let you drown.*

Without thinking, he reached for her. Pulling her onto his lap, he protectively wrapped his strong arms around her. He did not have to question if he had been too aggressive this time as she laid her hand on the center of his chest and rested her head in the crook of his neck.

"Sweetheart, if you want to see where this goes I'm willing to do the same."

"Are you sure? There is so much I need—"

Before she could finish her confession, he silenced her by putting a finger to her lips. She wanted to be honest and upfront about her medical condition. It was only fair that she tell him if she did not become pregnant within the next year or so her dream of becoming a mother would possibly be lost forever. What if he really did want children and she couldn't have them? Then what?

He truly hadn't understood the weight of his words. If only he knew she had a burning desire to oblige him, gladly giving him the six sons he teased her about earlier. Doing so would fulfill her deepest longing. This man just didn't know.

"Shhh. I've made my decision, nothing you can say will change my mind. I want this too. We can take our time. I don't need you to tell me everything about yourself in one night. I'm looking forward to getting to know you, okay."

"Okay."

A feeling of contentment enveloped Starr as she sat nestled in Kevin's lap. She could stay right here in his arms forever. One day she would tell him of the heavy burden he lifted from her tired, bruised shoulders. Relief bathed her at the thought of not having to tell him about her condition just yet. If she had done so, she would have been an emotional mess. Besides, what she wanted now more than anything was to get to know her husband. *Husband...I really have a husband.*

"Are you all right?"

"Yeah, I was just thinking."

"About?"

Leaning back, Starr gazed up at Kevin giving him a dimpled smile. "I was just thinking how should we start this new friendship?"

Taking a finger, he traced the outline of her lips. "Like this."

Starr waited with bated breath, as Kevin lowered his mouth on top of hers. She let out a soft moan as he explored the warmth of her mouth before their tongues began a seductive dance. When they were both thoroughly satisfied, the kiss was broken.

Struggling to catch his ragged breathing, he hoarsely whispered, "How was that for the start of our new friendship?"

"I like. Do it again."

Chapter 14

"I'm going to wring her scrawny neck!" Kevin hissed angrily between clinched teeth taking thunderous steps towards her front door. Trina had gone too far this time. Not only was she harassing him all hours of the day and night with phone calls, pages, emails, and text messages. She had shamelessly taken to bothering his elderly mother.

He could ignore the pages, delete the emails, phone messages, and text messages. But the harassing calls regarding his whereabouts to his momma, he would most definitely address. She had really crossed the line. Kevin would have bolted out of Starr's place the minute his mother called if what they were discussing hadn't involved their future.

Once his mother assured him she was all right, just irritated because, "that floozy" had interrupted her while watching *Law & Order*, Kevin decided he would deal with Trina later. Later had come and he wouldn't wait until tomorrow, as he had told his mother.

Banging a large fist on the door, Kevin didn't care it was after one in the morning. Didn't care he had probably waken her neighbors. However, he did care that her constant stalking tactics had interfered with his evening. For a second, he'd thought Starr was about to kick him out of her house because he had answered his cell phone. Thank goodness her demeanor dwindled from being royally pissed to understanding, when she learned it was his momma calling.

"Hey, baby!" Trina squealed as she pulled the door open modeling a white ultra sheer teddy leaving nothing to the imagination. Her perfume so thick, it wafted around Kevin's head tickling his nostrils. She waited all night after calling his mean, old crabby mother. Trina knew the old bat was Kevin's Achilles tendon. If she continued her unrelenting phone calls to the elderly woman sooner or later, he would come. Now that he was here, she was going to pull out every trick in her bag to get Kevin back in her bed.

Rubbing his hand over his baldhead in frustration, Kevin let out a harsh breath. *I knew it! She did this crap on purpose!*

The very sight of her contorted his handsome facial features into a mask of disgust. What used to turn him suddenly irritated the hell out of him as he scowled at a scantily dressed Trina.

"Don't 'hey baby' me," he hissed.

Rolling her neck, smacking her lips, she huffed, "What's wrong with you?" He had a nerve to have an attitude. Didn't he see how good she looked? All the trouble she'd gone through to look good *just* for him?

Not wanting to further cause a scene, neighbors were peeking out their windows, Kevin pushed pass Trina causing her to jump back before he bulldozed her over.

"Don't play games with me, Trina."

The angry glint in his eyes was unmistakable. He was angry with her for troubling his elderly mother. Closing her eyes, she didn't want to see his anger. All she could visualize was the pleasure Kevin would bring her aching body. Even though she had hooked up with a new bed partner less than twenty-four hours ago her body still craved satisfaction. It craved Kevin. He was the one man who could make her purr like a well-stroked kitten. If she wanted to purr, she'd better think of something real quick to soothe his anger.

Opening her eyes, with the innocence of a five-year-old child, she stared wide-eye questioning, "What?"

Shaking his head, he couldn't believe how in the world he had ever gotten himself involved with this manipulating woman. The little devil on his left shoulder snickered, *Idiot...the mind-blowing sex. Go 'head man, hit it this one last time. You know you want to.*

If this had been a month ago, he would have given into the crafty, wicked voice in his head, but not tonight. There were about to be some monumental changes in his life, and Trina was not one of them.

"Don't give me that dumb look. Why are you calling my mother looking for me?" he snapped.

Covering her mouth with a dainty hand, she giggled, "Oh that." She waved her hand as if dismissing her actions. "I thought you'd be there since I haven't been able to get in touch with you." For added affect, she pouted, "I've missed you."

Moments lapsed before Kevin responded. Was she really that dense? How many times had he conveyed to her that he was no longer interested? That what they had was over?

"Look, Trina, I've told you as nice as I could that it's over. So you need to stop calling me." His voice dropped an octave as he coolly warned, "And my mother…don't you ever call her again…understand?"

Snatching her head back as if she'd been smacked across the face, Trina blinked back the tears. Why was he doing this? All the other times they broke up and saw other people they always ended up back together when those relationships fizzled out. What was so different this time?

No it can't be! Anger replaced hurt feelings. Crossing her arms over her chest, tapping her foot, she shot daggers at Kevin. "Who is *she?* Who's the little slut you're banging?" Trina screeched at the top of her lungs.

Before he realized it, he shot back, "None of your damn business! And you of all people should not be calling anyone a slut!"

She had some nerve. The girl was running neck and neck with Kevin when it came to the number of notches on her bedpost. Hell, he admitted he was a man whore.

Trina sucked in a dramatic breath as her hand flew to her chest. She couldn't believe he all but called her a slut.

Again, with the dramatics, she stomped to the front door and flung it open. "Get the hell out of my house!"

"Best damn thing I heard all night!" Kevin bellowed as he stormed pass her nearly knocking her over.

Trina was beside herself. This is not how she planned on her night ending. She knew calling his mother would get his attention. After hanging up with his mom she'd put her plan of seduction in motion. She showered, sprayed perfume all over her body, slipped into some sexy, daring lingerie and waited. She banked on the moment Kevin laid eyes on her, that all would be forgiven. From there she would lure him into her bed. How wrong she had been. Instead, the man had treated her as if she had active tuberculosis.

Not wanting to give him the satisfaction of having the last word, Trina ran outside down the walkway, not caring that she was practically naked, and yelled, "You...you...baldheaded jackass!"

She became even more furious as she watched Kevin's broad shoulders shake from laughing at her hysterics as he flipped his middle finger.

Tears streaming down her face, she swore, "I'm going to get you Kevin Dawson if it's the last thing I do."

Chapter 15

In nervous anticipation, Starr chewed the inside of her cheek. Kevin had called early this morning asking her to come with him to meet his mother. Though she was nervous, she was giddy knowing he wanted her to meet his mother.

Lowering her eyes, she inspected herself, making certain the short-sleeved lavender linen dress she wore wasn't too short. Slightly leaning over, she peeped at sandal-covered feet checking for any chips of nail polish on her manicured toes. Flipping the visor down, she next peered into the mirror searching for any wayward strands of hair. Growing up her mother had always drilled into her, "Always put your best foot forward when meeting someone for the first time." According her momma that included being properly dressed and making sure your hair was in place and not a nappy mess.

Keeping his eyes on the road, Kevin reached over and flipped the visor back up.

"Hey, I was using that," Starr said trying to suppress the irritation in her voice.

"Baby, you look fine. Stop worrying," he assured her as he took her hand in his and kissed it.

A surge of heat and chills shot through her at the same time from his moist lips making contact with her skin. Finding her voice, she wanted to know, "Who said I was worrying."

Chucking he answered, "You've been restless ever since you got in this car."

Starr let out a soft groan. "That obvious, huh?" Of course, she was nervous. After all, she was meeting her mother-in-law for the first time.

Kevin smiled. "Uh-huh. Don't worry, Momma's gonna love you. Trust me."

She wanted to tell him that the last time she trusted a man she ended up with her heart broken in a million and one pieces. "Easy for you to say. And how you know she's gonna like me?" She grumbled crossing her arms over her chest.

"Because she will," he assured as he brought her hand to his lips again, this time kissing her wrist at the pulse point.

"Oh...okay," Starr stammered as her heart rate increased from the sweet caress of his lips.

"I told you she would like you," Kevin whispered in Starr's ear as they sat snuggled on the sofa with a photo album on their laps.

Upon introductions, the petite, elderly Mrs. Dawson drew Starr to her bosom in a motherly embrace. "It's so nice to finally meet you."

Finally meet me. Starr hid her surprise as she returned the embrace. She wondered if Kevin had told her of their haphazard Vegas nuptials. No, Kevin would have told her. He wouldn't let her walk in there blind...would he?

All of Starr's stressing had been for naught. Mrs. Dawson made her feel welcomed from the moment she invited her into her home. She had been the perfect hostess. First offering, then insisting Starr joined her in a glass of iced tea and a slice of her award winning lemon cake.

Kevin playfully feigned jealousy. "What? I don't rate some tea and a slice of my Momma's worlds' best lemon cake?"

Starr's heart melted when the little lady placed a tiny hand on each side of his face pulling his forehead down to meet her lips. "Of course Momma's baby can have some tea and cake."

The tender sentiment between mother and son was what Starr longed for. She wanted a man to love her and give her a wonderful son like Kevin. Ava was right. Looking at Kevin and his mother, she didn't want her child to be fathered by some unknown donor. A wave of sadness washed over her as she painfully wondered if she would ever have either. Just because they decided to be *friends* didn't mean he had fully committed himself. *Lord, please, all I want is a good man to love me and give me a child.*

Sitting across from her youngest son and his new lady friend gave Beverly hope. She studied the couple as they looked at old baby pictures of Kevin and his older brother, Richard Jr. A faint, demure smile touched her lips as she nodded her silver head. *She's the one.* Beverly was observant of the way the younger woman's eyes sparkled and how her laughter came out melodious as she ooh'd and ahh'd over the baby pictures. She noticed how each time Starr lightly tapped her son on the knee before saying, "Oh, look at you. You were such a cute baby." Or "Aw, look how chubby you were." And when she broke out into a fit of giggles hugging the photo album to her chest with Kevin attempting to pry the album from her clutches, Beverly knew she had stumbled upon, *the picture.*

"Momma, I asked you, begged you to take that picture out." Kevin groaned in embarrassment, his caramel coloring turning a tinge of pink.

"Stop being a baby. It's an adorable picture," Starr teased.

"Let me see." Beverly said reaching for the photo album although she was aware of the picture, which brought her son embarrassment.

Sticking her tongue out at Kevin like a five-year-old, Starr tugged the album from his grasp and handed it to Beverly.

A fond smile curved her lips as she looked at the toddler in the picture. She remembered that warm, sunny afternoon like it was yesterday. The day was an Easter Sunday. The then three-year-old Kevin had become irritable dressed in the little three-piece navy blue suit and dress shoes. As Beverly talked with the Pastor's wife, Kevin had maneuvered out of her line of vision. Sitting down on the lush green manicured lawn, the toddler proceeded to remove every stitch of clothing. Everything. Richard Sr.'s deep rumbling baritone laughter caught his wife's attention causing her to spin around.

"Oh, my Lord! Richard, this is not funny! Put that camera down and get *your* son!" Beverly yelped as she watched in horror her baby boy running stark naked squealing in delight on the front lawn of the church as his daddy snapped picture after picture.

Starr threw her head back and laughed until tears came from her eyes as his mother recanted the story of that afternoon long ago. Even Kevin chuckled though he heard the same version of the story a hundred times or more.

"Oh, my. Look at the time," Beverly noted out loud, as she looked at her watch. "My quilting club will be coming over shortly." Turning to Starr, "Do you know how to quilt dear?"

Starr shook her head. "No ma'am."

"Well, maybe Kevin can bring you over the next time my club meets and I could teach you."

Starr felt honored Beverly was inviting her into her circle. "I would love for you to teach me how to make a quilt."

Saying their goodbyes at the door, the elderly woman hugged the younger woman. "It was a pleasure meeting you." Although Starr had just promised to come back to learn quilting, the older woman emphasized with a sincere smile, "Don't let this be your last time coming to see me."

"It won't be. I promise."

Gently squeezing his mother in a bear hug, "I'll call you later pretty lady."

"All right son." Before she released her hold, she whispered, "I like her. She's good for you son."

Watching the couple stroll hand in hand, Beverly whispered a prayer of thanksgiving. "Thank you, Lord. You have answered my prayers. Starr's the one. I know she is." Closing her door, she was confident by next year this time she would be a grandmother.

Chapter 16

"You two stop that running!" She yelled behind the tiny balls of energy making a path between the throngs of shoppers. Dodging in and out between the sea of people was making it almost impossible to keep her focus on them. The last thing she needed was for some crazy, sick pervert to be within close proximity lurking in the shadows. If anything happened to those kids, she would have to hop the first plane out of the country to hideout in a cave.

The energized toddlers obediently slowed their running to a slight jog at the sound of the stern, yet loving adult voice.

"Okay, Auntie Ava." The two cherub faces sang in unison as they returned the few feet they had gotten away from their auntie.

Smiling down at the beautiful pair, she stretched out her arms prompting them each to take a hand. Ava loved spending time with her godchildren, NJ and Autumn. When Summer expressed she needed to "get these kids out of my hair" so she could shop in peace for a party dress, Ava jumped at the chance.

Taking the kids to the food court in the King of Prussia Mall for ice cream was the perfect distraction to allow her the time she needed to find the perfect dress to wear to Kevin's big bash. He was throwing a huge party announcing the official launch of Dawson's Investments. And she couldn't do that with two very active toddlers underfoot. She was grateful when Ava volunteered, "You go ahead in Nordstrom's, and I'll take the guppies to get something to eat."

Summer raised a suspicious eyebrow at her sister-friend. Yes, she was grateful; however, she wasn't totally convinced she should trust her babies with Ava. It wasn't that she was afraid of them getting hurt while in her care. She was more afraid of Ava allowing them to get into mischief. You see, Ava found everything the spirited tots did hilarious.

She would never forget the last time she allowed her to baby sit. The evening started like any other evening, godmother and godchildren enjoying their special time together. Ava fed the kids dinner, bathed them, and the trio retired to the family room to watch a Disney movie. After the movie, she had taken the kids to their room to read them a bedtime story. Halfway though the story, the telephone in the other room began to ring. Leaving the children for no more than a minute to answer the phone, she heard Autumn's high-pitched screams. Thinking something awful had happened Ava dropped the phone as she ran back into the kids' room.

Autumn was beside herself as she screamed bloody murder. Whether it was curiosity or good old-fashioned meanness, Ava wasn't sure. All she knew was once she saw the scene in front of her she fell to the floor on her knees turning beet red from laughing so hard.

NJ dumped almost an entire container of baby powder all over his sister's head, and was in the process of christening himself, as he vigorously shook the remaining powder coating his dark, thick, silky locks.

Poor Autumn kept slipping and falling on the hardwood floors coated in the powder as she hysterically attempted to make her way to Auntie Ava for shelter from her impish brother.

"What?"

"You know what," Summer responded, still eying Ava suspiciously.

Attempting to appear dumbfounded, "Noooo, I don't know."

Nodding her head, "Yeeees, you do, Ava."

NJ and Autumn looked back and forth between Mommy and Auntie. Both were silent, as if their young minds tried to comprehend what was going on. Mommy looked a little upset. Auntie Ava looked as if she wanted to laugh.

Throwing up her hands in the air, she huffed, "Come on Summer that was last year. I didn't know NJ was gonna turn Autumn into Casper the Friendly Ghost."

Crossing her arms across her chest, she pointed out, "And what about two months ago?"

Nervously, Ava shifted from foot to foot. She did have to bring up that little incident. See, this is the reason why she didn't have any kids and didn't want any. Spending a few hours with them and then giving them back to their momma was just about all she could handle. Unconsciously, she shrugged her shoulders. How was she to know that after watching *Finding Nemo* the little self-proclaimed abolitionists would free the expensive, colorful exotic fish from their daddy's aquarium?

"You know Nick is still pissed about his fish," Summer snapped. She had to put up with hearing him grumble and complain about his dead tropical fish for two weeks. Finally, she had to tell him, "Get over it! They're only fish!"

Rolling her eyes toward the ceiling, "I know. I know…I said I was sorry a hundred times already." Did she have to hear how pissed Nick was every time this subject came up? She truly was sorry and grateful at the same time.

She was sorry the kids had gotten into the expensive aquarium. What was she supposed to do? She couldn't hold her pee all night long. After all, people did have a right to use the bathroom! She couldn't help it if her godchildren were inquisitive.

Grateful Nick hadn't taken her up on her offer to replace the two fish, which met their early demise, thanks to the itty-bitty freedom fighters. Why in the world would anyone pay two hundred dollars for one fish? Certainly not Ava. Sista, had bills to pay. Lucky for her, they hadn't gotten to the other exotic fish in the tank, which were twice as expensive as the others.

"Summer, I got this, I promise."

Taking her friend by the shoulders, she turned her in the direction of her destination. Gently giving her a nudge, she said, "You go find your dress. I won't let my little guppies out of my sight." For good measure, Ava crossed her heart and hoped to die.

Letting out a little chuckle, Summer stooped down to eye level with her with her babies. Giving a penetrating stare, she looked from one to the other. "NJ and Autumn, I want you to be good for Auntie Ava…okay."

Bobbing their heads up and down, they promised, "Okay Mommy, we'll be good."

The penetrating, *you better behave yourselves or else,* stare was replaced by a genteel smile. "Good. Now give Mommy some kisses."

Tiny arms encircled Summer's neck as wet kisses landed on her cheeks before she went off on the search to find the perfect party dress.

Snuggly holding onto each tiny hand, Ava made her way through the throng of shoppers. Now that her little cherubs had full tummies, off to Build-A-Bear they went.

Browsing the designer dresses, Summer felt as if someone was watching her. However, every time she'd look over her shoulder she didn't see anyone. Hunching slender shoulders, she turned her attention back to finding the perfect dress.

Veronica Taylor slowly eased from behind the mannequin that concealed her thin frame. She couldn't help herself. She had to get a better look at the petite woman her coworker Amy all but knocked her over to get to.

All the sales associates were aware of the women who came into the designer dress department dropping big bucks. Though Veronica had never seen this one before, it was obvious that she was a spender since Amy literally charged after her like a raging bull. It annoyed Veronica when she did that. For once, she would like to benefit from one of the extravagant shoppers. She too, could use a big, fat commission. The extra money would definitely come in handy since her daughter was now in high school. Like all fifteen-year- olds, Tanya wanted the latest fashions her classmates sported. Whenever Veronica offered to design something nice for her, Tanya's response would be, "Mom, I don't do homemade clothes." Or "I'd rather go to the thrift store and get last year's labels." Remarks like those cut deep. How could she tell her daughter if she hadn't been deceitful and greedy she could have potentially been a top designer?

As annoyed as she was with Amy, she was glad this one time she hadn't been aggressive, approaching the customer, and taking the young associate's sale. She stood glued to the floor as Amy greeted the woman. "Hi, Mrs. Stiles, how are you today?"

Mrs. Stiles. It can't be. She looks so young...so beautiful. Veronica thought as she wondered if the petite woman was Nick's wife. She had heard that after all these years he had settled down and married.

As she eyed the beautiful woman, Veronica's stomach began to churn. If only she had played her cards right it would be her shopping at Nordstrom's, instead of working here as a part-time, weekend sales associate. She should have kept her big mouth closed and not brag to her ex-boyfriend at the time she was pregnant. Telling him she was pregnant with Nick's baby had backfired. It hadn't taken long for him to calculate that he may be the father of her baby after their one night of sex.

Veronica had been angry with Nick because he had cancelled on her again. And to make matters worse, he was neglecting her in the bedroom. Business meetings and late nights at the office had consumed him. Weeks had gone by since they had been intimate. Feeling neglected, out of spite, Veronica agreed to have dinner with her ex. Several drinks later, accompanied by bad judgment, she ended up in bed with her former lover.

Not once did she feel any regret or remorse. In her heart, at the time she felt justified by her actions. It was only a one-time thing, which would never happen again, is what she'd told herself.

Her ex, however, felt differently. Losing her once to Nick was enough. Accepting his offer to dinner and then making love to him was all the encouragement he needed.

Everything blew up in her face when the former lover kept stopping by her place of business and incessantly calling her on the phone. She wanted him out of her life. She had everything going for her. She was pregnant with her wealthy boyfriend's baby and he had just given her a sizable amount of money to open her first boutique. He was even offering marriage and the house with the white picket fence. Becoming frustrated with her ex's advances she blurted out, "You need to stay away from me. I'm pregnant with Nick's baby." She even went as far as to boast, "And even if this baby isn't his, he'll never know it."

Her blabbing was the beginning of the end for her. The bottom fell out when the ex-lover went to Nick telling him everything and demanding a paternity test. Not only had he revealed the one-night-stand, he told Nick how she had confessed that once she got her business up and running, she had planned on ending the relationship. He enjoyed adding more salt to the wound as he went on to tell Nick how Veronica only stuck around for the right opportunity to hit him up for the money she needed to open her boutique. Her pregnancy had been that golden opportunity.

The joyful, squealing of a small child brought Veronica out of her miserable musing.

"Mommy, Mommy…Daddy's here, Daddy's here!"

Veronica further concealed herself, as she watched a little boy no more than four years old enthusiastically run to the woman, hugging her around the legs. Her heart pounded in her chest. The child was a carbon copy of the man from her past.

The little boy was eager to tell the woman, "Him has Autumn. She sleepy."

The petite woman giggled as she threaded her fingers through his dark, curly locks gently correcting the tot's grammar. "NJ, it's 'Daddy has Autumn and she's sleepy."

The child formed his mouth in a perfect circle as he said, "Oh."

Not far behind the boy were two attractive women making their way to the woman and child. The pretty cocoa colored one with the short sassy cut gave her friend a kiss on the cheek before hugging her. As this was taking place, the fair-skinned one playfully yanked the toddler from his mother's legs and began tickling him.

Ugly envy coursed through Veronica as she watched the three women laughing and giggling as *Mrs. Stiles* continued her search for that special dress. The way she took dress after dress off the rack made Veronica sick. The woman didn't even bother to check the price tag.

"Which one do you think Daddy will like?" She heard Summer ask her son. The little boy pointed to the Nicole Miller dress she held up in her left hand. "This one?"

Bobbing his head up and down, the child said, "Uh-huh." Leaning down, she kissed the toddler Eskimo style. "Thank you, little man." Wrinkling up his nose the little adorable boy giggled. "You welcome, Mommy."

Turning to the sales associate, Summer smiled. "I'll try these two on, Amy."

Grinning from ear to ear, the young associate beamed. She would make a nice commission. The Nicole Miller and Just

Cavalli dresses each were over six hundred dollars. "Okay, Mrs. Stiles, I'll show you to your dressing room."

Uh-oh. Veronica swallowed hard as the fair-skinned woman with shoulder length dark hair made her way behind the mannequin.

"Hi, do you work here?"

"Yes." Veronica replied nervously, mentally kicking herself for being nosy. After all these years, she needed to get over it. It was her own fault things hadn't worked out between her and Nick. "Can I help you with something?" Hopefully she'll want to buy a dress too and not question her as to why she was snooping behind a mannequin.

"Yeah, are you hiring?"

An uneasy expression crossed Veronica's features. Was this woman trying to be funny? If she was a friend of Nick's wife, she most likely did not need a job as a sales associate.

"I'm not sure…why do you ask?"

"My cousin needs a part-time job, she's in college. Could use the extra money. Know what I mean?"

Veronica sighed. She wasn't trying to be funny after all. Just as she was about to respond to Ava's explanation, Veronica sucked in a gasp of air.

Immediately Ava swung around to see what had elicited such a reaction. That's when she noticed Kevin and Nick entering the dress department. Turning her attention back to the sales associate, she watched as the woman eyes followed Nick. He was carrying Autumn as she slept in his arms. His point of destination being Summer as he spotted her coming out of the dressing room.

The woman sucked in another breath of air as Nick stood before Summer towering over her. Briefly, they gazed lovingly at one another before he leaned down and she stood on the tips of her toes, meeting for a tender kiss.

Ava's eyes traveled to the nametag on the woman's chest. *Veronica T.* "Oh snap," she whispered loud enough for Veronica to hear.

Veronica wanted to faint right there on the spot. The woman she was talking to knew who she was. Knew all about her history with Nick. She had assumed correctly. The young woman was Nick's wife. And the adorable little boy and sleeping girl were his children.

All eyes turned on her when Amy yelled, "Veronica, Mrs. Klein would like for you to bring her a size ten. She said you would know which dress she was talking about."

With as much dignity and courage as she could muster, Veronica quickly moved to the rack and removed the size ten dress.

She could feel everyone's gaze on her as she made her way past the small group on her way into the dressing room.

"Is that Veronica?" she heard Summer question Nick.

"Yeah…that's her," he answered his tone frigid.

"Nick, baby…don't be like that." The woman looked as if she'd seen better days. She appeared really tired, weary, and beaten up by life. Which was a shame because if one looked at her closely one would see that she had once been a beautiful woman.

"Yeah, whatever."

Sucking her teeth, shaking her head, she chastised, "Boy, you're so mean sometimes."

Chuckling, he said, "You just worry 'bout if I'm mean to you or not."

"Humph…been there, done that," Summer sarcastically drawled out as she took her purchase to the register.

Veronica leaned against the opposite side of the wall humiliated. She had heard everything her former lover and wife had said.

Chapter 17

"Dude, are you still pissed with that woman?" Kevin asked as they sat in the family room of Nick's home.

"Naw." Nick chuckled, shaking his head. Taking a long swig of his beer, he added, "I was just shocked seeing her after all these years." He often wondered what he would do if he ever ran into her. It didn't matter now. In hindsight, Veronica's betrayal was the best thing that happened to him. A faint smile twitched his full lips as his beautiful wife and children flashed across his mind.

"Yeah, that was a long time ago." Kevin agreed as he remembered how crushed his best friend had been. For months, Nick drowned his wounded heart and ego in the bottle. The only thing that snapped him out of his drunken stupor was the threat of his own company being taken over by corporate sharks. That was a very dark period of Nick's life; not many were privy to it, not even his wife.

"Yup, sixteen years," he said thoughtfully as he sat the beer bottle on an end table.

"Damn, Nick you're getting old," Kevin joked.

Chuckling, he came back with, "Punk, we're the same age."

Grinning, his buddy pointed out, "You're four months older than me. Therefore, you'll always be older."

"Yeah whatever, man." Changing the subject, he questioned, "So what's up with you and Starr?"

Over the last several weeks, Nick noticed the two were getting closer, spending all their free time together. Today when he showed up at the office with her, Nick decided he would just come out and ask what was going on. No one knew better than him Kevin's track record with women. Heck, in their early years they had chased tail all over the tri-state area together. Having this knowledge made him nervous. Like it or not, his best friend's sole interest in women had been to satisfy his carnal cravings. The last thing he wanted was to see Starr get hurt since she had become like family to him.

"Come on man; don't look at me like that." Kevin all but pleaded with his friend. He knew exactly what Nick was thinking. He was thinking Starr was just another woman to temporally keep his bed warm at night. However, that wasn't the case. Kevin really wanted to see if he could make a future with Starr.

Feeling the need to defend himself, Kevin firmly stated, "I am being careful where Starr's concerned."

Nick raised a questioning eyebrow. "Like?"

Here we go. Unconsciously, he rubbed his head. "Like, I cut those other women off."

Not believing it, Nick's gaze held skepticism. "Word?"

"Word."

Nick titled his head, appraising his lifelong friend. After marrying the woman of his heart's desire, he repeatedly assured Kevin that being committed to someone you loved was a thousand times more fulfilling than having a different flavor each month. Kevin would always chuckle telling him, "Man, they're too many flavors out there I've yet to sample." Now here he was telling him he was no longer interested in sampling.

"So you mean to tell me you've given up all your skirts... including Trina?"

As far as Nick was concerned, he should have given that one up a long time ago. The girl was touched. Damn near crazy. He would never forget the time she showed up at a dinner party wearing a dress so short and tight you could see everything. The flimsy cloth left nothing to the imagination. When Kevin discreetly led her outside and told her to take her inappropriately dressed behind home, she had the audacity to demand, "What's wrong with what I got on?" Yeah, the girl definitely had a few loose screws.

Kevin let out a harsh, tensed breath. "Especially Trina." Pausing to take a sip from his bottle, he filled Nick in on her latest fiasco. "You know she had the nerve to call my Moms, harassing her about my whereabouts?"

"What? I know Moms was mad as hell!"

"Man, you know it. She told me, 'you better tell that gal to stop calling here bothering me while I'm trying to watch my shows. She keep messing with me I'm a take my strap to her."

Both men cracked up as Kevin imitated his elderly mother. Beverly Dawson was no joke. On several occasions, as out of control teenagers Kevin and Nick were introduced to Beverly's leather strap. The most memorable was the time they staggered in way past curfew smelling like a brewery. They quickly sobered up when Beverly appeared out of the darkness swinging her strap landing blows all over their lanky frames. After whipping their behinds, she made them stand in the corner the rest of the night like a couple of pre-schoolers.

After reminiscing about their many escapades as wild teens, Kevin announced, "I took Starr to meet momma."

This is serious. His man had given up his skirts *and* taken Starr to meet his momma. *Maybe he is ready to settle down.*

"How'd it go?"

"Good. She liked Starr as soon as they met." Which he found surprising since his mother was usually a little on the reserved side when meeting any of his female acquaintances. Most likely, because she knew nothing serious would ever come of it.

"Did you tell her she was meeting her daughter-in-law?"

"Naw"

Nick lifted a dark brow. "Why?"

"We agreed not to tell her just yet. You know just in case things don't work out."

"So you guys are going to try to make this work?"

"That's what we're hoping."

Nick was speechless for a minute. This was the same man who swore he would never marry, but by a strange turn of events, he ended up married to a woman who had never given him the time of day.

Finding his voice, Nick held out his fist. "Word?"

Holding out his fist, making the motion to complete the brotherhood pound, Kevin confirmed, "Word."

"That's what's up." Nick broadly smiled, giving Kevin his blessings. If there was one thing he was sure of, it was that Kevin was a man of integrity. If he made a decision to build a life with Starr, he would do everything humanly possible to make it succeed.

Chapter 18

"Girl, I don't believe it! I had no idea that chick was *Veronica* when I was asking her about a job for my cousin Kimmy," Ava swore.

"Summer, you didn't see her while you were looking for a dress?" Starr asked from her position on the plush loveseat in the living room next to Ava.

"Chile, please. You know when I'm on a mission shopping I don't see a thing. But, I did have a strange feeling like someone was watching me."

"She probably was watching you. That Amy chick kept yelling, 'Mrs. Stiles this, Mrs. Stiles that.' She was driving me crazy."

Laughter bubbled from Starr and Summer at Ava's imitation of the over zealous sales girl. "It's a wonder if everyone in the darn store didn't know who you were."

A sad expression overcame Summer. "Mmm, I feel sorry for her."

Her friends looked at her like she was crazy out of her mind.

"What?" Ava said in disbelief.

"Summer, why do you feel bad for her?" Starr asked incredulously. As far as she was concerned, Veronica only had herself to blame for her demise. As much as Marcus had cheated on her and then blamed her because of his wandering, she had no sympathy for cheaters when they got caught.

"Because I do. That's a shame what Nick did to her," Summer softly mumbled with compassion. Though she loved her husband and forgave him, she never forgot how terrible he had treated her when he found out she was pregnant with their son. No one knew better than she how cruel Nick could be.

Ava got up and sat on the arm of the chair Summer was sitting in. Putting the back of her hand to her forehead, she checked her for a fever. Summer had to be feeling ill. "Honey, I know you have a soft heart. But because of that woman your life was a living hell once upon a time." Giving her friend a pointed look with dark brown eyes, she reminded her, "And she did do your man dirty."

"Real dirty. I'm talkin' dirty, dirty," Starr piped in. "How could she stoop so low as to try and put that baby off on Nick, knowing good and well he wasn't the daddy? Scandalous, just scandalous." Starr went on wrinkling up her nose in disgust.

Lifting a perfectly arched brow, Ava again reminded, "And don't forget not only did she cheat on your man, she swindled thousands of his dollars."

Rolling her eyes towards the ceiling she thought, *Do these two ever listen when pastor preaches on forgiveness?* Cutting another look at them, she could tell by their around the-way-girl facial expressions they were holding firm to their thoughts about Veronica. *Apparently, they don't listen.*

"Okay, okay, enough of ancient history. I want to know what the deal is with Miss Starr and Mr. Kevin."

Letting out a small sigh, Starr knew this moment would come. No longer could she hide the fact that over the last few weeks she and Kevin were practically joined at the hip during their free time.

Without much effort, a small smile touched her lips as she thought about Kevin. The man took to courting her the old-fashioned way and was doing a darn good job at it.

At first she believed they would every once in a while talk on the phone or go out. But surprisingly, Kevin had taken her out on several dates. None of which *she* had to pay for. He was incredibly thoughtful. Each morning he would call to wish her a good day and then, later in the evening follow up to see how her day had went. Having a man express this much interest in her at times was a little unsettling. Old demons would come out to play and taunt her. *He's going to use you too. You better get out while you can.*

Brushing those thoughts aside, Starr was grateful that Kevin had been the initiator, relieving her of the awkwardness of making the first move. Now it seems almost natural for her to pick up the phone in the middle of the day wanting to know from him, "How's it going?"

Her world had become somewhat less intense thanks to Kevin. Getting to know him had definitely helped her to focus on more positive things instead of on her health issue. The one thing she loved about Kevin was his ability to be carefree and spontaneous. She discovered this when he called her three weeks ago on her day off at six in the morning.

"Wake up sleepy head I need some company. Be ready in forty-five minutes. Put on some sweats and sneakers."

An hour later, Starr found herself doing laps on LaSalle University's outdoor track with Kevin. Exercising three days a week at the gym certainly made it possible for her to keep her pace. And it most definitely didn't hurt that she had been on the track team in high school and in college. The only running she did now was on a treadmill, which was no comparison to an outdoor track. It felt good actually hearing and feeling the pounding of her feet on the ground, as she inhaled crisp air into in her lungs.

Since that morning, they agreed to a standing date twice a week for an early morning run. It was during their runs they talked and learned tidbits of information about one another.

With all of her musing, she hadn't noticed the other two women in the room with her throwing and catching questioning looks between the two of them. Neither one of them missed the dreamy look glistening in her dark eyes.

"Well?" Ava pressed, now curious more than ever.

Downing playing her involvement with Kevin, she shrugged her shoulders, "Nothing much."

"What? Whateva, Starr," Summer drawled out rolling her eyes. "Every time I call you you're never home or you're on the phone with him."

"I know that's right. Why you being all secretive? Like you don't want us to know?" Ava fired, turning her head in Starr's direction squinting one eye.

Playfully sucking her teeth and grinning from ear to ear showing off her dimples, she denied it. "I'm not being secretive."

Throwing a plush throw pillow, hitting Starr square in the face, Summer agreed with Ava. "Yes, you are. Now tell us before I pinch you."

"Nooo, don't pinch me," Starr whined, crossing her arms shielding her deltoids. Summer had perfected the art of pinching from Nita Jackson, which really hurts! The last time Summer pinched her she was bruised and tender for days.

"All right! I'll tell you two nosy hags!" Starr cried out as Summer stood advancing towards her working her fingers in a killer pinching motion.

Nudging Starr, Summer demanded, "Move over." She wedged Starr between herself and Ava. *Let's see if she weasels out of this,* Summer thought with a smirk on her face.

Feeling trapped, Starr didn't know if she should look to the left or the right. Either way her gaze landed, her dark eyes would reveal what she wasn't quite ready to admit, even to herself. She was falling for Kevin. Big time. So instead, she focused straight ahead avoiding eye contact that would reveal what she felt for him. "Kevin and I have decided not to annul our marriage. We're going to give this marriage a try."

Her friends nodded their heads in understanding. Starr didn't have to spell it out for them. Kevin was the hope she needed.

"You guys getting it in?" The one friend questioned with an impish grin.

"Ava! Why you so nasty!" Starr shouted, fighting to hold back a smirk.

Summer burst out laughing from the blunt query. *Ava is crazy!* Not only had she asked the question she too was dying to know. She had stood up and started gyrating her abs and hips in a snake-like move identical to a seductive belly dancer.

Shaking her head, Ava said, "Uh-huh, I ain't nasty…I just want to know."

"Summer, stop laughing and make her stop. They might come in here," Starr hissed between clenched teeth. She would be mortified if the men came in here and saw them acting raunchy.

"Girl, they're in there drinking beer and watching sports. They aren't coming in here." Standing doing the booty bounce dance, Summer teased, "Is he tappin' it or what?"

"No," Starr mumbled barely above a whisper.

Simultaneously both women stopped moving. "Huh?" They chorused as a mask of confusion slipped over their features.

Speaking a tad bit louder, "I said no, we ain't gettin' it in, he ain't tappin' it, and we ain't knocking boots, humping or anything else," Starr declared as she crossed her arms over her chest.

Still confused, Summer asked, "Why not? You're married. You haven't had any in years. What's the hold up?"

"There's no hold up. We're just waiting." That's all she was giving them. They didn't need to know she still had some misgivings. Until she could be sure, Kevin was absolutely certain that this was what he wanted; she wasn't sharing his bed.

"Didn't you guys do it in Vegas?"

Starr shot Summer a look, which she shrugged off. The three of them were best friends. They knew just about everything about each other. Why wouldn't she tell Ava about Vegas? It wasn't like Starr had sworn her to secrecy.

Again, Starr mumbled, "No" under her breath.

"Huh?" The two sung in unison.

"Look a here, you two are getting on my nerves sounding like idiots with all of your 'huhs.' I said NO! We didn't actually sleep together," Starr snapped out in a clipped tone.

Neither Ava nor Summer paid Starr's snapping any attention. They wanted to get down to the nitty-gritty of the situation at hand. "Exactly what do you mean by '*we didn't actually sleep together*'? Either you did or you didn't," Ava boldly stated.

Embarrassed, she dropped her face in her hands." Mumbling through her fingers she confessed, "Kevin told me after I nearly tore his clothes from his body; I was so stinkin' drunk by the time he got me in bed I had passed out."

After learning this, he went up another notch in her book. He could have easily taken advantage of her while she was in a drunken stupor, but he hadn't. Well…not exactly. He did admit to getting about four good strokes off. However, his conscious and the fact she was stiff as a corpse wouldn't let him go on. He told her it gave him the creeps that she was out cold like that. She had laughed when he told her he checked her pulse to make sure she was still living and hadn't died from alcohol poisoning.

Both Ava and Summer looked sadly at her. They wondered if she had been so hurt by Marcus that she couldn't fully give herself to her husband. Or was it she feared Kevin would turn out to be like her father?

"Don't look so sad." Giving them a weak smile, she added, "I'm fine with how things are going between us." Although she had her misgivings, she knew to some degree Kevin cared. Every time he kissed her, caressed her, and held her close, she felt his tenderness in each and every action.

"I really want to get to know him before sex complicates things." Even though the words she spoke were true, Starr wanted more than anything to share his bed. He had made her feel like the most desirable woman in the world. The long walks in the park holding hands, the candle lit dinners he prepared for them at her place, the cute text messages he sent to her cell phone and the late night phone calls wishing her a good night all showed how much he cared. Now she wanted more. She wanted to be his wife in every since of the word. But would she be able to handle another disappointing love affair?

All joking and ribbing came to an end. Both women were silent as their dear friend spoke. Neither woman missed the longing in her eyes as she told them about her relationship with Kevin and everything he had come to mean to her.

Chapter 19

Envy and hatred simmered in Trina's bones as she sat in her darken car on the corner of Broad and Locust streets. It seemed as though everyone was in attendance to celebrate the official launching of Dawson's Investments.

The women were beautifully arrayed in their designer cocktail dresses and evening gowns; and the men were handsomely outfitted in designer tuxedos.

"I should be in there!" She hissed to herself as she watched well-wishers, clients, and potential clients' mill into the Bellevue. She wanted nothing more than to be one of the women on the arm of a handsome escort…preferably Kevin's arm.

She couldn't believe how Kevin was treating her. They had an understanding. He had always taken her back into his bed, but to her dismay, not this time. But why? What or whom had captured his attention? Or maybe had she gone too far this time confronting his elderly mother? *The old windbag,* Trina thought as she held a pair of binoculars to her eyes searching for her target.

As a sleek black limo pulled up to the entrance of the grand hotel to a complete stop, she squinted, straining her eyes to get a better look despite the aid of the binoculars. She held her breath as a long leg clad in black extended from the vehicle as the driver held the door open. She sucked her teeth in disgust when discovering the leg belonged to Nick. Within seconds, he was taking Summer's hand helping her to exit the luxury vehicle.

Slightly pulling the looking device from her face, rolling her eyes, she mumbled, "Freakin' Black Barbie and Ken. Make me sick. Just look at 'em." She despised Nick. He probably was the reason Kevin refused to see her anymore. That damn Nick always looked down his arrogant nose at her like she was gum stuck to the bottom of his Italian leather shoes. She really didn't despise Summer as much, just envied her. She wanted everything she had…well not everything. No way was she about to *purposely* make her perfectly shaped body fat and scarred with ugly stretch marks from carrying a couple of snot-nose brats for nine months. However, looking at Summer's petite, shapely body in her expensive black evening dress gave her cause to reconsider.

An evil smile curled her lips. *Maybe, just maybe, I can trick Kevin into getting me pregnant like Summer did Nick. Then he'll marry me too.*

That thought evaporated into thin air as she watched in horror as the occupants exit the following luxury vehicle that pulled up at the curb.

Kevin and Starr were oblivious to the woman jumping out of the car across the street. With the excitement of the evening and the normal hustle and bustle of Broad Street traffic, the vulgar ranting and raving of the wild woman on the other side of the street could not be heard.

Continuing her demented ranting, Trina stared on in rage as her grip tightened on the binoculars. Starr was affectionately straightening Kevin's bow tie. Standing back, she checked for balance. Trina cringed when a satisfied smile graced Starr's lips before standing on the tips of her toes placing a soft kiss on Kevin's lips. The ranting came to an eerie hush as she watched him take Starr's hand and bring it to his lips for a gentle kiss.

Uncontrollable anger shook her as she witnessed the open display of affection Kevin showed the beautiful woman. *He never kissed my hand like that!* "That no good bastard. So that's what he left me for. I swear he's going to be sorry." Trina punctuated every word as she seethed plotting her course of revenge.

Jumping behind the steering wheel, she sped off running a red light nearly colliding with the Town Car turning onto Broad Street.

The elderly woman in the backseat of the sedan managed to contain the frightening scream from erupting from her lips. Getting a good look at the car, fright was replaced by annoyance as she recognized the vehicle. She would tell Kevin about this later. Tonight was his night and she wouldn't let the likes of Trina ruin it.

Shaking her head only like a mother could, she fussed, *I told that boy to leave that strumpet alone.*

Chapter 20

Entering the grand ballroom, Beverly Dawson went in search of her youngest son. She had a mind to snatch him by the ear, pull him down to her level, and give him a piece of her mind. She had warned him that one day, running around with so many women was going to come back and bite him in the rump. The deep creases that had formed in her forehead softened and relaxed when she saw Starr at Kevin's side as he engaged in conversation with a business associate.

Now Starr was the kind of woman her son should be involved with. She carried herself like a lady. Tilting her head to the side studying the lovely young woman, Beverly could tell her mother had raised her well.

Looking up from her champagne flute, Starr's eyes connected with those of her mother-in-law. The younger woman smiled acknowledging the older woman's arrival. For an eighty-three year old, she was absolutely stunning. Dressed in a full-length silver gown and her hair in an up do style, she looked regal, like royalty.

Tapping Kevin on the arm, getting his attention, she whispered, "Honey, your mom is here." Excusing himself, he took Starr's hand in his as they made their way across the room. He was overjoyed to see his mother. It wasn't often that she was out this late in the evening. At this hour, she was getting settled for the night. When he invited his mother to the event, he didn't expect her to make it, which he would have understood.

Pulling his mother to his chest, he gave her a gentle squeeze. "Momma, you made it." Happiness settled in his heart as he held his mother close. Although this was a paramount night for him as he set out to make his mark on the world, a bit of sadness tugged at him. His brother Richard, Jr. and his wife were unable to make it. He knew their absence couldn't be prevented. Audrey's father had survived a massive stroke a week ago. His condition was unstable and she didn't want to leave his side. Kevin fully understood his brother's place was with wife. If the tables were turned, he would have done the same. There wasn't anything he wouldn't do for Starr if she needed him.

Beverly chuckled. "Of course I made it. Where else would I be? I'm so proud of you, baby. I wish your father could be here."

Gently he rocked his mother as he swallowed the lump in his throat. It was at times like this he missed his father terribly. Holding his mother close, he felt her loneliness. Ten years had gone by since his dad's death, yet his mother still mourned for her one and only true love. "I know Momma. I wish Daddy was here too."

Standing close by, Starr heard the tender exchange. Her heart ached for Kevin and his mother as they wished for their beloved family member. In all the weeks she'd spent getting to know Kevin, she had never seen such anguish in his eyes.

Momentarily closing her eyes, Starr fought the overwhelming need to comfort him. She wanted nothing more than to hold and console him until the hurt went away. Just the thought of being close to his solid muscled frame sent shivers down her spine. She envisioned tangled limbs intertwined in heated passion. She wanted to fan herself, but she didn't because it might cause the simmering flame within her to burst into a full alarm inferno.

Breaking the embrace, Beverly turned to Starr. Starr happily greeted the elderly woman whom she was so fond of with a kiss on the cheek before she was enveloped into the warmth of a motherly hug. "Hello dear. You look lovely."

Thank you, Mrs. Dawson, you look lovely as well." Stepping back, she reached for her mother-in-law's hand. "I love your gown."

Playfully rolling her eyes, she said, "Oh, this old thing. I forgot I had it hanging in the back of my closet."

Starr giggled. "Well, maybe I should come check out the back of your closet the next time I need a new dress."

"You're more than welcome to do so."

"Don't play with me Mrs. Dawson. I just might take you up on your offer."

"Anytime dear, just let me know when you're ready. And stop calling me Mrs. Dawson." Hesitating for a second, Beverly tilted her head as she closely inspected the young couple. They were made for each other. With the wink of a sparkling eye, she smiled sweetly at Starr. "Call me Momma."

"Okay," Starr consented as her voice trembled. She and Kevin shared a quick, nervous glance. The mere fact that his mother suggested such an intimate title made them wonder, *Does she know?*

Loudly clearing his throat, breaking the uneasy air surrounding them, teasingly he inquired, "Did you two forget I'm standing here?"

Releasing Starr's hand, his mother patted his clean-shaven jaw. "Son, I haven't seen this pretty young lady since you brought her to meet me over three weeks ago. I'm enjoying her company. Now you go on over there and talk to your business associates while I get to know Starr a little better."

Shaking his head, Kevin let out a chuckle. His mother had never shown this much interest in any of the women he dated. Giving Starr the, *Is it okay if I leave look,* he smiled when she gave a slight nod of her head. His smile further deepened when she looped her arm through Beverly's leading her to the non-alcoholic punch fountain. The two women walked off chatting as if they were two old friends.

Lingering in the spot where he stood, Kevin knew life couldn't get any better than this. The two most important women in his life adored each other. What more could a man ask for?

"I see somebody's momma likes you," Summer commented with a smile playing at her lips as she sipped sparkling water from a flute.

Returning the smile, Starr agreed. "She does. And I like her as well. You know I was a little nervous meeting her."

"Why?"

"Girl, you know how momma's are about their boys. They usually don't think no woman is right for them."

"Well, honey, you don't have a thing to worry about." Summer giggled, "She already got you and Kevin off and married with a house full of babies."

Summer knew this for a fact because Kevin was always complaining to her and Nick about how Beverly was getting on him about settling down and giving her some grandbabies before she's too old to enjoy them.

Starr's eyes sparkled as she laughed. The way things had been going with her and Kevin, the thought of them having their own Dawson Bunch was a welcomed possibility. Never before had a man treated her with so much respect and tenderness. As she spent more and more time with him, she wanted to tell him of her baby dilemma. Fear kept her from doing so. The last thing she wanted was for their budding relationship to become strained or worse, come to an end before it had a chance.

"Tell me about it. One out of two ain't bad. The only thing we have to get working on is the baby part."

Shock registered on her friend's face at her admission as she squealed, "You mean you two still haven't done it!"

"Ow!" Summer yelled as Starr yanked and then pulled her by the arm into a corner close by.

"Do you have to announce it to the entire world? I swear you can be so loud at times to be so tiny," Starr hissed between clenched teeth. It's a good thing Ava had agreed to baby sit so Joan and Henry could attend the launch party. Otherwise, she would have two big mouths to deal with.

Rubbing the soreness from her arm, Summer apologized. "My bad. I just thought…you know."

"Drop it Summer, okay."

She was not about to discuss her sex life. Not even with her best friend. When she did do *it*, of course they would have their usual pow-wow. But until then Starr wanted the inquiries to stop. She would sleep with her husband when she was good and ready.

Just as the thought was fleeting through her head, she and Kevin made eye contact from where he stood across the room. Starr let out an agonizing groan of want and need as her eyes locked with his. She almost became undone when he gave her the sexiest smile and winked at her causing her to blush like a giddy teenager.

Oh, yeah…she was ready. Every time the man kissed or caressed her, she nearly went up in flames. She could not take another night of rolling around in the bed stuffing pillows between her knees and counting sheep to help her fall asleep.

"Okay, don't get all tissy with me Missy!" Summer snapped back playfully nudging her friend.

Feeling bad for talking rough to her friend, she hugged her and apologized. "I'm sorry Boo. I didn't mean to get like that.

Summer hugged her back. "No, girl, don't apologize. You have a right to tell me to mind my business."

"Oh, girl, it's not like that. You know I'm gonna tell you and Av when I get me a little somethin'-somethin'."

As they both giggled, Summer threatened, "You better tell us."

"Speaking of Ava, I wish she would've come tonight."

"I know, but she insisted on babysitting the kids. I don't know what's getting into her lately?"

Concerned, Starr questioned, "What do you mean?"

"It's like all of a sudden she's become attached to the kids, especially Autumn."

"Hmm, now that you say it, lately she's always taking them somewhere."

"I know," Summer said thoughtfully. Every weekend she had asked to do some activity with the kids.

Before the conversation could go any further, Starr said, "Our men are over there giving us the eye."

Slowly Summer looked over her shoulder, smiled and wiggled her fingertips in a wave at their husbands. She turned back around. "Come on let's go get our men." Knitting her brows together, she quipped, "Because that barracuda in the red dress keep circling your man."

"I saw her earlier, but I wasn't worried." Starr chuckled as she thought about her mother-in-law. "Momma has my back." Every time a female swooped in to make a play on Kevin Beverly somehow managed to block the swarming buzzard.

As they made their way over to their men, Summer agreed with her. "Yeah I saw how Mrs. Dawson shooed her and the others away. Girl, you in like Flynn. That Momma eagle ain't letting nobody come between you and her baby."

"Think so?" Starr asked wanting to believe her friend's observation.

"Girl, please, she was ready to take a heifer down."

Starr threw her head back and laughed. Summer was right. If Momma wasn't politely asking Kevin to get her a drink, she was whisking him off to meet a potential client. She and Summer snickered as they watched her discreetly feed her drinks to the nearby lush green planters. When she discovered she had been caught, she winked at the two younger women. "A mother's work is never done."

Advancing closer, Summer mused, *Girl, you're drought's about to end tonight,* as she peeped Kevin's seductive gaze roam over Starr. His gaze was bold and daring. *Yup, you in trouble girlfriend.*

"Why you got that simple smirk on your face, Summer?"

She sang in a singsong voice, "Nothing…oh nothing. Have yourself a good

night. I know I will."

Chapter 21

The tree-lined street nestled in West Mt. Airy rested in the tranquility of quiet darkness. The late night end of summer breeze aroused tiny goose bumps up and down Starr's arms. Excitement and fear coiled through her innermost parts as she put one foot in front of the other. She had agreed to this, and had even packed an overnight bag with enough toiletries and clothes for two days. So why was she now having doubts? Maybe it was because five years had gone by since she'd been intimate with a man. True, she wasn't a virgin; however, it had been a long time since she had been intimate with anyone.

Each day she prolonged *truly* consummating her marriage made her want Kevin even more. Wanting him was a deep ache that needed to be soothed, an itch that needed to be scratched. The way he looked at her, caressed her as he held her in his arms, and nibbled on her soft lips made her tremble with anticipation each time. However, holding steadfast and waiting to take their relationship to the next level was crucial. At thirty-two years old, Starr had no intentions of adding any more lovers to the number. Waiting and taking her time to get to know Kevin had been the right decision.

Thoughts of his large hands caressing and studying every naked inch of her lush body made her insides hum in delight. Never before had she had an overwhelming desire to be with a man. Now older and wiser, she knew her past encounters were based on a man making her feel wanted. With Kevin, she didn't have to worry whether he wanted or desired her. Everything he said and did was a bold declaration of just how hc felt. It was in each longing gaze, in each gentle caress, in each tender endearment.

For this reason, as excited as she was, fear and doubt snaked around her heart, constricting it. By her own admission, she was not as experienced as some women. It was no secret Kevin had shared his bed with many. Women, she was sure, who were gifted in the art of pleasuring men. Women, she was certain, who could satisfy his every carnal craving. Would she be able to measure up and satisfy him? Or would he find her lacking as Marcus had taunted, and use it as an excuse to end their relationship before it a chance to really get started?

Lost in her thoughts, Starr stumbled and tripped as she stepped up onto the first step leading to the large wrap around porch. If it had not been for Kevin's quick reflex causing him to reach out and firmly grip her by the waist, she would have fallen flat on her face.

"You all right, baby?"

Embarrassment burned her cheeks from her sudden state of clumsiness. "I'm all right." Smiling sheepishly, she said, "Just a little clumsy. Thanks for keeping me from falling on my face."

Gently, he placed his hand at the small of her back and led her to the front door. Standing close behind her, he inhaled the scent of her perfumed body as his solid chest pressed against her back. Reaching into his trouser pocket, pulling out a set of house keys, he whispered in her ear, "Now, you know I'm not about to let that happen."

Placing a large hand firmly on her flat stomach, fusing them even closer, he used his free hand to insert the key. Starr's heart did a rapid pitter-patter as she let herself go, melting into the heat of his solid frame. Tiny shivers ran up and down her spine as he placed soft, moist kisses along the center of her neck.

Pushing the door open, the couple moved as one unit into the foyer. A sudden gush of air assaulted Starr's heated body as Kevin disengaged his hold. Her body screamed in protest as he disarmed the alarm system, locked the door, and reset the alarm to home mode. She didn't remain in a state of protest for long. Within seconds strong, powerful arms were holding her. "Now where were we?" came the deep husky growl as kisses rained down the nap of her neck to the slope of her right shoulder.

The kindling sparks that had been firing off all night were building into an inferno. Kevin wanted Starr with every fiber of his being. He was certain she knew how bad he wanted her as his aroused manhood pressed into her backside. For weeks he lay in bed wondering what it would be like to have her underneath him writhing as he sunk deeper and deeper into the core of her womanly essence. Just the thought made him want to explode, losing it before they even got started.

Turning her around, he gazed down into her face. Pleasure like he never experienced flowed through him. The moonlight shining through the window illuminated the slow rising and falling of her breasts and slightly parted lips begging to be kissed.

Having on three-inch heels made it easier for Starr to leisurely drape her arms around his neck as he drew her closer, making them a perfect fit. The heaviness of her breasts and tingling nipples tortured her, as she wantonly pressed even further into his male firmness. She did not recognize her own voice as she achingly moaned, "Kiss me, Kevin."

Happy to oblige her, his mouth swooped down on hers. He had meant for the kiss to be sweet, tender. That was until she pressed even further, making his hardness ever more strained, searching to be buried in her hot moistness. Cradling the back of her head in his massive palm, he deepened the kiss eliciting a series of soft moans from the woman he held. Each delicious moan pushed Kevin closer and closer to the edge.

Abruptly breaking the kiss, he swept her up in his powerful arms. With the keen night vision of a large feline, his movements were agile as he made his way through the pitch-dark living area. His strides were long as he took the stairs two at a time with his destination being the master bedroom.

Making his way down the long hallway, he came to a sudden stop, standing at the entryway of his bedroom. *I can't make love to my wife in that bed.* Reversing his steps led them to the guest bedroom. There was no way he would, nor could he make love to his woman, his wife, in a bed that had been soiled with past lovers. He needed their coming together to be on undefiled ground. Starr meant too much to him to disrespect her in such a manner. For once he was about to make meaningful love and not have meaningless sex.

"Wasn't that your room back there?" Starr whispered in the still, dark house.

Gently laying her on the queen size bed, he gazed deep into questioning eyes. Bending down he placed butterfly kisses on her forehead, nose and then lips. "Baby, you're my wife. I can't make love to you in my bed." He hesitated and then added, "It wouldn't be right."

Nodding her head let him know she understood exactly where he was coming from. As her gaze continued to hold his, an indescribable emotion swept through her as tears moistened her eyes. *He really does care about me.* Not only had he been patient, never pushing her further than she was willing to go. Now he proved the measure of his worth, as well as hers, as he refused to take her to a tainted bed. A bed he shared with more women than she wanted to think about.

Sitting up on her knees, Starr made her way to the edge of the bed. Reaching out she pulled Kevin close, wrapping her arms around his neck. Bringing her lips close to his she could feel his sweet, warm breath, she whispered, "Thank you for respecting me as your wife."

Kevin groaned in sexual agony when instead of kissing him, she nibbled on his bottom lip as if it were the most delectable treat she'd ever tasted.. "You're welcome. Now turn my lip loose. You're killing me, Mrs. Dawson."

"Sorry…I…can't…help…my…self…Mr…Dawson...you... have...sexy…lips." She softly whispered in between tasting his sweet, tender flesh.

I can't take this torture. Kevin stepped back from the seductive web she was weaving around him. As he stared at her, gazing up at him begging to be loved, he knew once he was deep inside of her he would be consumed with possessing her forever, never wanting another man to touch her again. Just the thought of some other man's hands on her, set off a rumbling growl deep in his throat, as his jaw clenched and his large hands curled into tight fists. The sudden impact of his emotions took him by surprise. Never before had he cared what a woman did after leaving his bed. Why all of sudden did it matter? Could it be because his feelings ran deeper than what he realized?

Kevin's sudden change in demeanor frightened Starr. She didn't like the menacing mask her wore. "Did I do something?"

His expression remained fixed, as he answered, "No."

"Then why are you staring at me like that?" Starr whispered, past insecurities coming back to haunt her. Self-consciously she wrapped her arms around her waist that wasn't a size two.

Stepping back into her space the hard mask slipped away as he gently commanded, "Come here, baby."

Easing off the bed, she made her way to stand in front of him. Starr stood still not knowing what to expect as Kevin took panther like strides circling her body as he silently appraised her. No longer did his dark piercing gaze frighten her. It suddenly gave her a sexual charge that caused her body to quiver from head to toe. Her breath came out in short uncontrollable pants as he slowly and completely disrobed her.

After shedding her clothing, he took his time visually caressing every soft, sexy curve. When he spoke, his tone held an air of finality. "I don't want another man to see you like this. To do the things to you I'm about to do. After tonight, you *belong* to me. Do you understand?"

Feeling lightheaded, Starr swooned not so much from what he said, but from the deep possessive, seductive pull of his words. Gazing up at this beyond sexy being, her eyelids rapidly fluttered as she struggled to regain her equilibrium. Never in her life had a man outright told her that he wanted her for keeps. Her trembling voice came out on a breathless sigh. "Yes, I understand."

As he continued to drink in Starr's rich cocoa, creamy flawless skin, he seductively licked his lips as he contemplated what she tasted like.

Starr sucked in a breath as Kevin reached out and circled a nipple with the tip of his finger. Immediately her body responded to his glorious touch causing the deep, dark chocolate tip to pucker and pout. When he dipped his head, using his tongue in the place of his finger, Starr's knees slightly buckled. Kevin's large hands automatically splayed her hips to keep her steady. A long, satisfying purr vibrated in the back of her throat as he drew the chocolate tip between his lips and firmly suckled it sending the hidden treasure between her thighs into an uncontrollable throb.

Eyelids rapidly fluttering, Starr thought she would die when he moved to the other breast giving it equal attention. Surely, she had died and gone to glory when suckling was replaced with hot, wet kisses as Kevin leisurely took his time trailing from her breast to her flat stomach. A wanton moan escaped her lips as a slick, wet tongue dipped into her belly button. Her heartbeat kicked up an alarming rate as her legs were gently parted by strong hands giving her tormentor free reign to place delicate butterfly kisses and nibbles, up and down the interior smoothness of her thighs.

"Kevin." His name floated from her lips in a husky, passion-filled whisper that was foreign to her own ears. This man, *her* man, made love to her like no other had ever done. He was about to venture where no other man had ever gone.

When he didn't answer and the hot, searing kisses and nibbles moved closer to her pulsating womanhood a wave of panic overwhelmed her.

"Kevin...don't...please...stop."

Between sensual kisses, he mumbled, "Baby, I can't. Don't ask me to."

He had to have all of her. Taste all of her. He dreamed about it night after night. Hell, to be honest he thought about it during every wakening hour. Without further hesitation, Kevin indulged his every fantasy.

Digging perfectly manicured nails into bulging muscled shoulders, soft sighs of ecstasy bubbled from the depths of Starr's being. Her mind was in a sensual haze, as she could not believe the intensity of his intimate kiss. Never before had any of her former lovers been so generous, so attentive.

Soft sighing lingered into purring moans as her trembling body shattered into a million pieces giving her body the most exquisite pleasure she'd ever experienced. Again, for the second time she didn't recognize her own voice as she screamed Kevin's name as her sweet release consumed every inch of her, leaving her weak.

Cradling Starr's limp body, Kevin gently placed her in the center of the bed. Taking a few steps back his eyes held hers in a smoldering gaze. All he wanted to do was love her like he never loved another. He wanted to brand her and to make her his woman, forever.

Not wanting to waste another second, he began to unbutton his shirt. "You know this would go much quicker if you help me," he told her as a mischievous grin tugged at the corners of his lips.

Not wasting any time, she went to her husband. She wanted him just as bad as he wanted her. Moving his hands away from the front of his shirt, she finished the task of removing his shirt. Anticipation made her hands trembled as she went to his slim waist and unbuckled his belt, and then unfastened his trousers. She was shocked when he gently grabbed his wrist. "I'll take if from here." He couldn't stand how agonizingly slow she was removing his pants. He needed to be inside of her. *Now*!

Slightly moving a few inches back, Starr watched as Kevin quickly shed his pants and underwear in one clean swoop.

"Are you okay?" Kevin asked concerned as Starr took in a deep gasp of air.

Anxious, Starr bit down on the corner of her bottom lip. "I don't know…"

"You don't know what baby?"

"If that's gonna fit," Starr nervously answered as she pointed to his proud manhood standing at full attention. By all means was she no virgin, but neither Marcus nor Stephen was so well endowed. *Have mercy.*

Advancing forwarding, Kevin steered Starr until the back of her legs grazed the bed.

"What's the matter? You scared?" He teased.

Starr gasped again. This time somewhat taken aback by his cockiness. Brotha was confident with what he was working with. "I beg your pardon?"

"You don't have to beg. I'm gonna give you what we both want."

Momentary irritation fizzled as Starr demurely lowered her eyes and then swept them up to gaze directly into his, softly demanding, "Well, stop talking and give it to me." *What in the world! Where did that come from? I sound like a hussy in heat! Heck, I am a hussy in heat!*

Aw, hell! This woman is going to be the death of me. Before she knew what hit her, Kevin picked her up and had her on her back hovering over top of her. When his head dipped down and captured her mouth in a passionate kiss, Starr returned the kiss with just as much heated fervor.

Kevin gently nudged her legs a part with his knee as he positioned himself at her center. With one powerful thrust of his hips, he entered her.

Starr winced from the bold intrusion. Kevin went completely still.

"You okay?"

Nodding her head, she mumbled embarrassed, "It's just been a really long time."

"I'll take it slow," he promised gently kissing her forehead.

Once her body adjusted, Kevin slowly sunk further into Starr's moist heat. With slow measured movements he went deep, filling her to the hilt only to retreat to the point of almost withdrawing. It only took her a second or so to pick up on his rhythm, once she had, their movements were fluid and symbiotic. Each time he withdrew to sink back into her, she lifted her hips welcoming him home. Yes, this was his home, a place where no other would be welcomed but him.

Becoming daring, she wrapped her legs around his waist, drawing him in deeper as she boldly stared into deep eyes that mirrored everything she was feeling; a blazing, consuming passion that she had never before experienced. Placing her hands on each side of his face, she pulled his mouth to meet hers. Her tongue invaded every region, desperately trying to extract every essence of sweetness as she stroked, tangled and suckled his tongue. The kiss only added to the explosive heat of their coupling, causing them to frantically pick up the pace of their lovemaking. Each delicious stroke ripped moans of pleasure from places deep within them they both never knew existed.

When she felt herself tumbling over the edge, Starr did the only thing she could do. Give into the turbulent waves that were lifting, taking her higher and higher.

Sensing she was nearing completion, Kevin urged in a deep, sexy whisper as he buried his head in the crook of her neck, "Baby, come with me."

It was his sensual coaxing that finally pushed her over the edge, sending her crashing into the waves. Kevin had no choice but to be pulled along as he threw his head back, letting out a primitive growl as Starr's body writhed and quaked beneath him. It necessarily wasn't the writhing nor quaking that did him in, but rather the incredible force in which her feminine muscles contracted and squeezed him, her body shattering into a million pieces as she screamed his name with her release.

Collapsing on top of Starr, Kevin enveloped her in a tight embrace before reversing their positions. The repositioning of their bodies automatically led her to rest her head on his broad chest as her lower body nestled between sturdy muscular thighs.

It had taken a few minutes for their pounding heartbeats and labored breathing to return to normal. The room held a comfortable, satisfying stillness, wrapping the lovers in a cocoon of sheer contentment.

"You okay?" Kevin asked in a deep, husky whisper.

Smiling, Starr without shame admitted, "I couldn't be better."

Wow, I never knew orgasms could be so…so…darn incredible!

Kevin chuckled. "That good?"

"Mmm hmm, now be quiet so I can go to sleep. You've exhausted me."

He chuckled again. "Oh, so this is how you gonna do a brotha?"

Slightly pushing herself up, she placed a tender kiss on his lips. "Just tonight, I promise."

"A'ight, I'm holding you to your promise."

Smiling, Starr snuggled herself back against his broad chest. "Please do, Mr. Dawson."

"You can count on it, Mrs. Dawson."

It wasn't long before Kevin felt Starr's breathing go shallow as she softly snored. Gently kissing the top of her head, he repeated to her slumbering form, "You can most definitely count on it, Mrs. Dawson."

Chapter 22

"Glad you could make it," Ava snickered in a hushed tone to Starr as she and Kevin slid into the pew next to her.

"Better late than never," Starr whispered back not bothering to hide the sassy smirk dancing across her lips.

"Mmmm hmmm."

A few feet down the pew, Summer leaned up just a bit trying not to look too obvious, shot them a look that sneered, *About time y'all showed up.* Sitting back, she flipped over the church program and scribbled, *Look what the cat dragged in.* Nudging Nick, she passed him the program.

Glancing down the aisle, he gave Kevin the *What's up* head nod before winking at Starr. He was tickled pink from the way she blushed in embarrassment, giving away their reason for being late for Sunday morning service.

Taking the pen from his wife's hand, he scribbled underneath her note, *Mind your business,* then handed her back the piece of paper. His broad shoulders slightly shook from silently laughing. In a huff, Summer sucked her teeth and shifted her position on the pew so her back was partially facing him. *Get on my nerves.*

Joan loved cooking Sunday dinner for her new family. Who would have ever thought being Nick Stiles' housekeeper for years would be such a blessing? Certainly not Joan. It was a blessing, which brought her more happiness than she had ever expected. She had pretty much resigned herself to the notion that she would never have a family. Never have anyone to really call her own. But all that changed a few years ago when Summer's pregnancy shook up Nick's life and hers right along with it.

After the birth of NJ, Summer pleaded with Nick to reconcile with his estranged father. Henry was all too happy to have another chance at being a father and a grandfather. Determined to be the best grandpop, Henry practically became a permanent fixture in his son and daughter-in-law's home. Naturally, he and Joan became familiar with one another.

Initially, Joan brushed off Henry's flirting as just being friendly. No way would he, a judge, be interested in a lowly housekeeper. However, to her amazement, he was very much interested. He told her he liked her spunk. One date led to another and before long, he proposed, she accepted, and now they were a happily married couple.

Closing the oven and leaning up from basting the delicious, smelling roasting chicken, her eyes glanced around the warmly decorated kitchen. It definitely had the feel of a grandmother's kitchen with its bright yellow walls, grapevine borders and antique hutch that perfectly matched the walnut cabinetry. The hutch stored a beautiful set of pink glass dishes her grandmother brought during the depression when folks couldn't afford to buy china but wanted something nice to use for special occasions. Another nostalgic touch Joan added to her favorite room in the house was a modern sink that had the appearance of an old-fashioned pump sink.

Ava and Summer sat at the large, round country table positioned in the room's center. Ava prepared the cucumbers, red onions, mushrooms, and tomatoes for a garden salad, while Summer busied herself with the task of shredding cheese for baked macaroni and cheese. At the counter, Starr stood stirring sugar into a freshly brewed pitcher of iced tea.

Hovering over the young women like a momma chick, Joan's heart filled with so much love. She loved each of them as if they were her own daughters. Since she couldn't have children of her own, she claimed Summer, Ava and Starr as her children. Although Nick worked her nerves, she loved him like a son prior to becoming his stepmother. Kevin wasn't left out of the bunch. She loved him too, and constantly fussed at him about his frisky ways with women, as any caring mother would.

And her grandbabies! Lawd, she just loved herself some NJ and Autumn something fierce. She and Henry along with Nita and James spoiled those babies something terrible. Yes, they did. Didn't care what Nick or Summer had to say about it, either. After all that's what grandparents were for.

Shifting her gaze between the three young women she tried to decipher which one it was. You see, the other night she had a dream about fish; a whole bunch of little fish swimming everywhere. A strange dream it was. The little fish were in the kitchen sink, bathroom sink, bathtub, washing machine and toilet. Wherever there was a source of water in the house, the fish magically appeared.

Slowly nodding her head, *somebody's pregnant or is about to get pregnant. Lawd, I hope it ain't that Summer. NJ and Autumn are a hand full as it is.*

"Why she looking at us like that?" Ava whispered.

"What's that Miss Growny?" Moving over to the pantry Joan removed flour, shortening and baking powder from the shelf. "Girl, get to that refrigerator and get me some milk."

Ava got up, taking the long way around to the fridge. She knew Momma Joan was quick with a dishtowel. One good flick of the wrist and you'd have a welt for days.

"Just 'cause I'm old, don't think I can't hears ya." The older woman chuckled, setting down the ingredients for her melt-in-your mouth biscuits, on the counter.

"Momma Joan, you got some good ears," Ava commented sliding the milk on the counter praying Momma Joan wouldn't get her.

"No, she doesn't. You just can't whisper worth nothing," Summer teased.

Starr laughed. "Summer, you ain't right."

"She sure ain't. And that Ava ain't no better. The both of them 'bout to make me take a switch or this here dishrag to their behinds for sassing me."

"You know we're just playing, Momma Joan," Ava said, affectionately kissing the older woman on the cheek.

Joan smiled warmly at the younger woman. "Baby, I know y'all just messing with an old lady."

Reaching inside the cabinet, she took a bowl down and placed it on the counter. "Starr, leave that tea alone. Ya been stirring it forever." Pointing to the cabinet near the stove, "Go over yonder and get my biscuit pan."

Obediently, Starr went to retrieve the pan. On her way back to the counter, she shot her friends a look as they sat snickering at her. *Humph, I'm not telling them nothing now since they want to cackle like a bunch of hyenas.*

"Come on, chile, ya moving too slow! Get the lead out!" Joan fussed.

Instead of shooting another nasty look, Starr smirked at the snickering hens. Yeah, she was moving slow, but loved every bit of the reason why. Early this morning she was awakened by Kevin suckling the nipple of her left breast. Of course, he hadn't stopped there. After he took his time suckling, kissing and nibbling every inch of her, bringing her body fully alive, he gently flipped her over on her stomach. Her center began to pulsate as she relived him pulling her up on her knees in a kneeling position just before he entered her slowly. Just thinking about it made her tingle as a smile spread across her lips.

Ava kicked Summer under the table. The dreamy dazed look followed by the smile that boasted pure ecstasy, made their mouths drop open as they gawked at one another. They didn't even have to ask, they knew. Starr had gotten her swerve on! And what a swerve it must have been! No wonder she and Kevin came schlepping into church all late.

"Starr, sweetie, just don't stand there. Bring me my pan so I can show you how to make these here biscuits." Joan shook her head. *Chile is somewhere in outer space. I guess that's what good lovin' will do to ya.*

"I'm sorry, Momma Joan." Passing her the pan, "Here you go."

As soon as the pan was in the older woman's hand, Starr started to the table. Her mind wasn't on learning how to fix biscuits. She was reminiscing about her early morning tryst.

Before she could move two paces, Joan reached out and grabbed her hand. "I said get over here so I can show you how to make these biscuits. You know that man of yours loves my biscuits. I'm gonna show ya how to make them for him just like Momma Joan's."

Blushing from Momma Joan's statement, she followed her like a small child to the ingredients on the counter. Every time someone mentioned Kevin being her man, it gave her a warm rush all over. He *was* her man. And it felt so darn good.

After being with Kevin all night, Starr decided to follow her heart. She was letting go of her past and moving on. He was a good man and did not deserve to be compared to those other jackasses she'd been involved with. No, she would not let ancient hurts and disappointments come into play ruining their relationship. *A clean fresh start, that's what we're going to have. I want this so bad and I'm not going to let anything mess this up for me.*

"Now you just can't throw all this in the bowl together." Joan's motherly voice pulled Starr from her quiet thoughts. "You have to do it like this." Joan went on to instruct as she showed Starr how to combine the flour, baking soda, salt, shortening, & milk into a perfect mixture of dough.

As Joan watched over Starr, Summer wanted to know as she munched on some of the cheese she'd just shredded, "Momma Joan, why were you looking at us all weird a few minutes ago?"

Seeing that the younger woman was doing just fine, she left her to take a seat at the table. Ava and Summer eyes were glued to hers as they waited in anticipation of some great news. Joan had to swallow back a giggle. *Lawd, I don't know which one is the nosiest. 'Bout ready to snatch the words clean out my mouth.*

Nonchalantly shrugging a shoulder, "Not much, just had me a dream the other night."

This little tidbit of information made Starr stop her task to turn around and face the others. She had to give her full attention to the details of this dream. Whenever Momma Joan dreamed something, ninety percent of the time it came true. It was downright spooky how accurate her dreams were.

"What you dream about?" Starr questioned almost in a whisper.

"Baby, I dreamt about fish." Waving her arms in the air with dramatic flare, "A whole bunch of 'em too! They were everywhere I'm telling you. All in my sinks, the bathtub, washing machine and even in the toilet."

The older woman's excitement dwindled. She eyed each of the childbearing aged women. Lifting a brow and in a conspirator low tone, she asked, "Y'all do know what this means? Right?"

Throwing up her hands as if surrendering, Ava yelled, "It's not me! I'm not doing a thing." Shaking her head, "I'm like a nun! Ain't had none, ain't seen none!"

Summer didn't mumble a word, just looked around the room from Joan, then to her friends. Wasn't any need for her to get so dramatic like crazy Ava. At the rate she and Nick were going, she was liable to pop up pregnant at anytime.

Any other time she would have laughed at Ava's little off Broadway production. But Starr was too busy bracing her weight against the counter as she became dizzy and swayed. She and Kevin hadn't used protection last night or earlier this morning.

What if... No, she wasn't going to think it. Didn't want to get her hopes up. Although she and Kevin joked about having kids, they never had a serious conversation on the subject. What if he really didn't want kids? Or what if he thought she was trying to trap him? Then what? Letting out a deep breath, *I need to talk to Kevin...tonight.* This was no way to start a relationship. She'd have to let him know the next time they needed to be more careful, especially if he didn't want children right now...or ever.

"You all right, baby?" Momma Joan inquired, her wise eyes penetrating into Starr.

"I'm fine. Just thinking about how your dreams are always so on point." She answered slightly shifting from foot to foot as her gaze bounced between each person in the room. Three pair of eyes gazed back. She knew what each of them was thinking. Breaking the awkwardness of the moment and getting the attention off her, she blurted out, "Everybody knows it's Summer." Starr nervously giggled and threw over her shoulder as she put the pan of biscuits in the oven, "Y'all know she's as fertile as a kitty cat."

As melodies of laughter filtered around the room, the delicious aroma of roasting chicken tickled Kevin's nose as he entered the kitchen.

None of the women was aware of his presence until they heard his deep baritone voice. "Who's more fertile than a kitty cat?"

The moment the question left his lips, Starr turned to acknowledge his presence. The second their eyes connected her stomach did a series of flip-flops. He was standing in the doorway, his hands in the pockets of well fitting jeans, gazing at her with the sexiest grin.

She was grateful the all-wise Momma Joan came to the rescue. After just thinking about all the ways he pleasured her, she couldn't stand to have him looking at her like that in front of everyone. It was downright scandalous. If he kept it up, she just might have to cut dinner short. "Boy, get your tail out my kitchen before I take a stick to ya!"

Backing up from harms way, Kevin chuckled, "Don't shoot the messenger. Pop Henry sent me in here to check on dinner. Says he's starving and you haven't fed him since Friday."

Joan laughed. She loved that man of hers. "You tell that 'ole fool of mine to stop telling them lies. Dinner will be ready in about thirty minutes. Don't take long for the macaroni and cheese to bake.

Kevin chuckled again. Momma Joan was a mess. "All right, I'll tell Pops what you said."

Making sure he wasn't in hearing distance, the older woman predicted, "Yes, lawdy I need a stick for that one. A switch won't due. He's a big man." Winking at Starr, nodding her head towards the other room, "Baby, I hope you can handle that there man. If you can't, just come to Momma Joan. I'll tell you what to do with 'em."

The younger women gasped in surprise at the older woman's wanton words. One of them shrieked, "Momma Joan!"

"Momma Joan my foot! As you young folks say, 'You better recognize!' Why you think that old man in yonder ain't had nothing to eat since Friday? He ain't need no food when he had me."

Starr, Ava, and Summer fell out laughing at Momma Joan as she sashayed across the floor swaying her round hips from side to side.

Chapter 23

"Hey, what's wrong?"

Starr had become extremely quiet once they returned to her house. Usually as they watched a movie, the couple snuggled on the sofa. But tonight, Starr seemed content with sitting at the other end.

She bit the inside of her mouth. Why did she have to let it show something was bothering her? Why did she have to wear her feelings on her sleeves for all to see? The entire time they were at the elder Stiles' home for dinner, she had told herself repeatedly she would have this conversation with him. But now she was suddenly apprehensive, afraid of what he might think or do.

Her mind was scrambling with her thoughts. She couldn't figure out what she wanted to say now that Kevin had scooted next to her and started to play with the soft curls at the nape of her neck. The seductive caress had her wanting to straddle his lap.

Still caressing, he used his opposite hand to lift Starr's chin. She didn't resist when he gently guided her face to meet his gaze. "You gonna talk to me or what?"

Concern fell over Kevin when she eased away for his touch. Standing to claim the nervous energy running through her, she smoothed the non-existent wrinkles from the front of her skirt as she began to pace.

Watching her pace, concern gave way to dread. How had she found out? He thought he had hid *it* out of her view. The first thing he had planned on doing once he made it home was to get rid of *it*. Anger set his jaw tight. He was going to choke the life out of that trifling Trina.

After he and Starr finished making love Kevin did like he had done every Sunday morning for years. Opening the front door, he stepped on the front porch inhaling the crisp morning air as he bent down picking up the Sunday Inquirer. Thoughts of the sleeping woman he left in bed fizzled. To his horror as he lifted the paper from the cement floor a familiar pair of red, lacey thongs twirled to the ground from the early morning breeze. Confusion, then anger marred his handsome features. "What the hell..." he hissed under his breath.

"What are you doing out here?"

Startled by the soft, feminine voice behind him, he nearly tumbled off the top step of the porch. With a deft flick of his slipper-shod foot, he kicked the offensive fabric to the step below out of view.

Recovering quickly, he turned flashing a sheepish grin as held up his reason for leaving her warm, nude body, "had to get my Sunday morning paper."

Leaning against the doorway in his dress shirt from last night, she was a beautiful sight. So what, her hair was a complete mess; and strands were going every which way, but the right way. His stomach tied into knots when she smiled demurely, running her fingers through the mussed curls on her head. "Come on. I'm ready to take my shower."

Kevin let out a deep, nervous breath. He was thankful Starr's invitation was offered thrown over her shoulder as she made her way back up the stairs. The second she was out of sight gave him the discreet opportunity to kick the thong under a nearby shrub before dashing off after her.

Now he wasn't so sure he had been discreet enough. What if she had seen the offensive scrap of fabric on their way out this morning to church? If she had seen what he had attempted to hide, would she understand? He couldn't be a hundred percent certain. She had years of hurt and mistrust bottled up inside.

During their many late night phone conversations she revealed how growing up her father had been in and out of the picture. It killed him to hear the pain and sadness in her voice as she shared the most intimate details of how her father always made promises to stay with his wife and daughters. However, every time he came back with promises of being a better husband and father, he ended up leaving and breaking their hearts.

One evening Starr revealed old hurts that had been buried deep within her soul for years. After she had unloaded some serious stuff, she was an emotional mess. Kevin found himself on his cell phone soothing her while she shed uncontrollable tears as he drove over to her place. Once he was on her front door step, in a tender voice, he pleaded, "Open the door, baby." The moment she opened the door, he swooped in and picked her up in strong arms. Closing the door, he leaned against it for support as she clung to him purging her battered soul.

He had rushed to her in the middle of the night after her quiet sniffles had become gut-wrenching sobs as she told him of her mother's depression. The poor woman had been so depressed; she attempted to drown her sorrows in a bottle of wine and sleeping pills. He could literally hear her body shaking over the phone when she hissed, "I hate him for doing that to my mother... to me and Karen." She just graduated from high school and was excited about going off to college. Fear and worry kept her from leaving home. That fall, she enrolled in La Salle University's nursing program instead of going off to Howard University.

Six months after the attempted incident of suicide, Donna Avery went into seclusion. Her daughters believed she did this because she felt like a failure as a wife and a mother. The only time Starr, Karen, and the children went to visit their mom was on Mother's Day. They refused to let her shut them out and be alone on that special day. She lived in a small log cabin in rural Virginia. Literally in the middle of nowhere.

His heart bled for Starr. She had gone through so much in her thirty-two years. He didn't want drama from a previous relationship to bring her more heartache. He didn't, however, want to hide anything from her, either. How was he going to explain Trina's craziness?

"We didn't use anything."

"Huh?" He was caught off guard by the statement as she cut into his thoughts of how he would tell her about Trina.

Slumping back down in the space beside him, "I said we didn't use anything."

Taking a second, her words registered their meaning. Relief bathed him from the inside out. Letting out a deep sigh, he asked, That's what got you so quiet?"

"Yes. What if—"

Putting a finger to her lips, he silenced her.

"I'm cool. I get tested every six months."

Frowning, she slapped his hand from her lips. Rolling her eyes and sucking her teeth she said, "I know that. That's not what I'm talking about."

Now it was his turn to frown as he lifted a thick brow. *Women talk too much.* He knew big mouth Summer told her that he and Nick used to get tested on a regular. Now that Nick was a happily married man, he didn't leave his buddy hanging. When testing time rolled around, Nick tagged along for moral support. Although Kevin was always careful, he'd be on pins and needles until the results were in.

Starr duct her head…*busted!* Summer was going to kill her! And Nick was going to kill Summer if it got back to him that she told Starr about his and Kevin's STD testing ritual.

Trying to clean up the mess she made, she stammered, "Umm, what I met was…what about a baby?"

Chuckling, he found it amusing watching her wiggle and back peddle out of her slip up. "What about a baby?" he teased, a smirk dancing along his lips.

"Stop playing with me, Kevin."

Lifting his hand, he lightly began stroking the back of her neck again. Tiny shivers crept up the length of her spine from his touch, nearly making her squeal out in delight. "I'm not playing."

"Yes, you are." She murmured as his mouth descended upon hers kissing her senseless. She wanted to tell him to stop it, and to get serious. She didn't want to play games, not now. Not when she was ready to tell him her heart's desire. But the way he was kissing her and caressing her was making her lose her mind.

Breaking the kiss, "No…I'm not," he whispered against her

moist lips.

Pulling Starr to her feet, he gazed deeply into her eyes. What he saw tugged at his heartstrings. Never before had he ever dreamed of a woman making him want to give her his all. For years, he expertly played the field telling himself one woman would never be enough for him. There simply were too many beautiful ones out there to sample to be tied down to just one. Heaven help him. He had been wrong. Dead wrong. Starr had become his everything. No longer could he see his life without her being its nucleus.

Every body part trembled with anticipation as Kevin slowly stripped her of her blouse, skirt and bra, leaving only her panties on. Her nipples puckered and begged to be caressed and suckled as his large hands tenderly grazed their sensitive tips. She didn't have to beg long. A quick inhale of air filled her lungs when he dipped his head, capturing a pouting chocolate tip between his teeth. Soft moans floated on airwaves when his tongue laved, then circled the pebbled flesh right before he suckled it.

Moving to the pay homage to the other breast, his fingers toyed with the hem of her satin panties. Her abdominal muscles twitched as long, strong lean fingers dipped inside stroking her ultra sensitive pearl. She barely had enough strength to step out of her panties as he glided them past her hips, down her legs. She was glad she didn't have to worry about removing her shoes since the first thing they always did was kick them off. Goodness knows, she would've lost her balance and toppled over on the floor.

The pink tip of her tongue darted out to moisten her suddenly dry lips as she stared at Kevin removing his clothes. Her southern region throbbed in expectancy as thick muscles rippled and flexed with every lazy movement he made. The man was simply built like a Greek god.

Splaying her waist with both hands, he gingerly backed her up against the nearest wall all while nibbling on her earlobe driving her insane. Once secured against the solid surface, he huskily whispered, "Baby, hold onto my shoulders" as he effortlessly lifted her off her feet. Doing what came natural to her, she wrapped her legs around him as he pressed the palms of his large hands against the wall for leverage. Taking her moist lips in a hard kiss, he entered her with a quick, hard thrust of his hips.

Starr's sweet groans of passion were intercepted and swallowed deep in Kevin's chest as he deepened the kiss, while pumping in and out. Sturdy well-defined quadriceps and hamstrings gave him the strength to measure out long, deep, powerful strokes.

Needing to come up for air, breaking the kiss, Starr tightened her grip on his broad shoulders. The electrical atmosphere surrounding them in raw sensuality drew their eyes in a heated gaze. Each lover was feeling what the other was saying with their body, yet wondering if they were speaking the same language.

Making certain they spoke with the same ancient tongue, their hearts desiring the same blessing, Starr tilted her pelvis enticing her Nubian King to take full possession. *Mmmm* was the purred elicit response floating from her lips. The slight shifting of her pelvis magnified the pleasure she was feeling. Every part of her body began to tremble as she climbed the stairs of ecstasy.

That little move, right there, had him on her heels climbing behind her. "Dayum…girl… what you doing to a brotha?" Kevin gritted out between clinched teeth right before his body was hit with a bolt of lightening, sending him into a wave of spasms. The first wave slammed into Starr sending her spiraling into an orgasmic haze of pure, titillating pleasure.

Bodies drenched with perspiration, the lovers remained in a sensual tangle of heated limbs. Neither was ready to break the intimate contact just yet. If they could be suspended in time, this is where they would want to be…forever. What they'd just shared was beyond incredible.

"That was something else," Kevin whispered, planting a path of soft wet kisses along her jaw traveling down her neck to the curve of her shoulder.

Fully satiety Starr purred, "I know that's right."

"Starr?"

Lazily she answered, "Hmm?"

"Have my baby."

Chapter 24

What in the name of hell's fire is going on! Starr silently screamed in her head throwing her hands up in the air. All week long crazy stuff had been going on around her. Monday morning as she left her house, two flat tires greeted her, one on the driver side, and the other on the rear right passenger side. It really pissed her off because she hadn't noticed the flat tires that morning when she walked Kevin to the door an hour before she left for work. To avoid being late for work she had to take public transportation, which she detested with a passion. People were downright rude. Somebody always had to sit next to her, sneezing or coughing spreading their germs, too trifling to cover their mouth. Not knowing the bus and train schedules added to her mounting aggravation. She ended up being over an hour late for work, despite her efforts to make it in on time.

Later that afternoon her mechanic called darkening the black clouds that were already hanging overhead. He'd informed her that the flat tires were the results of a slash job. Dumbfounded, she couldn't imagine who in the world would deliberately want to slash her tires. Although she did have a run in with Betty, one of the nurses on the unit about leaving unfinished paperwork, she didn't think the woman would go to the extreme of vandalizing her car.

True, Betty was angry with Starr because she reported her to their supervisor. Betty had repeatedly failed to perform her job duties, leaving her coworkers to complete the bulk of her work, and oftentimes putting patients at risk. Many of the other nurses on the unit complained about Betty actions, yet none of them had the guts to report the lazy nurse because she was a longtime employee of the hospital.

Armed with documented proof of the nurse's neglect, Starr approached the unit's supervisor. The supervisor had no choice but to give Betty a written warning. If she received a third warning, she would be in danger of termination after being a nurse on the unit for over twenty years.

When the bitter nurse heard about the slashed tires, she smirked, "That's what that little snitch gets. Serves her right."

If she had not been concerned about her professional integrity, Starr would have slapped the snot out of Betty. One thing was for sure, *if* she found out that dried up prune laid a finger on her car, to hell with professional integrity, Betty was getting a beat down at the end of shift.

To make matters worse by the time Wednesday rolled around everything at work was a chaotic mess. Two nurses had called out on night shift, which meant a ton of work was left for the day shift nurses. One of the patients' long lost sons decided to pop up for a visit antagonizing his three older brothers for putting their father in hospice care. Things got so out of hand the staff had to call security to have the son removed. Everyone felt bad for the dying patient. He definitely did not deserve to have his sons bickering over him while on his deathbed. And to add fuel to the fire, the staff was in an uproar when the supervisor announced she would be resigning her position in six to eight months. Her husband's job was transferring him overseas in eight weeks. The only reason she had extended her stay was because their home had to go on the market and the kids had to finish out the school year.

Needing to get away from the madness, Starr asked another nurse to cover her patients. The nurse she asked the favor of didn't have a problem with it, but of course, a few of the other nurses grumbled, "Why she gets to leave for lunch?" Starr didn't give two shakes of a lamb's butt about their grumbling. By law she was entitled to a break that didn't consist of sitting in the nurse's lounge being bothered every five seconds. On days like these, she seriously contemplated moving on like her girls had done. Ava was now a school nurse and loved her new job. Who wouldn't love having off all major holidays and the entire summer? And Summer worked part-time, three mornings a week in a Family Medicine practice in Germantown.

Enjoying the warm, sunny fall afternoon, she took her time walking to K-Mart on Tenth and Market Streets. She wanted to get a few packs of those new energy conserving light bulbs. The second her cell phone began to ring, Starr nodded her head to the beat. The ring tone was set to Mary J's big hit, *Just Fine.* Pushing the glass pane door open, making her way to the house wares aisle, she flipped the small device open. Normally, she'd pay attention to the 'unknown' display on the cell phone, but she was too busy jamming to Mary J. "Hello" she sang to the unidentified caller.

"Hi honey."

Abruptly coming to a jarring stop, Starr cringed. After all this time, what could *he* want? She had spent years getting over his betrayal. Hadn't he caused enough damage? Why was he bothering her now when her life was finally coming together? No thanks to him.

"What do you want?" she hissed through clinched teeth, anger twisting and knotting her insides.

"It's been a long time." The caller paused. "I just wanted to see how you're doing." The male voice had a nerve to come across the line sounding concerned.

"Not long enough. Don't ever call me again."

Flipping the small device closed with a sharp click, Starr was fuming. How dare he call her? Did he think she was still the same young, naïve girl? That girl that wanted his love so bad, she believed every one of his conniving lies. Well, he had better think again, because if that's what he thought, he had another thing coming.

Her good feeling mood disintegrated, taking the bounce out of her step. No longer interested in the energy conserving light bulbs, she reversed her steps and headed back to the madhouse.

Again, she wanted to know what in hell's fire was going on as she stood on the sidewalk, her mouth hanging open, looking at what used to be a beautiful flower bed. She had been so proud of her handiwork. For three weekends straight at seven in the morning, she had dragged herself after working all week to Home Depot to take gardening classes. Now some imbecile had destroyed everything. Flowers, grass and mulch were all over the place. Someone had ripped up every beautiful flower that had been planted.

Planting her garden had made her feel close to her mom. It made her think of the vibrant, loving woman her mother had once been. Growing up, the one thing she vividly remembered was that her mom was always her happiest while gardening. She would hum and talk to her flowers telling them how beautiful they were going to make world. The first sign of her mother going into a deep depression was her lack of interest in her garden. With no zeal to make the world a beautiful place, weeds chocked the life out of her small paradise. Starr didn't like remembering that version of her mom. So she created the one thing that had brought her mother joy, a beautiful garden.

Feeling totally defeated from the events of the week, she dragged the few steps to her front door. Before she could get inside Mrs. Virginia stopped her. "Starr, I tried to stop them. But by the time I got back with a piece of paper and pen to write down the license plate number they were gone."

The elderly woman proceeded to tell her a dark car pulled up across the street about an hour ago. There had been two people in the car. The driver was described as a young black woman and the passenger a teenage boy. Mrs. Virginia knew this because the boy jumped out the car with two huge vicious dogs leading them to Starr's lawn. Letting the beasts loose he gave them the "Attack!" command.

Mrs. Virginia was downright appalled as the hooligan doubled over laughing as the dogs brutalized the beautiful flowerbed. She hadn't meant to let the screen door slam shut as she hurried to get pen and paper.

"I heard that woman yell, 'Hurry up! Get them so we can get out of here!'" Sighing Mrs. Virginia apologized. "I'm sorry I slammed the door. I was in a rush to get something to write down the plate number."

Starr gave the older woman a weak, tired smile. It wasn't her fault someone had destroyed the one thing that kept her connected to her mom. "Don't be sorry, Mrs. Virginia. It's not your fault. Have a good night."

Gently closing her front door, she racked her brain trying to figure out who would slash her tires, and then trash her flowerbed. Other than dried up Betty, she hadn't had any run-ins with anyone else. Quite honestly, there wasn't anyone for her to have any run-ins with. She got along with all the other folks she worked with. And her time while not working was spent with her girls and Kevin.

Flopping down on the sofa, Starr was miserable. It was official…she had had the week from hell. The only thing that kept her sane was that she and Kevin talked every night on the phone. Having to prepare for a major presentation to land a multi-million dollar firm had tied him up. They hadn't seen each other all week. Sure, she enjoyed their talks. However, she wanted more. Just talking wasn't enough. She wanted to wake up each morning in his arms after a thorough night of being made love to.

Leaning her head back she closed her eyes, inhaled deeply, then exhaled slowly. *In with the good and out with the bad.* Starr repeated this mantra several times as an attempt to forget this week's madness. As a sense of calmness began to claim her, she let her mind travel to the last time she was with Kevin.

Later that night as they lay in bed, limbs tangled in a sweet embrace she whispered, "Did you really mean what you said? Or was it the heat of the after moment that had you talking?"

Untangling himself from the embrace, he pushed up on his elbow. Gazing down at her he gently traced her bottom lip with the tip of his finger. "Baby, I would never mislead you about something as serious as us bringing a child into the world."

Her heart skipped several beats. Was he serious? All she'd been thinking about for weeks was having Kevin's baby. Every night before she fell asleep, she imagined what their baby would look like. Would it have her dimples? Or Kevin's beautiful caramel complexion? Would it be boy or a girl?

"But what if I can't get pregnant?" She softly asked, her eyes filling with tears.

Kevin's fingertip stilled. "What are you saying?"

Swallowing the lump in her throat, willing the tears to stay behind her lids, she shared with Kevin every detail of her medical history. He listened intently as she relayed her condition and prognosis as told to her by Dr. Neil.

When she finished her story, he wiped the lone tear that escaped sliding down her cheek with the pad of his thumb. "Baby, don't cry. We'll have a baby. I promise."

"You promise." She sniffled wiping a tear away.

Lying back down on the bed, Kevin pulled her to his chest kissing her forehead. "I promise."

Kevin's statement was made with such conviction. He had faith. He was living proof that God was still in the miracle business. Now all he had to do was convince Starr not to give up hope, but to put her trust in the Lord.

Nodding her head, she snuggled against his chest. Kevin was going to make everything all right. She thanked God that for once she had a man that had her back. A man that supported what she wanted. When she told him she dreamed of being a mother since she was a little girl, he hadn't gotten all crazy on her. Instead, he promised to make her dream a reality.

Covering her mouth, she yawned. “Night Kevin.”

“Night baby.”

Closing her eyes, Morpheus called to her and she followed. All night as she lay contently nestled in her husband’s arms, visions of sweet cherubs cooed and gurgled at her until dawn.

A broad smile spread across her face as she remembered Kevin’s promise and her dream. Not even the horrendous week she had could take the joy away she was feeling at this moment. Placing her palm over her flat belly, she whispered a prayer. “Please let a little one be growing inside of me.”

Chapter 25

Three Months Later Saturday Afternoon

"Girl, you know I love you." Kevin grunted out between gasps. Starr was working him over big time.

Straddled atop her man she was riding him like a jockey aiming for the finish line in the Kentucky Derby.

The ride started off as a nice easy trot, the banging of the headboard, *tap…tap…tap,* keeping in rhythm with the trot. Soft feminine fingertips glided over hot, taunt abdominal muscles outlining a well-defined six-pack. Maintaining the easy pace Starr leaned forward, her tongue following the path of her fingertips.

A rush of air exploded from Kevin's lungs. Wet, butterfly kisses were lovingly planted over the expanse of his torso before settling over a pebbled male nipple. Returning the favor from earlier, Starr drew the nipple between her teeth. A throaty, female giggle filled the air as Kevin hissed a passionate expletive. The way in which she was suckling him was driving him insane.

No longer able to take any more of her wicked torturing, strong fingers threaded through soft curls. Starr groaned in protest as he pulled her away. "You better behave yourself Mrs. Dawson."

"I am behaving," she softly challenged; the motion of her hips, moving up and then coming down.

Needing something to do with his hands, Kevin filled his palms with firm breasts. Starr's head fell back as experienced, confident fingers circled and massaged her. A sensation of warmth grew in the pit of her stomach, spreading throughout her limbs. Her body crying for release, she removed Kevin's hands from her breasts and placed them on her hips.

Gripping her waist, he got the message she wanted to take him on a fast and furious ride. Planting delicate palms on his sturdy chest, Starr moaned as she gradually picked up the pace. The leisurely trot gave way to a full speed gallop. *Tap-Tap-Tap-Tap-Tap!*

As the first wave hit, Starr's hands flew to grip the ones firmly holding her hips for stability. The second wave severely arched her back, while the third and final wave had her screaming Kevin's name as her toes curled and her body bucked out of control.

His dark eyes glued to this wild woman, he marveled at the intensity of pleasure sweeping through him as he meant her powerful strokes. Never before had any woman made him feel like this, made him feel that his whole universe depended upon her existence. The moment her body bucked above his was the turning point where he lost all control. Giving one final upward thrust, he tumbled over the cliff, crashing into an orgasmic wave.

Falling forward, collapsing on his chest, she whispered, "You know I love you too, boy."

And she did love him. She loved him more than she thought humanly possible. Having been hurt by men practically her entire life, she was determined not to fall head over heels in love with Kevin. Yes, she enjoyed being with him, the idea of them having a baby together and having someone she could share all her fears, hopes and dreams with. She had even resolved to give their relationship a chance and not judge it or him according to past experiences. But to love him, she refused to allow her heart to do so. She told herself they could stay married and raise a family without being in love. Heck, folks have been doing it since the beginning of time.

She believed she could have a safe relationship with Kevin if she didn't allow her heart get in the way. Yeah, right! Kevin was the most romantic man she'd ever known. Not in the traditional sense of romance like buying decadent confectionaries, flowers, or jewelry. It was little things like sending her text messages at work offering to make her dinner. Or instead of getting store brought cards, he'd pay his next-door neighbor's granddaughter a couple bucks to make adorable, homemade cards out of construction paper and color markers. And when her garden had been massacred, every Saturday morning he was side by side with her digging and replanting until it was restored to its former beauty.

What really won her heart over was the evening he blindfolded her and led her into his bedroom. Once the blindfolds were removed and she took in her surroundings, she squealed in pure delight. The master bedroom had been completely redone. The old wallpaper had been pulled away. Remnants were sand blasted to a smooth finish. The walls were freshly painted in cream silk, with the crown molding, windowsills, baseboards, and archway done in ivory mist. His old furniture had been replaced with Ethan Allen furniture crafted from rich mahogany.

Starr leaped on the massive sleigh California king size bed bouncing up and down like a kid. Leaping back off the bed, she jumped in his arms wrapping her legs around his waist, showering kisses all over his face. "I can't believe you did this!"

"Anything for my Queen." Kevin knew it bothered Starr that he had yet to make love to her in his own bedroom. She didn't have to say anything, he noticed every time they made their way to the second floor her eyes would travel to the closed master bedroom door.

How could she not love a man like this? However, every single time she wanted to tell him she'd fallen in love with him, the words refused to come out. As hard as she forced herself to say the words, she just couldn't make herself confess what her heart was feeling. It was the unknown, which kept her feelings locked deep inside. Every man she'd ever confessed her love to, had recklessly trampled over it..

An astute lover, Kevin was aware of her full inability to put her trust in him. He very well understood that his past womanizing ways possibly added to her leeriness. He'd been aware every time she wanted to confess her love, but held back. He'd been aware of every kiss, touch and caress that attested to how much she indeed loved him. He'd also been aware of how stubbornness held her back, waiting for him to be the first to make a declaration of love.

Putting an end to her struggle, one evening as they strolled hand in hand window-shopping on Main Street in Manyunk, Kevin came to a stop. Peering into the large glass window of a fashionable maternity boutique, he wrapped an arm around Starr's waist. He wondered if she truly comprehended how much he loved her and wanted her to be the mother of his children. Didn't she have any idea that she was the only woman he wanted? Many nights as he held her he'd questioned God, *Why didn't I meet her sooner*? A still quiet voice would gently remind him, *You weren't ready.*

Leaning down, he whispered the words that made her heart quiver. "Starr Dawson, I love you."

Dazed and confused she'd thought she misheard him. "Huh?"

Pulling her to his chest, he wrapped her in his arms, engulfing her in a tight embrace. Kissing her forehead, he whispered, "I said I love you." Giving her a few moments to let his confession seep into her heart and soul, he added, "And I can't wait for the day you're carrying my baby."

Burying her face in his chest her body shook as she silently sobbed. He loved her. He'd actually told her he loved her and wanted her to be the mother of his child. Had he any inkling of how she prayed he'd be the first to say those words? How she was so afraid of letting her guard down, only to have him tell her he didn't feel the same. With much trepidation she also confessed, "I love you, too."

After confessing their love, they no longer felt it necessary to keep their marriage a secret. Beverly Dawson was all too thrilled to have Starr as a daughter-in-law. She didn't even give her youngest child a good tongue-lashing for running off to Vegas to get married. The elderly woman was too enthralled admiring the emerald cut diamond with tapered baguettes totaling three carats set in platinum gracing Starr's ring finger. Kevin sheepishly blushed as his mother took his hand in hers rubbing her thumb over the plain platinum wedding band which matched his wife's.

Neither of the newlyweds had the heart to correct the elderly woman. Nor did they want to tell her they'd gotten hitched in a drunken stupor. She was happy for the young couple so who were they to put a damper on her happiness?

Initially she had been hesitant on telling her own mother. Starr desperately wanted to, but wasn't quite sure how her mom would take the news. For years she made it very well known that she was anti-men. According to her, they were all the same, "worthless." It would break her heart if her mother thought that of Kevin.

However, her sister, friends and Kevin encouraged her to call her mother. To her surprise, Donna was in an upbeat mood. Usually when Starr did make contact with her mom, she was pleasant, yet somewhat withdrawn. She couldn't help but to beam when her mom told her, "Baby, you deserve to have a good man's love." And when Donna requested to speak with Kevin Starr was as giddy as a child seeing Santa on Christmas morning.

After the ice was broken with the necessary pleasantries, Donna and Kevin went on to have an engaging conversation. Every now and then Kevin would erupt into a fit of laughter over something Donna had said. Knowing her mother had immediately accepted Kevin filled her with so much joy and happiness.

Lying on their sides facing each other Kevin reached out and gently stroked the side of Starr's face. She smiled and returned the tender gesture. "You're too good to me," she softly whispered.

"That's because I love you more than life." Telling her this came as natural as breathing.

Scooting closer to her husband, she snuggled against him. "I love you more."

Chapter 26

Pacing back and forth, she wanted to throw something against the wall. If she hadn't been at work in her boss' office, she would have. However, such an outburst would get her thrown out in the street on her butt, the minute he'd return from his weekly Monday morning meeting. When her smug coworker dropped the paper on her desk, nearly hitting the tip of her nose, she smirked, "Did you see this?" Trina shot up from her desk and ran straight into her boss' office, locking the door.

How could he do this to me! She had loved him for years. Never made any demands, always went along with *his* program. And now he had the audacity to let someone else take her place as his wife.

Anger violently shook her as she stared at the happy couple in the Lifestyles section of the Sunday Inquirer. The headline boasted *Philadelphia's Most Eligible Bachelor Secretly Takes A Bride.*

Ripping the paper in shreds, "I should be his wife!" And she would have too, only if she hadn't left him that last time to be with that jerk Tyrel Timmons.

When the handsome, larger than life professional football player came along showering her with beautiful gifts and taking her to the hottest clubs in the tri-state area, Trina forgot all about Kevin. She'd told herself she didn't want to be bothered with that bourgeois Negro anyway. With Tyrel, she didn't have to worry about if her dress was too short, or if her blouse was cut too low. He didn't care. Matter of fact, he'd always fawn all over her telling her how good she looked. But that damn Kevin and his stuck up, insufferable friends always looked down their noses at her when it came to what she wore.

Humph, it wasn't like Kevin was trying to be with her for real anyway. He only wanted her because the sex was off the hook. Probably the best he'd ever had. That's why most men latched onto her like a leech. Trina had some serious bedroom skills.

In the beginning, that's how it was with Tyrel. He couldn't get enough of her either. They had met at the end of the season during a time when his schedule wasn't as demanding. No longer traveling from city to city, Tyrel became obsessed with his new conquest. At first, she thought the attention was flattering. It didn't hurt either that he was constantly buying her designer label clothes, shoes and handbags along with weekend getaways to the Caribbean. She was living large at his expense and loving every minute of it. You couldn't tell her she wasn't Miss Thing. It hadn't even bothered her that Kevin hadn't tried to contact her, which he usually did during their on again, off again relationship. In the past, she anticipated his calls and wouldn't hesitate running to him. The sex was just that good. Although the sex with Tyrel was blah, even if Kevin had called, she wasn't about to mess up her gravy train by jumping back in his bed. Shoot, Trina was living the lifestyle of the rich and famous and she wasn't about to give it up for him or any other man.

The more money Tyrel lavished on her, the more his attitude changed. And it wasn't for the better. No longer did he help her in and out his super expensive sports car. When she protested, standing on the curb with her arms crossed over her chest and glossy lips in a pout, he'd yell, "Come on and get in if you want to go!" Letting out an expletive, "You ain't crippled so move it!" Now instead of opening doors for her, he was going through them first, rudely leaving her to lag behind.

The icing on the cake, which made her come to her senses, was the night he accused her of coming onto another player while at a team party. "What are you doing, Tyrel?" she hissed between clinched teeth as he roughly yanked her by the arm, dragging her outside through a crowded room. She had never been so humiliated in her entire life.

Once outside he barked, "What the hell do you think you're doing?"

Trina stared at him dumbfounded as she looked up into his face contorted in anger. "What are you talking about?" She questioned, attempting to pull away from his firm hold of her.

Tightening his grip, he all but growled like a rabid dog, "Why you all up in my teammate's face?"

Okay, he was losing his mind. Yeah, he had taken her to the party; however, once there he left her alone, ignoring her while he went off chatting with his buddies. What was she supposed to do? The other girlfriends and wives hadn't welcomed her into their little clique. So when his teammate struck up a conversation with her, she indulged him. What was so wrong with that?

"Well, what was I supposed to do? You left me all alone!" Becoming angrier by the second, she mustered up enough strength to snatch away from his grip. "And those stuck up witches in there act like they're too good to talk to me!"

Tyrel let out a harsh laugh. "They probably thought you were up in there trying to take their men. Look at you." Disgust curled his upper lip, as he sneered, "Looking like a ho. Dress all up your stank behind."

Stunned, Trina's lips trembled and her eyes watered. Before she knew it she drew back, and a loud crack rippled through the night air as her right palm made contact with his left cheek.

If it hadn't happened so fast, she wouldn't have believed it herself. *He smacked her back!* The stars floating in front of her eyes and blood trickling from her nose made her a believer. Not to mention that the six-foot six, two hundred ninety pound maniac was screaming so loud, the others came outside to see what was going on. In a daze, she watched as several of the men rushed over escorting Tyrel back inside. "Come on man, what's wrong with you hitting that girl like that in public?" the team's quarterback admonished as they rushed Tyrel inside looking over their shoulders making sure no one had witnessed the scene. Not one of those bastards even bothered to come over to see if she was okay.

The next day Tyrel left frantic message after message apologizing. "Listen, baby I just got a little jealous. I didn't mean to hit you...Come on pick up the phone." This went on for days until he finally got tired and stopped calling.

In the meantime, Trina wasn't about to let grass grow under her feet. Uh-huh, nope. She was through with Tyrel. Her main mission in life had become to set out on a campaign to win Kevin back. She had pulled out every seductive trick to get him back. But it was to no avail. He just wasn't interested in her anymore. She knew she had crossed the line on more than a few occasion.

Each time he was furious with her demanding she stay away. The last time he showed up banging on her door she thought he had gone crazy. When he pushed past her throwing a pair of red lacey thongs in her face and ranting about slashing some tires on his new woman's car, she denied everything.

"Trina, you're such a liar!"

"I don't know what you're talking about!"

"Yeah, whatever, Trina." Stalking to the door, he stopped, turned and glared at her.

"I've warned you."

"What's wrong with him?" Trina's cousin Keisha asked, turning up her nose as Kevin pushed past her, storming out the door as she was coming in.

Flopping down in the chair in front of her boss' massive oak desk, her face fell in her hands. "My life is such a waste. Why did I have to mess things up with Kevin?" she sobbed. As hard as it was for her to admit, she had lost and there wasn't a thing she could do about it. Or was there? Lifting up her head, Trina dried her eyes. She remembered something her cousin had suggested. Smiling, the wheels in her head begin to turn. "If I'm miserable you're going to be miserable right along with me."

Skipping out of her boss' office, Trina dumped the remains of the newspaper in the trashcan. It was time for some sweet revenge.

Chapter 27

"So, Missy how are you enjoying married life?"

Starr's dark sparkling eyes lifted over the brim of the menu she was studying to peer at her sister. Although she hadn't gotten pregnant yet, life was good. After the announcement of their marriage, Starr moved in with Kevin. Now that the cat was out the bag, it didn't make sense for them to reside in different locations. Heaven was smiling on Starr. Ava agreed to move into her place taking over the mortgage payments. This worked out well for the both of them. Starr didn't have to pay a mortgage on a place she no longer lived. And Ava had a whole house to herself with payments less than the one bedroom condo she was renting in center city.

Starr smiled. "It's not as bad as I thought." It didn't bother her one bit that Kevin bordered on the side of being slob. Nothing major, just little stuff like leaving those itsy-bitsy pieces of hair in the sink after shaving or leaving the tube of toothpaste on the bathroom sink every time he brushed his teeth. Why he couldn't just wash the small piece of hair down the drain and put the toothpaste back in the cabinet was beyond her. As much as this drove her crazy, she could certainly live with the minor annoyances.

He wasn't by any means a demanding husband. He respected the fact that she worked a full-time job, too. She had been a nervous wreck the first time he'd come home and dinner wasn't ready. Dinner not prepared by the time her father came home in the evenings was one of the many reasons for arguments between her parents. She recalled her father's ranting. "Damn, woman! I work all day and you can't have a decent meal on the table when I come home!" He hadn't cared Donna had just rushed in from work and had the tasks of preparing dinner while helping two small children with homework.

Out of nowhere, Starr went into apology mode…just like her mother. Scurrying between the refrigerator and freezer pulling out anything to throw a quick meal together, she rushed out, "I'm sorry dinner isn't ready yet. It'll be done in about twenty minutes. Thirty minutes top."

Walking over to his wife, Kevin removed the frozen bag of vegetables from her hands and flung them on the countertop. Pulling her in his arms, he said, "Hey, its okay. I know you're just getting in from work. Let me go upstairs and get out this suit and I'll be right back down to help you."

Watching him leave the kitchen Starr let out a heavy sigh. Her father would have never offered to help her mom. Instead, he'd cuss and rant as he stormed out the house, sometimes not coming back for days.

Ordering their food, they passed the menus back to the waitress. "Bad as you thought? What did you think would happen?"

"I don't know. Like maybe he'd change."

"You guys only been living together for a couple of months. What could change so fast?"

Shrugging a shoulder, she mumbled, "Like maybe get tir—"

Before she could finish, Karen held up her hand, stopping whatever she was about to say. "Uh-huh, baby sis, don't go there. Kevin isn't Daddy or Marcus. Can't you see that that man loves you? I don't think he could ever get tired of being with you."

"I know, but—"

Karen blew out a frustrated breath. "But nothing, Starr. I swear sometimes I could just shake you."

This is what Karen was afraid of. Starr was allowing their father and Marcus' hateful and deceitful behavior to come between her and Kevin. She was happy for her sister. It had been years since she's seen her so carefree. Without question, she was convinced her new brother-in-law was the reason for her sister's newfound happiness. She just prayed Starr wouldn't allow her insecurities to get in the way of her marriage.

Frowning, rolling her eyes, Starr huffed, "What a minute girl and let me finish before you start jumping all over me. Geesh, I was going to say before I was so rudely interrupted…" Shifting in her seat, softening her tone, she told her sister, "I just get so scared sometimes this is all a dream. I never had a man love me like this." Not even when Marcus pretended to love her when it suited his needs could he compare with the way Kevin loved her. "You know…he told me even if we can't have a baby of our own we could adopt."

Reaching across the table, Karen took her sister's hand in hers. Smiling she confirmed, "See, I told you that man loves you. He's crazy about you." Taking the cloth napkin from her lap, Karen dabbed at the corner of her mouth. "You love him too, right?"

Feeling the lump rising in her throat, she tried to swallow it back down. Yes, she loved her husband with all her heart.

She also knew he loved her. However, it still troubled her that her man used to be a major playa. The first month they lived together, she had to get adjusted to the sporadic female callers. For the most part, they were polite and got the message Kevin was off the market and stopped calling. However, one caller was determined to test Starr. As they eased into their second month of living together as man and wife, the little trick had the nerve to call again questioning Starr. "Who are you?" She demanded to know as if she had a right. When Starr told the little snot she was Kevin's wife, the heifer had a nerve to laugh. "Okay…yeah right. As much as that brotha likes to sling that thang around… don't believe the hype…yours ain't the only honey pot he's dippin' in. Trust me; I know what I'm talkin' about."

Kevin arrived home that night greeted by Starr yanking clothes off hangers and snatching undergarments from bureau drawers, dumping the garments into a suitcase. Perplexed, he inquired, "Hey, what you doing, baby?"

"Don't baby me! I'm outta here!" She snarled as she glared at her husband.

Dumbfounded, hunching broad shoulders, throwing his hands up in the air, he demanded to know, "What I do?"

She told him every detail of the conversation with the taunting heifer. The caller had even gone as far as suggesting they were still seeing each other.

Furious, Kevin exploded using every filthy cuss word one could imagine. Her own anger began to dissipate as she watched him snatch the phone out the base scrolling through the caller ID. He dropped the F-bomb, his eyes becoming slits as he glared at the display. Hitting the call button, he dialed the number. Starr's jaw unhinged allowing her mouth to drop open. She couldn't believe this gentle giant had transformed into the Incredible Hulk. She had never heard anyone get so thoroughly cussed out before as he growled every word out like an uncontrollable beast.

Hanging up the phone fury continued to consume him. Starr was taken aback by his abrasive demeanor when he finally turned to speak to her. "Look I can't change my past. It is what it is. I'm sorry you got that call. But how many times do I have to tell I hadn't been with anyone months before we got married? You're my life now. I want you and no one else."

Drained from a hectic day at the office and now having to deal with an angry woman, Kevin dragged both hands down his face. Every day he worked like a dog to build his business up, to increase his wealth, so when the time came she could stay home and take care of their children. He didn't want her to have any worries as to how the bills were going to be paid. Each night he faithfully came home to her. What more could he do to prove he was a hundred percent committed to her and their life together? "I love you and I need you to trust me."

Remembering that night and all the ways he showed her she was his universe, Starr nodded her head. "Yes, I love him."

Karen smiled at her sister. She wanted her to experience the same kind of love she had with her high school sweetheart, Gregory. If she could, she would move heaven and earth to have him back. Since that fatal day five years ago, Karen hadn't given thought to loving another man. Her life was too busy raising her children and working part-time as a dental hygienist.

Gently squeezing her sister's hand, she said, "Good. You better love that man with everything you got."

Starr returned the squeeze. "I will. I promise."

♥♥♥

Whack...whack...whack... Running, swinging the racket, Kevin hit the ball with great force against the white walls in the enclosed glass court. Taking his frustrations out on the ball, he had his opponent working double time trying to keep up with him as adrenaline pumped through his veins.

Trina was still up to her old tricks. Just that morning she had showed up outside his office building. Anger coiled through him as he thought about how she'd called his home talking trash to his wife. She had better be glad his momma had raised a gentleman; otherwise, he would have knocked her into next year.

Not in the mood for her mess, he gritted out between clenched teeth, "What do you want? I thought I told you to stay away from me and my family."

"Look I just came here to apologize. I didn't mean to get the wifey all worked up." Trina looked up at Kevin her eyes wide with innocence. "I didn't know you were married." she smoothly lied. If she couldn't have him, then she would make the one who did, life a living nightmare.

This was stupid. Kevin's best bet was to walk away before he lost control and did something he would be sorry for later. Not giving her another second of his time or attention he threw over her his shoulder as he headed towards the building's revolving door, "Well now you know. So leave us alone."

Trembling with anger, she wanted to jump on his back and pound his baldhead. Reigning in her emotions, she called out, "Kevin."

Why did he turn around? Trina stood on the sidewalk in broad daylight fondling her breast, taunting, "You know you miss this."

Curling his lip up in disgust, he didn't know who he was angrier with, himself or Trina. How had he allowed himself to get so involved with a nut case like her? Why hadn't he listened to his mother when she told him to "leave that one alone?" He was too busy thinking with his little head to hear anything his wise mother was telling him.

Rage and embarrassment turned his face crimson as her wicked laughter floated after him. The fact that he had been seen talking with her, no matter how brief, by everyone going into the office building totally humiliated him. Shaking his head, he mumbled under his breath, "Why didn't I listen to Momma?"

Losing all three sets, his opponent collapsed to the floor. Kevin had taken being an aggressive racquetball player to a whole new level.

Sweat pouring profusely down his face, burned his eyes. Grabbing the front of his shirt, he wiped his face and rubbed his eyes, soothing the burning. He couldn't wait to take a nice cold shower to cool off and then sit in the sauna to help soothe the muscles he knew would be sore tomorrow from playing so hard today. Seeing his opponent attempting to get up from the floor, he reached down firmly grabbing the man's hand helping him to stand. Once on his feet, Kevin gave him a firm pat on the back as they made their way out the enclosed room. "Good game, Bob."

Bob chuckled. "Yeah, considering you tried to kill me."

"I was kind of hard on you."

"Ya think?"

"Sorry dude. Just had to work out some aggression."

"Ya think?"

Both men erupted into laughter. "Come on man let me make it up to you. I'll buy you a beer."

"Now that's what I'm talkin' about."

Chapter 28

"Oh, man, that feels so good."

"You like that?"

"Yeah, baby. Don't stop…please don't stop."

"Only if you're a good boy."

"I promise I'll be a good boy."

Starr sat on the edge of the claw foot tub massaging Kevin's aching, sore shoulders and back as he soaked in hot water and Epsom salt. He couldn't believe how bad he hurt the next day. He thought sitting in the sauna yesterday would help loosen his muscles, but it hadn't.

Starr leaned her body in to give her hands greater pressure against his muscles. "What had you playing racquetball so hard? You are one big knot."

Eyes closed, enjoying the deep massage, he took a deep breath. His anger was finally ebbing away. As much as he loved his wife, he didn't feel like rehashing Trina showing up outside his office building. Every time he thought about her outrageous behavior, he wished he had pushed her into the oncoming morning rush hour traffic. Keeping the angry acid burning in his gut from eroding a wall through his stomach, he had resorted to popping Tums all morning. A hundred times he thought about calling Starr, telling her about his visit. But he decided against it when he remembered her reaction to the jeering phone call a few weeks ago. The last thing he wanted to do was to cause her any unnecessary worry about where his affections lye. She was his life now. Nothing his former lover said or did could sway him from the comfort of the world they were building. It was a world that promised years of love, companionship, and lots of babies. Therefore, there was no reason to trouble her with Trina's nonsense. So instead of upsetting his wife and committing murder, he pretended every time his racquet encountered the ball that it was Trina's head he was whacking.

"Just had a hell of a morning waiting for me when I got to the office yesterday." Before a twinge of guilt could gnaw at him, he pushed it far away. He was doing the right thing by not coming clean about Trina. Wasn't he?

Kissing the top of his shiny baldhead, continuing the skillful pampering with her hands she offered, "You want to talk about it?" She had sensed something was up when he came home yesterday evening. Usually when he came in the house, he greeted her with, "Honey, I'm home." Instead, he let his briefcase drop to the floor with a loud thud right before kicking off his shoes. If she hadn't gone into the dining room to get a dish from the china cabinet she wouldn't have known he was home. It was the loud thud from his briefcase that had alerted her he was there.

When she asked if every thing was okay, his response had been, "Yeah, baby I'm just a little tired." She didn't push, just gave him a soft kiss on the lips and led him to the kitchen table where his dinner was waiting.

Later that night, while making love, he had been aggressive. Starr could barely keep up with his pounding thrusts as she held on for what felt like forever. When his thunderous release finally came, he squeezed her tight, nearly cutting off her oxygen supply. If he hadn't afterwards cradled her kissing her damp forehead declaring, "Baby, you are my world. Please believe that," she would have sworn the man was trying to kill her. If she could walk in the morning, it would be a miracle.

"Nope, I don't want to talk. This is what I want." Without warning, he snaked his arm around her waist. With a loud splash, followed by a high pitch yelp, she fell into his lap fully clothed.

Starr's fiery protest was quelled the instant his tongue slipped into her warm mouth. She moaned as he coaxed her tongue to dance with his. Another soft moan escaped her mouth floating into his as his hand gently cupped a firm breast, his thumb stoking the nipple into a hard pebble. Sighing from his sweet caress, she no longer cared he'd just ruined a new pair of Ralph Lauren slacks. His tongue and hands were driving her insane. Who had time to worry about something as trivial as clothing?

How he had so quickly disrobed her she didn't know. Frankly, she didn't care as she sat in the warm water between muscular thighs resting against his broad solid chest. All she cared about is that this felt right. It felt like home.

Trailing kisses along the side of her face, he gently captured an earlobe between his lips. "You mad at me?"

Giggling, she squirmed as he tortured one of many erogenous zones. "I should be mad at you."

"Oh baby, don't be like that."

"Well, I am. I just brought those pants and you know it," she pouted, stroking a muscular thigh.

"You saying you don't like being in here with me?"

"No. I'm saying you could have asked a sista to take off her clothes," she spat with attitude.

Kevin chortled. "Starr, baby, that is so corny. You know I don't do corny."

Turning to face him, she splashed water in his face. "Don't you dare call me corny." She laughed when he squinted like a little kid and shook his head. As soon as he opened his eyes, she attempted to splash him again. Grabbing her by the wrist, he pulled her to his chest until their lips touched. Her body shivered when he whispered against her lips, "If I were you I wouldn't do that again."

He could feel her lips spread into a smile against his. "And what if I do it again?" she taunted swiping her tongue over his bottom lip. He groaned as he felt his sex come to life. This was one woman he would never get enough of. "Then I'll just have to put you over my knee and spank you."

Imagining a naughty spanking with feathers, she purred, "Mmmm, I just might like that husband."

Starr became aware that the verbal foreplay was turning Kevin on as she felt his erection pressing up against her. Leaning back, she looked at him lifting an arched brow.

Kevin laughed from the expression her face held. "What you expect with you all up in my face purring like a sex kitten?"

Gasping, feigning offense, Starr placed her hand on her chest. "Me, acting like a sex kitten?"

"Yes, you." A sexy, devilish smirk danced across his lips. "You are what you are."

He didn't give her time to come up with a quick comeback to their playful bantering as he pulled her closer bringing her breasts up close and personal. Her eyes closed and her head fell back when the tip of his tongue circled a berry tipped nipple.

When he gently tugged on her hips, she knew what to do. She knew what he wanted. She wanted it too.

Holding onto his shoulders she gingerly lifted herself up so that his warm mouth wouldn't lose contact with her breast. Once positioned over him, she slowly impaled her throbbing womanhood, not caring that water was being splashed everywhere. Delicious moans bubbled from her throat as she filled herself. Starr took her time loving her man. Savoring every stroke.

Coming downstairs to get a glass of water she could hear Kevin's muffled voice as he talked on the phone. Since he would be up for at least another hour or so, she decided to wait until he got off the phone so she could talk to him. Earlier he distracted her with some awesome lovemaking as she tried to get him to talk about what was going on with him. Though he denied anything was wrong, other than having a bad day, her gut told her otherwise. Something was troubling him and she was determined to get to the bottom of it.

After drinking her water, she navigated herself to his office. Easing up to the door her heart pounded and she suddenly felt dizzy. *Oh, God...please...no. Please... God...no.* She begged as she struggled to breathe. *But why? Why is she coming to his office? Why did he see her?*

Not able to hold it in any longer a strangled cry erupted past her lips. She wanted to run, but couldn't move. Her legs were cemented to where she stood.

Swinging around in his chair his gaze collided with hers. His heart sunk as she stood in the doorway her hand covering her mouth, tears sliding down her face. "Nick, man I gotta go."

Abruptly hanging up the phone, he stood quickly crossing the room. "Starr, baby let me explain."

Shaking her head, Starr slowly backed away. What could he say to her? Hadn't she asked him more than once what was bothering him? And he'd come up with some excuse about being tired and having a hard day.

Quickening his step, he reached out to take her hand. His action was halted by anger and hurt flashing in her dark eyes. The look she shot him screamed, *You better not touch me.*

Rubbing his hand down his face and then over his clean head he hissed out a curse. *I should've just told her when I started to.*

Putting her hands on her hips, she yelled, "I know you ain't cussing! I should be the one cussing you out!" She couldn't believe he had the nerve to be cussing because he had been caught up in some mess.

"I'm not cussing at you."

She let out a short brittle laugh as she dashed away her tears. Crying time was over. He had made a commitment to her. And if he wanted to weasel out of it, she wasn't going to make it easy for him. He was going to face her like a man. "Oh, I know you're not cussing at me. But what I want to know is why you didn't tell me about Trina showing up at your job yesterday? What? You wanna be with her now?"

"Come on baby, let's go sit down in the living room," he coaxed as he gently put his hand at her waist leading her into the other room. The way she was stabbing him with piercing eyes, he wanted to get her as far away from the kitchen as possible. Kevin wasn't a punk; however, he wanted a safe distance between them and the knives. He'd watched enough episodes of *Snapped* to know when a woman was pushed to the edge she was capable of doing some strange, deadly things. All her life Starr had been disappointed and hurt by the men who were supposed to love and care for her.

He had to make her understand that Trina was a huge mistake, one he wished he could permanently erase. He had to make her see that if Trina was the last woman on earth and humanity depended on them to survive, the human race would become extinct.

She was so angry with Kevin; she knocked his hand from her waist as she stomped into the living room plopping down on the sofa in a huff. All she knew is that he had better hurry up and explain why this chick kept popping up out of thin air. Furthermore, he'd better recognize she could do without another cheater in her life and in her bed. Husband or not, it didn't matter. She loved Kevin, however, she would be damned if she sat back while he ran around on her. Been there, done that. Wasn't doing it again.

Kevin sat on the opposite side of the sofa. Suddenly the collar of his tee shirt felt like it was choking him. Reaching at the collar with his index finger, Kevin pulled the cotton fabric away from his neck before he spoke. "Baby, I just want to apologize to you for having to overhear about Trina. I know I should've told you she came by the office."

You damn right you should've told me. "Why didn't you?" Arms folded over her chest, her legs were crossed, an angry foot madly swung back and forth, as she waited for his response.

"Baby, I wanted to. I even picked up the phone several times to call you but I didn't want to upset you. I had to vent to somebody so I called Nick."

"You didn't think my finding out this way would upset me? Trust me I understand you and Nick are tight, but I'm *your* wife. You should have come to *me*." Irritation laced her words as she spoke in a leveled tone. She was his wife and he should have trusted her enough to come to her with this information. But instead, he decided to go to his best friend with his problems. If he wanted her to trust him then he had to be upfront with her about everything. "Even if you thought it was going to upset me, you still should have followed your first mind and told me."

Letting out a deep breath, he agreed with her. "You're right, I should have told you. I just thought you were still a little uptight about the phone incident. Honestly, baby I didn't think it was necessary getting you all worked up over a woman I wish would disappear from the face of the earth." His facial features scowled into a tight mask. "I should have left her alone years ago. Believe me when I tell you if we weren't married Trina still wouldn't have a snowball's chance in hell."

Starr's gaze slipped from his. Embarrassment flushed her cheeks as she thought about her behavior that night Trina called taunting her and now tonight. In both cases, she had over reacted not giving Kevin a chance to explain himself. Immediately in her mind, she had thought the worse and accused him of being a cheater like Marcus. If she hadn't been so wrapped up in comparing him to her ex, she would have given him half a chance. Though she promised herself she wouldn't compare the two men, she miserably fell short. *Why do I keep doing this to him? It's so unfair.*

If she had really paid attention, she would have known he wasn't the least bit interested in that woman. Goodness gracious, the way he yelled and cussed at her a few weeks ago should have told her that he really didn't want any parts of Trina. And when he shared with her how Trina had totally humiliated him outside his place of business, she felt awful.

Breaking into her musing, he whispered, "Besides, being all riled up can't be good for you if we're trying to have a baby." Scooting over he pulled her onto his lap. Tracing her bottom lip with his thumb, he again apologized. "Baby, I'm really sorry. I promise from this point on I won't hold anything back from you. Okay."

"Okay. But I just have to know something."

Caressing the back of her neck with the pad of his thumb, he said, "What baby?"

"Why did you stay with her so long?" What she really wanted to ask him was why he gotten involved with her in the first place? She'd often wondered how did a hoochie momma end up dating a Wharton Business School graduate and Investment Banker? It wasn't that Starr looked down on people or where they'd come from. Heck, her family was as dysfunctional as you could get. For all she knew Trina could have come from a really good, solid family and went buck wild once she became an adult.

Shrugging massive shoulders, he simply said, "Convenience."

"Convenience?" Who did he think he was kidding? "You mean it was the sex," she dryly stated.

Kevin chuckled. "That too." He wouldn't deny Trina had skills. The girl could sho' 'nuff make a brotha holla.

Playfully punching him in the chest, she warned, "Boy stop playing with me. I'm trying to have a serious conversation with you."

He rubbed his chest as if wounded. "No, you're just trying to be nosy."

When she went to hit him, again he caught her small fist in the palm of his hand. Laughing he said, "All right, I'll tell you."

She listened as he told her about his and Trina's on again, off again relationship they'd had for years. The relationship was convenient for him because he had never had any intentions of settling down with her or anyone else. Whenever she wanted to take a break and see someone else, he never objected since he was doing his own thing anyway. However, around the last time she went off to date her football player was also around the time he began to notice Starr. This also was the period he was knee deep in getting Dawson Investments off the ground and had taken a hiatus from dating. When she came back crying and all upset wanting to crawl back into his bed, he refused her.

Patiently she waited until he stopped talking. Twisting her mouth to the side as if in deep thought, she stared at him for a few seconds. "Okay, that explains a lot. But why are you so angry with her?"

Dropping his head on Starr's shoulder, he mumbled, "You sure you want to hear this?"

Stroking the side of his face, she nodded her head. "Yup."

Lifting his head, he let out a harsh breath. "I think she's the one who flattened your tires and tore up your yard."

Starr shot up off his lap like a rocket. "What!"

Kevin nodded his head. "And the nut was harassing Momma."

Starr stomp her foot. "What! No!" *That no good hussy harassed Momma!* Starr didn't care about the tires or the garden. That stuff was replaceable. But harassing an eighty-three-year old woman was different. Starr loved the ground Beverly Dawson walked on. The witch had crossed the line. *I'm gonna get her. A sure as my name is Starr Avery Dawson, I'm gonna get her.*

"And she put her funky thongs in my Sunday morning newspaper."

Starr stopped pacing as she swung around staring bug eyed at him like another head sprouted from the side of his neck. Her voice came out in high pitch squeal. "That nasty, stank, heifer put her thongs in your newspaper!"

He couldn't help it. Couldn't contain it. Kevin's massive body fell over on the sofa as he roared with laughter. He had never seen his baby so mad. She was a hilarious sight.

Marching over to the sofa, she pulled on his arm trying to upright his huge body. This was no laughing matter. Girlie had trespassed. Big time.

"Come on boy and sit up!" She popped him upside the head to get him moving. "This ain't funny. Where does that trick live?"

"Ouch!" Sitting up, rubbing the back of his head, he reminded her, "You know I ain't got hair to cushion your blows."

Covering her mouth with her hands, she glanced at Kevin's baldhead and cringed. She hadn't realized she popped him so hard. She had left a red mark on his head. "Oops, I'm sorry sweetie. I didn't mean to hit you so hard." Bending down she kissed the red mark before pulling his head to rest against her breasts. "Feel better."

Kevin wrapped his arms around her waist and grinned nodding his head like a five-year-old little boy. "Huh-uh."

After petting the top of head like he was a puppy, she disengaged the embrace. "Good. Now tell me where she lives."

Lifting a brow, he asked, "Why?"

Huffing, throwing her hands on her hips and rolling her neck, she snapped, "Why do you think? So I can go kick her butt."

"You know Kevin," Starr ranted ticking off each offense on a perfectly manicured finger. "It's one thing slashing my tires, sending two vicious demons from hell to tear up my beautiful garden I worked hard at bringing to life, and I'll even give her showing up at your office. Because I really now know that you don't want her stank, raggedy tail. But messing with Momma and leaving her nasty drawers in my man's newspaper is a horse of a whole different color." Pointing her finger at Kevin, she threatened, "You're gonna tell me where she's at…because she's going down…Big time."

Beaming from ear to ear, he wanted to jump up, grab her and give her the biggest, sloppiest kiss. She finally got it. It had to take her to get furious to realize that he was over Trina. Now on second thought, he was glad things had worked out the way they had. Well, with the exception of his wife threatening to beat his ex to a bloody pulp. No way in the world would he tell her where Trina lived. He could just see it; he and Nick would have to bail the terrible three out of prison. Ava, Summer and Starr were thick as thieves. Anyone that was foolish enough to come up against one of them had it coming. Although they were grown professional women, they weren't above rolling on Trina.

Noticing his grin, Starr quieted her squawking. "What?"

Standing he sauntered over to where she stood. Looking down at her, he lifted her chin and tenderly kissed her lips. "I'm not telling you where Trina lives because I don't want you to get yourself along with your crazy friends in trouble." Kissing the tip of her nose, pulling her to his chest, he said, "I'm just glad you finally realize I don't want her. It's you I want forever. Understand?"

"Yes, I understand. But the next time I see her I'm going to bust her in the mouth."

Kevin chuckled. "Let's hope you don't see her anytime soon."

"Humph, how about never."

Taking a small step back, she looked up into his face. "One more question."

"Yes, nosy box."

"Shut up and just answer the darn question."

"You haven't asked it yet."

Starr rolled her eyes. "Keep playing with me and no more loving for you for a week."

Grabbing his chest staggering backwards, he gasped, "No, please not that."

Shaking her head, she laughed at her crazy husband. "Did Nick ever try to convince you to break up with her?"

Kevin gave her cocky smirk. "You mean how you and the other pit bull tried to do my man and his woman?" Starr swatted at Kevin like a cat at its catch, but missed her target when he jumped back laughing at her.

She and Ava were highly offended when Summer told them of Nick's pet name for them. Although they were on good terms with him by then, that hadn't stopped them from giving Nick a piece of their minds the next time they saw him.

"Where the hell do you get off calling us some damn dogs?" Ava pounced, her hands on her hips ready for a verbal sparring.

"Yeah! Nick, you are so wrong," Starr cosigned. The entire time Summer sat in the background sniggering. Her girls had blindsided Nick and she was enjoying every minute of it. Ava had been so riled up she hadn't waited for him to put Autumn down, who was an infant, before she pounced. They became even more outraged when he roared with laughter in their faces.

Handing the sleeping infant to his wife, Nick made his way to the twisted face twins. Throwing a massive arm around each of their necks, he drew them into a tight brotherly embrace.

Kissing each on the forehead, "Y'all know I was only joking."

Starr chuckled as she remembered that day. "Well, Nick was a mess back then. We didn't want him to hurt our girl any more than he had already done."

"Yeah, I hear you. Nick is my brother, but he was straight up trippin'."

"I agree. But now that I know the whole story, I understand where he was coming from." Starr shook her head. "I can't tell you how many times we begged that girl to tell Nick she was pregnant."

"The poor girl was terrified. Nick can be one beast you don't want to go up against if he thinks you've crossed him."

"Yeah, tell me about it." She said covering her mouth letting out a yawn. She was suddenly drained from all the events of the night. A small sigh escaped her lips as she remembered how the evening began.

Mimicking her, he too, covered his mouth letting out yawn. Kevin took Starr by the hand. "Come on baby, it's been a long night."

Finishing their talk as they walked hand in hand up the stairs to their bedroom, Starr pointed out, "We got off track and you never answered my question. Did he try to talk you of dating her?"

"Naw, not really. But I knew he wasn't crazy about her. He would just say, 'Dude you like living dangerously, don't you?'"

Each pulled down the spread on their side of the bed and climbed in. "It didn't bother you that he didn't like her?"

"Nope. Just like it didn't bother Nick that you and Ava didn't like him."

Sucking her teeth, she said, "That was different. We liked him until he started acting a fool."

Groping for his wife in the dark as she talked, Kevin pulled her hips to his groin. His muscular arm snaked around her waist. Without hesitation, Starr snuggled against him until she was comfortable.

"Starr?"

"Huh?"

"Go to sleep. I'm tired of talking about Trina." Nudging her bottom with his male hardness, he told her, "If you're not sleepy I got other things you can do besides talk."

Nudging him back with the curve of her firm bottom, she teased, "Boy, in the last two nights, you got enough to last you for the rest of the week."

Chuckling, he kissed the side of neck. "Night, baby."

"Night, my love," Starr whispered.

Hearing his wife's soft snores brought a smile to his lips as he held her close. It felt good knowing he had won her trust. Getting her to love him had come easy. Getting her to not compare him or their relationship to what she had had with her ex had been difficult, almost impossible. Kevin had learned a very valuable lesson tonight. Never would he hide anything from her again. Never did he want to see doubt in her eyes again. Or to have her think that he had been dishonest with her. Even if he feared her worst reaction, he would be honest and tell her the truth. More than anything, he wanted her trust. Whatever challenges were in their future, they would face them head on together. *No more secrets.*

Chapter 29

"Girl, you ought to be ashamed of yourself," Ava lazily mumbled as she and her friend lounged in massage pedicure chairs.

Opening an eye peeping at Ava, she miserably agreed. "I know, I know. I acted like a brat."

Ava switched the massage setting to high on the kneed mode. Her back was killing her. She didn't know if she needed a new mattress or if it were the restless nights she was having.

"I'm not talking about that. But humph, you did better than me. I would've started throwing things and breaking stuff up."

Starr laughed. If it had been Ava, everything breakable would've been broken. "I know that's right." Settling back into the soft leather, vibrating chair closing her eyes, Starr asked, "What are you talkin' about?"

"Oh, just the fact that *you* didn't come clean with your man."

Cringing, Starr couldn't deny her friend's rebuke. Here she had gotten all bent out of shape, throwing a temper tantrum because Kevin had withheld information, while she wasn't completely honest herself. Well, she hadn't actually lied. She just hadn't told him that her father had all of a sudden dropped back on planet earth from who knows where and had called her.

Starr had thought about changing her cell number because the man had the nerve to contact her again. He gave some lame excuse about needing to talk to her and Karen about something "very important." He was babbling some mess about family business they needed to discuss. As far as she was concerned, she didn't care if he'd hit the lottery and wanted to give her millions, she wanted nothing to do with him. After the third call, she vehemently told him, "I will have you arrested for stalking me if you don't stop calling me." He pleaded, "Sweetheart, just let me explain—"

Not hesitating to cut her father off, she hissed between clenched teeth, "Explain to me how you could turn your back on your wife and daughters time after time. Explain how you could make promises knowing you weren't going to follow through on them. Explain how you sent my mother into a depression so deep she'd almost killed herself and left me and my sister to fend for ourselves. I was barely out of high school and Karen was still in college."

By this point, Starr's chest was heaving as silence answered her. She wanted him to say something, anything that would show he had an ounce of regret. She didn't want to hear some nonsense about him being her father, and because of their biological connection, all should be forgiven. When he didn't answer, Starr wearily mumbled almost in tears, "Yeah, that's what I thought." *Click.*

It was sad to admit, but the truth was her father was so insignificant to her, she hadn't thought twice about telling Kevin. But now that her friend had brought it up, she realized she had been wrong to withhold her father's recent attempts to meet with her. Bending down, she pulled her purse onto her lap.

Giving her a quizzical glance, Ava watched Starr fumble through her purse. *What in the world is she doing?* Starr had taken everything but the kitchen sink from her handbag. Finally, she pulled out the cell phone that had been buried under all the stuff now sitting on her lap. "Who you are getting ready to call?"

"My honey, so I can apologize. Av, you're right. I should have told him when my Dad called the first time."

"Mmm hmm. Handle your business."

Ava closed her eyes trying to relax as the technicians sat at the end of the pedicure chairs pampering their feet. She drowned out Starr's voice as she confessed her little transgression to Kevin. She didn't have time to be nosy; she had other things on her mind. Lately, her painful past was coming back to haunt her. She wanted to talk to someone, but didn't know how to go about doing so. Over the years, she had shared every secret with her two best friends, except for this one. Too ashamed of what she had done, she didn't know how to go about telling her friends, her dirty little secret. *What will they think of me?*

Flipping the phone shut, Starr grinned to herself. Kevin hadn't been upset with her at all. To her surprise, he had told her, "I know you would have told me if things had gotten out of hand." Sheepishly she confessed, "Things may have already gotten out of hand."

Starr was furious with Karen when she learned she had met with their father to discuss *family business.* She was flabbergasted to learn their father wanted to reclaim his family. The man clearly believed they were still impressionable children who would be thrilled to have him back in their lives.

As always, the man had an ulterior motive. The only reason he contacted them was because Donna had tracked him down and served him with divorce papers, which he refused to sign.

During his meeting with Karen, he carried on and on about how he was a changed man and wanted his family back. When Karen didn't buy into what he was selling, he became irritated and threatened to track their mom down when she refused to tell him Donna whereabouts.

Livid, Starr decided to give her mom a visit to warn her of his threat. The last thing she and Karen wanted was for *that* man to track their mom down and sweet-talk her out of divorcing him. For some reason neither of them understood, their father had a strong hold on their mother. They often wondered if he had roots on her. It wasn't unreasonable for them to think he would be able to worm his way back into their mother's life after all these years. He'd done so in the past on several occasions.

After briefly talking things over with Kevin, they decided to drive down to Virginia to visit her mom. Starr didn't want her blindsided in the event her father did tract her down. The last time she had talked with her mom on the phone, she was happy. Getting away from Philly and the painful memories it held had done wonders for Donna. No way was Starr going to let that shiftless man destroy her mom's life again.

Hearing Starr flip the phone shut, Ava asked, "Everything okay?"

"Yup. We're going to drive down to see my mom next weekend."

"I thought y'all only went to see her on Mother's Day?"

"We do. But my dad is threatening to track her down. Says he wants her back."

"*What*?" Ava jerked her foot, nearly kicking the technician in the face as she applied nail polish to her toes.

The technician huffed, rolling her eyes as she shot daggers at Ava for smudging three of the toes she'd just painted.

"Sorry," Ava mumbled.

Sucking her teeth at Ava, Starr apologized to the technician. "Please forgive my friend. She hasn't had her medication today."

The woman ignored Starr's apology. Grumbling in Russian under her breath, she yanked Ava's foot as she removed the smudged polish.

Starr firmly held Ava's hand, shaking her head no. Ava balled her fist up ready to strike the grumbling woman on top of her head. She hadn't taken too kindly to the woman yanking on her foot."Can't take you anywhere. Don't know how to act," Starr teased.

Ava laughed. "Shut up girl and tell me why your pops is talkin' crazy."

"He's refusing to sign the divorce papers he was served. Talkin' about he need to find my mom to talk some sense into her. Karen said she got so sick of him going on and on about us still being a family." Starr sucked her teeth still annoyed with Karen. "I told her that's what she gets for meeting with that foolish man."

"Ain't he a piece of work?" Ava sarcastically drawled out.

"Girlfriend, you ain't neva lie."

Each woman fell silent in her own private thoughts. One wondered how she was going to deal with the nightmare of her past, while the other prayed a master manipulator wouldn't bewitch her mother.

♥♥♥

"It's not working," hissed the female voice.

"What do you mean it's not working? You said you had everything covered." The irritated male voice snapped on the other end of the phone as he watched the two women leaving the day spa on Germantown Avenue.

It had only taken a few months of sweet-talking and a quick romp in the sheets to win over the plain Jane bank teller at Starr's bank. After one night in the frumpy teller's bed, she sang like a canary giving him all of Starr's financial information. He was blown away by the amounts in her checking and saving accounts. The one surprise he hadn't been prepared for was that she had married. Initially he was furious, that is, until he figured out how this new inconvenience would work out to his advantage. With a little more digging, it wasn't hard for him to learn she had married well and had access to her new husband's accounts.

After using the bank teller to get what he needed, he dropped her like a bad habit. Now if he could get the bimbo on the phone to do her part, he'd have the money he needed and then some.

Huffing with an attitude, she snapped, "Like I said, it's not working."

"Well, you better make it work. If you can't get that punk Dawson out of the picture one way, then you'd better do it another way." A deathly pause hung between the phone lines before he spoke again. "Not unless want your cousin going to prison."

Fear quickly replaced her attitude. She knew she should have walked away when he caught her slashing Starr's tires early that morning. Instead, he had talked her into joining forces in destroying Kevin and Starr's relationship. He made it all sound so good. "We'll both get what we want. You'll get Kevin and I'll get Starr."

She had been so caught up in having Kevin she hadn't been thinking straight when she pulled her younger cousin into her schemes. In a million years, she would have never dreamed the man she was scheming with was an officer of the courts. Lady Luck definitely wasn't on her side. The guy was her cousin's probation officer. When she contacted him a few weeks ago telling him she was having second thoughts, he wasn't too pleased. "You know all I have to do is call your cousin in for a piss test and switch the specimens."

Dumbfounded, she yelled in disbelieve, "You wouldn't do that. Aren't you an officer of the courts?" Because her cousin had a drug offense, any positive testing for drugs meant going back to jail serving out the remainder of the sentence. His sinister chuckle sent chills down her spine. "Try me."

Voice trembling, she begged, "Please, I've done everything I can do. He's not interested."

"You got one month."

"But—" The phone went dead before she could finish pleading her case.

One month was all he had to get the rest of the fifty thousand he owed. Juggling women with his charm was beginning to get on his last nerve. None of them had enough money for him. A hundred dollars here and there wasn't getting it. He needed someone with a substantial bank account and Starr fit the bill. Once he got that punk of a husband out of the way, he'd swoop in to save the day with empty promises of forever. Heck, to get at that hefty nest egg she had chilling, collecting interest; he'd be willing to marry her this time right after she divorced Dawson, taking with her a nice sizable settlement.

Pulling off from the curb, he smugly chuckled to himself. “Once I get in those panties, she’ll give me anything I want.

Chapter 30

Grabbing the collar of her coat, Starr wished she had worn a scarf. The cool early December air was brisk, chilling her to the bone. Shivering she prayed, "Come on, please open the door."

No sooner than the prayer left her lips, the door swung open.

"My, isn't this a wonderful surprise." Holding the door open, the sweet woman beckoned, "Come on in here out the cold, sweetie."

Starr quickly stepped into the warm living space. Closing and locking the door, she embraced the older woman. "Hi Momma, how are you?"

Returning the warm embrace from her daughter-in-law, she beamed, "I'm find honey. To what do I owe this wonderful visit?" Beverly loved having one of her daughter-in-laws living so close by. As much as she loved her sons, she'd always wanted a daughter. Her sons had chosen well. She adored their wives.

Since that night Kevin had shared with her, Beverly had been harassed, Starr had taken to calling her every day and popping in on her regularly. She wanted to make sure she was okay and hoped she would catch Trina lurking. She was still itching to get hands on her one good time.

"I just wanted to stop by to see you before Kevin and I go visit my mom this weekend."

"That's good you're going to see your mom. I hope everything works out." Starr had mentioned to Beverly what was going on with her father. Though she never met the man, she didn't like him. What decent man would treat his wife and children that way? Going into the other room she mused *they sure don't make them like my Richard anymore.* She thought it was wonderful how protective Starr and her sister were of their mother. She prayed if their mother showed the slightest hint of going back to a man like that, that Starr and Kevin would be able to dissuade her if possible. Beverly let out a small sigh. *Love can make you do some crazy things.*

Taking off her coat and hanging it in the hall closet, Starr went into the kitchen where she was sure Beverly had gone and was waiting for her. They had set up their own little routine every time she came over. After washing her hands, she proceeded to take down two mugs from the cupboard then handed Beverly the canister containing several herbal tea bags.

"What flavor?"

"Vanilla."

Beverly smiled, "Good choice."

The two women worked in comfortable silence enjoying each other's company as they prepared their tea.

"Momma, do you have any more of that lemon pound cake?"

Beverly softly giggled. "Your husband ate the last of that the other night when he popped up over here."

Beverly was so blessed. Many of her friends' children could care less about their elderly parents, let alone coming to visit. Most of their children had spouses who pressured them into throwing their parents into state managed nursing homes because they are less expensive than privately owned elderly assisted complexes. Thank goodness, Beverly didn't have to worry about that. Her children understood how important her independence was to her. What her husband's pension didn't cover, her sons gladly paid the difference without hesitation.

"But there are some chocolate chip cookies I baked earlier in the cookie jar." Beverly had sensed Starr would be coming to visit when she called earlier wanting to know if she would be busy later in the evening. Wanting to have a snack prepared for her, she baked her secret recipe chocolate chip cookies.

"I tell you that son of yours eats like there's no tomorrow," Starr joked as she removed two cookies from the snowman on the counter. It's a good thing Kevin was active and worked out on a regular basis, otherwise he might end up as round as the snowman on the counter. If she didn't watch it, she would end up the same way, too. That's why she only took two and not three or four of the sweet treat.

"He's always had a healthy appetite. He was the greediest baby and chubbiest little thing. When he started walking he would topple over because he was so fat." Beverly chuckled, "Little legs could hardly hold him up."

Starr laughed imagining the chunky baby from all the pictures she looked at falling on his rump every time he tried to stand. "Well, he better cut it out before he becomes a chubby old man."

Biting into the thick cookie with huge chunks of chocolate, Starr moaned. "He couldn't help but to be a fat baby with the way you cook and bake." She knew it was rude to talk with your mouth full, but she couldn't help it. Beverly cookies were delicious. "Momma you've got to give me the recipe for these cookies."

"It's a secret. Momma can't give you the recipe right now," Beverly said as she brought the mug to her lips hiding a smile. Starr looked rejected by her mother-in-law's refusal to give her the recipe.

"Why?" Starr asked in a pitiful voice.

Beverly sat the mug down looking directly into the younger woman's eyes. "Well, because it's not for you."

"Oh," Starr mumbled dropping her gaze, feelings hurt, wondering what she had done to the older woman.

Placing her hand onto top of Starr's to soothe her hurt feelings. "I said I wouldn't give you the secret recipe now. You want to know why?"

Nodding her head, "Yes, ma'am."

"I can't give it to you until after you have my first grandchild." Gently squeezing her hand she added, "That's the only way you'll get my secret chocolate chip cookie recipe is to make them for my grandbabies."

Relieved, Starr smiled. "Not even for my big baby, your son?"

Chuckling, shaking her head, "Nope. Not even for our big baby. My recipe is for a new baby." Lifting her brow, she inquired, "Y'all are working on some grandbabies for me… aren't you?"

Blushing with embarrassment Starr lower her gaze again, she didn't want to tell this sweet elderly woman they were going at it like a couple of rabbits. That would be downright tacky.

Starr mumbled in total humiliation, "Yes, Momma we're working on it."

Beverly stood up and wrapped her arm around the younger woman's shoulder. "Sweetie, you don't have anything to be embarrassed about. There's nothing wrong with loving your man and making some grandbabies for me in the process. I'm an old lady. I'm just trying to make sure y'all aren't sleeping on the job."

Standing, Starr laughed all embarrassment fading as she hugged her mother-in-law. "Believe me we're trying real hard to give you those grandbabies."

Stepping back from the embrace Beverly's keen eyes zeroed in on the spot on Starr's neck right above her collarbone. With a wink, she teased, "I see how hard the two of you've been working."

"Momma!" Starr squealed embarrassed as her hand flew to her neck shielding the passion mark.

Starr twisted and turned, trying to get comfortable, but it was no use. No matter what positioned she settled into she couldn't get comfortable. Most of her restlessness was because her mother didn't know she was coming. She intentionally hadn't contacted her because she was afraid she would've refused her visit.

After talking with Karen, Summer and Ava, they all agreed the element of surprise would be best. However, she was now second-guessing her decision. She hoped this didn't blow up in her face. Or better yet, that her father hadn't gotten to her mom first. Starr would just die if she got there and her father was already there with his feet propped up, acting like he owned the joint.

Taking his eyes off the road briefly, he glanced over at his wife's restless form. "You all right baby?" He could tell something was up with her from the time they hit the road. The entire time she was supposed to be sleeping, she was fretful.

Opening her eyes, she rolled her head to the side and studied her husband before she spoke. Realizing how blessed she was to have a man to support her was giving her the strength needed to confront her mom. She had so desperately wanted her sister to come with her. The two of them together had a better chance of getting through to their mother if their dad had showed up working his voodoo.

However, she understood Karen would have her hands full with Kyle and Alicia's weekend activities. When she insisted on getting a sitter for the kids, Starr assured her she would be able to handle things. She wouldn't ask her to sacrifice her children. That just wouldn't be right.

Needing to draw comfort from him, she rested her hand on his thigh. Letting out a deep breath, she voiced what was troubling her. "What if my mom gets upset when we show up unannounced?"

"Why would she be upset?" He asked quickly glancing at her, briefly taking his attention away from the road. He hadn't said anything before because he didn't want to pry, but he wondered why Donna would only see her family once a year. He just couldn't shake the feeling that she was somehow punishing them because of her husband's past sins. He prayed that wasn't the case.

Hunching her shoulders, she truthfully answered, "I guess she likes to be alone, away from everybody."

Slowly he nodded his head as if he understood when he really didn't. "I see."

Starr frowned bunching her perfectly arched eyebrows together. "No, you don't."

Kevin chuckled. He couldn't put a thing past Starr. "You're right, I don't understand."

Feeling a wave of sadness wash over her, she confessed, "I don't understand myself Kevin why I'm so nervous about popping up seeing my own mother. I know part of it is because I'm terrified that she may want to work things out with my dad. I can't tell you how many times we've been down this road before. Now that mom has finally got up the courage to serve him with papers, he wants to talk this *we're a family crap* again."

Placing his hand on top of hers, he gently squeezed her hand then brought it to his lips for a tender kiss. "Baby, I don't know what to say other than I'm sorry you and Karen had to go through all of that growing up and still have to deal with it as adults."

He paused for a second trying to organize his thoughts before he spoke again. He prayed Donna wouldn't succumb to her husband's sweet talk and finally kick his sorry butt to the curb. However, he was a realist; there was a possibility that she may allow him back into her life. As much as it would hurt her, he needed Starr to realize this as well.

"Baby, you know you're mom might decide she wants to try again with your dad."

Dropping her face into her hands, she moaned, "I know. That's why I'm so scared."

Lifting her head up, tears threatening to spill over the lids, she whispered, "I don't want her to see us coming down here as interfering in her life. I don't think I could take it if she thinks I'm trying to stand between her and my father." Wiping away a tear, her voice quivered. "I never told this to anyone but sometimes I think my mother blames me for my dad leaving."

Kevin maneuvered the car to the side of the scarcely traveled dirt country road. Turning on the hazard signals, he put the vehicle in park and turned off the ignition. Leaning over he curved his hand around the back of Starr's neck and rested his forehead against hers. Tenderly kissing her lips and massaging the side of her neck with his thumb, he wanted her to understand something. "Baby, don't do this to yourself. You were an innocent child and there's no way you could've been responsible for the actions of two grown adults. It was your mother's choice to keep letting a man back into her life time and time again, who did nothing but abuse his family's love." Again, he paused carefully selecting his words. "I'm not saying your mom blames you, but if she does, it still doesn't make it your fault. Baby, you can't carry that burden. It's too heavy." Kissing the tip of her nose, he said, "I won't let you carry it."

Wrapping her arms around his neck, she gazed into his eyes. She shivered from what she saw in their dark depths…Love and protection. Not only was this man willing to love her, he was willing to protect her, even from herself. For years, she carried the guilt of having played a role in her parents' rocky marriage. Many times she thought if she hadn't been born and Karen remained an only child, things would have been different. Perhaps they would have been happy without the pressure of having to raise another child.

Pressing her lips to his, she whispered, "Thank you for loving me."

"You're welcome," he huskily whispered back as he traced the outline of her lips with his tongue, and then gently pried her mouth open. Starr let out a soft moan as he rolled his tongue around the tip of hers and then lovingly suckled it. When his hand traveled up the front of her blouse and squeezed a firm breast, she grabbed his hand pulling it away like a shy teenaged virgin girl.

"What's wrong?"

"They lock you up around these parts for making out on the side of the road."

Kevin laughed as he started up the car, pulling away from the side of the road. "Let's get moving then. A brotha can't afford to get locked up."

Starr laughed. "I know that's right."

Chapter 31

"Starr." Kevin whispered as he leaned over softly kissing her forehead. He hated to wake her; she had finally drifted off into a restful slumber. This trip was weighing heavier on her than he thought it might. It had been difficult for him to see her so uptight and worried about this visit; about how Donna would receive her. Kevin swore to himself if she said anything out of the way to Starr, he was respectfully going to say his peace. And what he had to say, she wasn't going to like.

"Hmmm." The short catnap was just getting good when she heard her name being softly called. A lazy smile touched her lips as she looked at Kevin through heavy lips. Running his finger along the soft curve of her cheek, he returned the smile.

"Wake up sleepy head, we're here."

Stretching to loosen up her stiff limbs, Starr looked out the car's window. The small cottage in the tiny rural Virginia community was the only dwelling for two miles. Donna's nearest neighbors, the Smithfields, were further down the stretched dirt road. *Why in the world does Mommy want to live way out her?*

"Come on, baby. Let's get out." Kevin needed to stretch, too. Driving for so many hours had just about every muscle in his body stiff and achy. Stepping out the car, he rolled his massive shoulders then reached his hands high above his head. Walking around to the passenger side, he rolled his head from side to side working out the crook in his neck.

"Okay," Starr murmured, her stomach tied in knots. *Here we go.*

Pulling open the passenger door Kevin offered his hand. When she hesitated for a second, he reminded her, "Baby, it's going to be all right. I'm here with you."

Placing her hand in his, she stepped out the car. "Thanks, I appreciate it."

Surveying the land, the place looked different than it had last spring. Gone were the vibrant flowers, thick emerald shrubs and lush green grass that so beautifully adorned the grounds of the cottage. In their stead were Christmas ornaments. Starr swallowed the lump forming in her throat as she peered at the nativity scene. About three feet from where they stood, the wise men were on their donkeys bearing gifts as a shining star suspended from a two hundred year old oak tree led them to the baby King in the manger.

Fighting to keep the tears from falling, Starr put one unsteady foot in front of the other as she held onto Kevin's hand. Her mother had always dreamed of recreating the nativity scene, however, could never afford to purchase the expensive props. The scene was absolutely breathtaking. It had her mom's creative handiwork all over it.

Standing at the front door, Starr bit down on her bottom lip as she looked over her shoulder. Kevin gave her a reassuring nod. Resting his hands on her shoulders, he whispered in her ear, "Baby, I'm right here with you."

Starr nodded, accepting his assurance. *I can do this.* Curling her right hand into a fist, she lifted her fist to tap the door. However, before she could knock the door swung open.

Surprise made her eyes go wide as saucers. She had the right house, didn't she? Had her mother moved and hadn't told her? Fear seized her as she wondered what had happened to her mother. *Oh, No! Did Daddy get to her before me? Did she run off with him?*

"You must be Starr," the deep voice stated.

Blinking she was wondering how this mammoth man knew who she was. If he hadn't had warm, twinkling sky blue eyes, she would have been terrified. His full height had to be well over six feet and his weight at least two hundred fifty pounds. The two long, salt and pepper braided ponytails and thick beard, made him look like a proud card carrying member of Hell's Angels.

Starr felt Kevin nudging her in her lower back. "Baby, the man is talking to you."

"Huh? Oh… I'm…I'm sorry. I'm looking for my mother," she stuttered.

"Honey, who's at the door?"

"Mommy?" *That is my mother, isn't it? What is this man doing here? And why is mommy calling him honey?*

Biker man stepped aside allowing Donna to step in front of him.

"Mommy," was all Starr managed to choke out before she burst into tears going into her mother's outstretched arms.

♥♥♥

Snuggled in Kevin's arms, on the pull out sofa bed in her mother's comfy den, she couldn't believe all that had transpired earlier today. Who would have ever guessed her mother had *really* moved on with her life? She and Patrick Wahl had been dating for over a year and were ready to get married. The only thing holding them up was her father's refusal to sign the divorce papers. As usual, he was being a real jerk. He had actually been in contact with Donna and knew of her plans to marry Patrick. Starr was furious when she connected the dots figuring out that that's why he had come around with his *wanting to be a family* crap. Donna had moved on, wanted no parts of him and was now finally happy with a man that truly loved her. And her father couldn't stand it.

It had been so long since she'd seen her mother so happy. Every time Patrick looked at her mom with so much love shining through those sparkling blue eyes of his, she fought to keep tears of happiness from spilling. As hard as she fought, the floodgates came rushing forth when Patrick adamantly let it be known, "That bastard can shuffle his feet all he wants, he's not getting my woman. I'll kill him first!"

Donna didn't know what to do as her youngest child bawled her eyes out. She looked to Kevin for guidance. All he did was hunched his broad shoulders. He hadn't the slightest idea as to what was wrong with her.

Embarrassed by his outburst, Patrick turned red as a beet. He hadn't meant to upset his future stepdaughter. He was still pissed because that idiot father of hers was being a jackass. It had taken him years to find a good woman like Donna. He'd be damned if he let her no good, deadbeat husband waltz back in her life and try to take her away.

"Baby, come with me," Donna tenderly whispered, taking her child by the hand. Once in her bedroom, she motioned for Starr to sit on the bed. She had kept her relationship with Patrick from her daughters because she wasn't sure how they would take her being involved with a man *like* him. She knew the two of them were an odd couple, but she didn't care. Patrick loved her and made her feel desirable. Something she hadn't felt in over thirty years.

Clearing her throat, Donna's voice came out in a nervous tremble. "Sweetie what's wrong? Why are you upset "?

Taking the box of tissues her mom handed to her from the nightstand, Starr whipped her tears away and then blew her nose.

"Mommy, I'm not upset."

"Then why are you crying?"

"Oh, mommy these are tears of joy. I'm so glad you finally have a man to love you. I haven't seen you this happy in a long, long time."

Donna let out a sigh of relief. She thought her baby was upset because Patrick had lost his temper. "I thought you were upset because of what Patrick said."

Starr laughed. "Shoot, I'll help Patrick kill him myself."

Shaking her head, Donna put on her best, motherly stern face. "Now, Starr Michelle Avery Dawson, that man is still your father."

Starr dryly drawled out, "Oh joy, joy for me. Please don't remind me."

Wrapping her arms around her baby girl, Donna laughed sending the both tumbling backwards on the bed. "I see that mouth of yours is still fresh as ever."

Laughing, she denied her mother's accusation. "Uh-uh, Mommy."

Donna felt so free. Continuing her laughter with her daughter, she nodded, "Uh-huh, Starr."

After a few seconds, the bubbling laughter faded. Mother and daughter held hands as they lay on their backs staring at the peach color ceiling. Starr enjoyed the comfort of being so close to her mother. She hadn't felt this close to her mom since she and Karen were little girls and they would pile in bed with her. Hearing their mom crying, they wanted to make her feel better. Although too young to understand why she was so upset, they would crawl into her bed, snuggle real close and tell her, "Mommy please don't cry. We love you." She remembered how her mom would wrap an arm around each of them, her crying tapering off to a painful whimper.

Donna rolled on her side and wrapped her arms around Starr. She pulled her close to her like she was a little girl again. A tear rolled down her check as she softly spoke. "This reminds me of how you and Karen used to climb in bed with me when you were little. Not knowing what was going on, but knowing enough to know I needed your love." Reaching out she gently stroked Starr's cheek. "I don't know what I would have done without you and your sister." It was their love that made her get up every morning to face another day.

"You really mean that Mommy?"

"Of course baby. Why do you ask that?"

Hunching her shoulders against the mattress, she decided *I might as well tell her*. "I thought you blamed me for Daddy leaving. I believed if I had never been born maybe he wouldn't have left."

Starr willingly went as her mother drew her even closer into her embrace. Resting her head against her mother's bosom, the tears began to flow again.

"Oh baby, you and your sister are the best your father ever gave me. I would never blame you for what he did. But after a while baby, I just couldn't take being hurt anymore. As you and Karen grew older and more independent, I withdrew more into myself. By the time you girls were old enough to take care of yourselves, I had to get away from my old life. Baby, I never stopped loving you girls. I was just so angry and bitter I didn't want how I felt to have an impact on you. Can you understand that?"

Listening intently to every word her mother spoke, years of guilt seeped deep from out of her soul. Her mother hadn't blamed her, nor had she abandoned her and Karen. She did what she had to do to survive because she was dying a slow death.

"Yes, I understand." Pausing for a moment, she wanted to know, "Mommy, are you really happy? I'm mean are you really, really happy?"

Gently she pushed her daughter out of her embrace to look her in the eye. "Baby, I haven't been this happy in years. Patrick is so good to me and for me." Searching her daughter's face she asked, "Does it bother you that he's white?"

Starr sat up, Donna followed. Grabbing her mom's hand, she gently squeezed it. "I don't care if he's purple, as long as he makes you happy and treats you right."

"Oh, baby he does all those things and more." A wide smile spread across Donna's warm brown face showing off dimples identical to her daughter's. "Wanna hear how we met?"

"You know I do," Starr said getting comfortable as she crossed her legs waiting to hear a good story.

Donna giggled. "I see you're still nosy as ever," she teased as she began her tale of the great Patrick Wahl.

♥♥♥

"You want a beer?" Patrick offered. He and his houseguest had been sitting alone for quite sometime.

"Sure." Kevin followed him to the kitchen taking a seat at the table as Patrick grabbed a couple of beers from the fridge.

Joining Kevin at the table, Patrick asked, "What do you think they're talking about in there?"

Twisting the top off the bottle, Kevin replied, "Who knows. They probably have a lot of catching up to do. I'm sure they'll be out in a little bit." Chuckling to lighten things up he said, "They better not forget us out here. You know how women are when they get to talking." Kevin made his hands move like a puppet's mouth. "Yak, yak, yak, yak."

Patrick attempted a smile, but failed miserably. "Do you think I upset, Starr?"

The concern in the middle-aged man's eyes didn't go unnoticed by Kevin. He felt bad for the poor guy. "Naw, man I don't think she's upset." Lifting the bottle to his lips, he took a swig. "Probably just got PMS. You know they grow three evil heads during that time of the month." Kevin chuckled at his own joke.

The older man threw back his head and roared. Pointing his finger at Kevin he warned, "You better not let the women folk hear you talking like that. I don't know about that woman of yours, but if she's anything like her momma, you better watch yourself." One of the things he loved about Donna was her feistiness when something or someone ruffled her feathers. The first disagreement they had, she out flat made it be known, "In my younger days I took a lot of crap off of people. I'm not the same Donna. I'm not taking anything off of you and nobody else!"

Kevin grinned at his beer-drinking partner. Patrick was cool people. He couldn't deny, he too, was shocked when Patrick opened the door. He chuckled remembering Starr's stunned reaction to seeing him towering over her. He was also taken aback by Donna good looks. Pictures hadn't done her justice. The woman was absolutely gorgeous and had the warmth of sunshine. *Starr's pops is an idiot.* It was plain to see that any man who captured her heart was blessed.

"You best believe it. My baby can be a firecracker when messed with."

"Yep, mine too." Patrick nodded his head in agreement proud of the woman he loved. When he first met Donna, she was withdrawn and leery of him. Initially he'd though it was because of his overwhelming presence. As he pursued her, he learned it had nothing to do with his size or the fact that he was white. It was because he was of the male species.

Several months would go by before she would even consider having coffee with him at the small diner in town. After that, it took him another eight months to convince her that he was romantically interested in her.

"Does Donna squint her eyes and tremble like she's about to explode from the top of her head when she's ready to take your head off for something you've done?" Kevin's eyes twinkled with mischief as he asked the question. He was guilty of agitating his beautiful wife just to get a rise out of her. He'd tease and pick until she couldn't take it anymore. Just as she was about to snap he'd pull her into his arms and kiss her until she was senseless.

"No, way dude!" Patrick's loud voice boomed. Both men chuckled, raising and clinking beer bottles in midair.

"Yes sir. She's just like her momma that's for sure."

Coming down the short-carpeted hallway the two women stopped. Looking at each other Donna and Starr softly giggled as they overheard the men laughing at something that was obviously funny to them. They were out there having a grand 'ole time together.

Donna wrapped her arm around Starr's waist as they headed to where the men were. "You have yourself a good man, baby."

Starr beamed at her mother. It felt good to know she truly hadn't given up on men. "I know, Mommy."

Entering the kitchen, Starr asked, "What's so funny?"

Both men swung around, answering in unison. "Nothing."

Each woman placed their hands on curvy hips, lifting an arch brow as if choreographed. They had a funny suspicion that they were the topic of humor. It didn't take long to prove they were right.

Kevin shifted his gaze trying hard not to make eye contact with Patrick. Earlier before the women came out, they compared notes on how similar mother and daughter were. Not only did they share physical attributes, but mannerisms as well.

However, it was a lost cause when his gaze bounced from Donna, to Starr and then back to Patrick. As the two men eyes connected, both grinned, reading the other's thought before erupting in laughter.

Donna shook her head masking a smile pretending to be annoyed. "Look at them acting like twelve-year-old little boys."

Making a tsking sound with her tongue against her teeth, Starr agreed. "Yup, twelve-year-olds."

Cocking his head to the side, Kevin asked in amazement, "Starr, how do you and your mom do that?"

Wrinkling up her nose, she said, "Do what?"

Standing, Patrick imitated the women's identical gestures. "You know, putting your hands on your hips and doing that thing with one eye brow."

Waving a hand, both women said, "Oh that."

Mother and daughter spun facing each other. Bursting into laughter, Donna hugged her child again, for what seemed like the hundredth time. "What can I say? She's mine through and through. Wait until you see me with both my babies together," Donna bragged. She was so proud of her girls. Despite their having a rocky childhood, overall they had grown up into wonderful adult women.

"Now that will be something. I can't wait to meet Karen."

"Patrick, you'll love my sister and her two rug rats, Alicia and Kyle."

Moving over to Patrick, Donna wrapped her arms around his waist. "Maybe we can go visit Karen and the kids sometime soon."

Patrick affectionately gave Donna a gentle squeeze. "I'd like that sugar."

Standing on the tip of her toes, Donna kissed Patrick on the lips. "Good, maybe we can see them soon."

Just as Starr grinned at Kevin as they looked on at the older couple's display of affection, her stomach growled like she hadn't eaten in months.

"Okay, I don't mean to break up this little love nest but I'm starving."

She hated to break up the happy couple, but she was beyond starving. She hadn't had anything to eat in hours and now she was feeling nauseous with a fierce hunger headache trying to attack her. If she didn't get food soon she was going to be one sick puppy.

Patrick chuckled. "All right little ladies and gent, get your coats so we can get you fed. I know you guys are hungry after that long drive and talking all afternoon."

Grabbing their coats, everyone headed to the door. Donna and Kevin were the first to leave out. As Starr was about to follow suit, Patrick gently tugged at her elbow prompting her to stop. Facing him, she looked up into bright blue serious eyes.

"Starr, I hope I didn't upset you earlier with what I said about your father and all."

Starr tenderly smiled at the older man, wishing her mom's path had crossed with the gentle giant years ago. Taking a step closer she wrapped her arms around the huge man's middle. When his arms embraced her, she let out a small sigh. Though she only met this man a few hours ago, for the first time in her life, she felt a true father's love as he held her. *Why couldn't you have been my real daddy?*

Stepping back from the embrace, she took his large hands in hers. "Patrick, you didn't upset me. Those were tears of joy. I'm just so glad my mom is finally happy." Pausing for a second, she looked him directly in the eye. "And I know you're the one responsible for her happiness."

Patrick swallowed the lump in his throat. He had been worried that Donna's children wouldn't accept him. That's why it had taken them so long to tell Starr and Karen about their relationship. Then when Donna's long lost husband came back demanding he wanted another chance, he feared her children would try to talk their mother into reconciling with their father. He could have danced on air when Starr made it known that she and Karen supported Donna in her decision to finally end a marriage that caused her nothing but misery and pain.

Gently squeezing the small hands that held his he thanked her. "I'm glad you approve. Donna makes me just as happy. I don't know what I would do without her."

Tilting her head to the side, she gave him a puzzled look. "Why wouldn't I approve?"

Uncomfortably, the large man shifted from one foot to the other. "Well…Because I'm white."

Hugging the large man again, she laughed. "Listen here, Poppa Patrick, this is the last time I want to hear this color foolishness from you and Mommy. If she makes you happy and you make her happy, it doesn't matter if she's green and you're blue." Giving him a teasing, scolding glare, she said, "Understand?"

Giving her a tight bear hug, Patrick laughed. "I understand Sugar Two."

"Uh, Poppa Patrick?"

"Yeah, Sugar Two."

"I can't breathe."

Releasing his hold, he threw his head back and laughed. Sometimes he didn't realize his strength. "Come on let's go. They're waiting for us."

Starr laughed accepting his hand as they walked hand in hand out the house, down to the sidewalk.

Standing on the sidewalk Kevin wrapped an arm around Donna's shoulder as they witnessed the exchange between Starr and Patrick. "Everything is going to be all right."

Looking up into the handsome face smiling down at her, Donna agreed. "Yes, everything is going to be all right."

Closing her eyes, Starr snuggled even closer to her snoring husband. Her life had changed dramatically over the last twenty-four hours. Years of feeling hurt and disconnected from her mother had begun to heal as they promised to never allow anything to weaken their bond again. No longer would she have to worry about her mother's happiness because she knew in her heart she had found her soul mate in Patrick Wahl. A man that would give her mother all the love she needed and deserved. A wonderful man who so willingly wanted to be something her own father didn't want to be…A father to her and Karen and grandfather to her niece and nephew.

Who would have thought a thirty-two year old woman would be so giddy with the idea of having a new daddy?

Chapter 32

Walking down the street arm in arm, these four women, beautiful and well dressed, represented Philly's very own version of Girlfriends. Pedestrians passing by eyed the foursome as they gaily talked and laughed taking up the sidewalk as they strutted along Chestnut Street.

The morning had begun with Christmas shopping in Chestnut Hill, as the small group went from shop to shop in search of the perfect Christmas gifts. Karen and Summer repeatedly admonished Ava and Starr each time they purchased clothing or toys for their children. At the rate the Aunties were going, neither mother would have a single gift of her own to put under the tree.

Whenever Karen or Summer protested, they were coolly reminded, "Leave us alone. It's our prerogative if we want to buy our godchildren every toy in the store." Both mothers simply rolled their eyes and walked away before becoming irritated.

By lunchtime, they had hit almost every shop and boutique. Hands sore from carrying large bags, tired and hungry, the next stop was the small pizza shop across the street from Borders Bookstore. Scanning the pizzeria, the place was packed with starving Christmas shoppers.

"We'll never find a place to sit," Summer complained as her stomach began to rumble.

"Ah, God is good." Karen mumbled under her breath as she spotted shoppers vacating a table in the corner. Making eye contact with the last person leaving the table, she gave a pleading look as if to say *please don't let anybody take that table.* When the man smiled, nodding his head in acknowledgement of her plea, she sent him a radiant smile. "Come on y'all, that guy is holding a table for us."

Quickly weaving through the tables, the women resembled the eighties arcade game Centipede. Dropping heavy bags in the corner, each woman profusely thanked the kind man for holding the table for them. If he hadn't been so kind, they would've been standing and waiting for at least another hour.

"No problem, anything for such lovely ladies." The stranger smoothly voiced, his eyes fixed on Karen.

"Thanks." They all sang out at the compliment as they waved goodbye.

After a filling lunch, the foursome dropped their packages off at Summer's house in Chestnut Hill. Wanting to stick to their goal of completing Christmas shopping in one day, they piled into Ava's SUV, jumped on Lincoln Drive, and headed downtown to do some more shopping on Walnut Street.

Five hours and several shopping bags later, the discussion of food was brought up again as bags were loaded into the back of the SUV.

"I'm hungry."

"Dang girl, what you got a tapeworm?" Ava teased as she strategically arranged the bags from prying eyes that might try to peep through the tinted windows. The holidays always brought out the worse criminal elements. It didn't matter that the SUV was parked in a lot; if someone wanted to go from vehicle to vehicle in search of *free* shopping there was nothing stopping them; certainly not the security guard at the booth making ten dollars an hour. The last thing any of them wanted was to have their gifts stolen that had collectively cost them thousands of dollars.

Leaning against the side of the door, Karen said, "I was thinking the same thing, Ava. Starr, honey, you've been eating up a storm lately."

Pursing her lips, she contemplated what Ava and Karen were saying to her. Now that she thought about it, it did seem like she was eating a lot. For some reason, she just couldn't get enough to eat. She didn't even want to think about how many pairs of pants she had tried on this morning until she found a pair that comfortably fit her waist, hips, and thighs. Not to mention that when she tried on a skirt earlier at Ann Taylor the size twelve didn't fit, the size fourteen had a nerve to feel a little snug and finally, the sixteen had the audacity to fit perfectly! Starr made a mental note to get her behind back to the gym at least four times a week. With Kevin busy taking on new clients, they hadn't been able to get their early morning run in. The man was bone tired. Lately, he had been working fourteen hour-long days. The last thing he wanted to do was get up at five in the morning to go running. Luckily for him, there was a fitness center in his office building where he could get his three times a week workout in. Starr concluded she would have to do the same thing.

Moving in with Kevin, she had to make some major adjustments. She now had a husband and an elderly mother-in-law to think about. She went from keeping a small house spotless to a large, four bedroom, two and half bathroom home. Also, she had to get accustomed to doing laundry for two, preparing meals for two, sometimes three, if Beverly came over for dinner, in addition to all of the other activities she did before getting married.

With all of this new activity going on, something had to give until she could adjust. Unfortunately, her regular workout schedule had been sacrificed, but not anymore. First thing Monday morning, Starr decided that she was going to leave for work an hour earlier and hit the gym. This extra weight had to go.

"You got something to add?" She asked her other friend since everyone else was commenting on her current eating habits. Why hadn't they commented on her weight, too? If they had noticed how much she was eating, surely they noticed the spreading hips.

Summer looked at her, and then shrugged a slim shoulder. "No, I don't have anything to say. You've been eating a lot lately. What's the big deal?"

Starr grinned at her petite friend. She could always count on her to be the free thinker of the group. If the others said, "go right," she would say "go left." This time she was going left with Summer. She was hungry and didn't particularly give a hoot about her spreading hips. *I'll get to the gym first thing Monday morning.*

"Well let's go then. I'm starving, where to?"

"How about that Brazilian Steakhouse?" Summer suggested, tapping her top lip with a leathered gloved finger. "Shoot, what's the name of that place? Nick and I went there a few months ago."

"You mean, FOGO DE CHACO on Chestnut Street?" Ava threw over her shoulder as she slammed the trunk door of the vehicle.

"Yeah, that's it. Ooh, Starr you'll love this place. It has a salad bar to die for."

"That's what I heard. One of my coworkers had lunch there and said the food was absolutely incredible," Karen chimed in.

Linking an arm through Karen's and then Ava's, Starr said, "Well, FUJI DEL COW it is."

The other women cracked up laughing. Starr was forever jacking up a name. It's "FOGO DE CHACO crazy lady," Summer teasingly corrected as she linked her arm through Karen's making them an unbreakable chain as they exited the parking garage.

Closing her eyes, slowly chewing, savoring the tender lamb chop, Starr was in heaven. She had never been to a restaurant that served a selection of so many mouth watering succulent meats. Everything from the pork roast, to the filet mignon, top sirloin, chicken breast wrapped in bacon, sausage, pork and beef ribs, and leg of lamb was scrumptious. Stuffed, she couldn't remember all of the fifteen different savory, fire-roasted meats she sampled. All she knew is that every last one of them were beyond delicious.

Rubbing her tummy, she had to undue the button on her slacks. Not only had she tasted every meat, she went to the salad bar four times. Summer hadn't lied when she said the salad bar was awesome. Everything from crisp fresh vegetables, ripe and juicy fruits, gourmet cheese, all types of greens, fresh baked breads, cured meats and fish adorned the larger than life salad bar.

Letting out a satisfied sigh, she closed her eyes and thought, that *food was soooo good! I definitely got to get my tail to the gym on Monday.* At the rate she was going, her hubby wouldn't be able to effortlessly pick her up anymore. *Uh-huh, I can't have that happening.* Nothing thrilled her more than being picked up and carried to the nearest spot to be made love to. Whether it was a bed, a table, or a chair, it didn't as long as Kevin was the one loving her.

"Starr?" Hearing her name being called she lazily opened her eyes.

"How you just gonna stop talking to us in the middle of a conversation?" Summer huffed turning over the round disc from green to red signaling the waiter to keep moving. If another thing were put on her plate, she would have to be rolled out the door.

"Sorry, Boo." Starr smiled ignoring the three pair of eyes boring into her. It had been over a week since she and Kevin had come back from visiting her mother and new stepfather. With their busy schedules, this was the first opportunity she had to tell them the entire story in detail, with the exception of Karen.

Picking up where she'd left off, word for word she recited her mom's story of how Patrick landed on her doorstep in a severe thunderstorm. He had walked for miles in the thick mud pushing his Harley when he stumbled upon Donna's small country cottage. A combination of cracking lightening, thunder, and pounding at her front door had scared the living daylights out of Donna. Against her better judgment, she felt sorry for the Hell's Angel look alike. Letting him in, she provided shelter until the storm was over and a tow truck could be called to take him and his bike back to his log cabin some fifteen miles down the road. The following week Patrick showed up with a bouquet of flowers and an offer to join him at the local diner for a cup of coffee. Donna kindly accepted the beautiful flowers, but refused the cup of coffee. The gentle blue-eyed giant kept coming around with flowers and his offer to go to the diner. Finally, one day she broke down, climbed on the back of his Harley and off they went.

Elbowing resting on the table, chin propped up in her palm Karen smiled. "I can't wait to meet Poppa Patrick." After talking with her mom's new husband for hours on the phone, she too, felt an immediate connection with him. When Starr called her the next morning after she and Kevin had arrived at their mom's, she asked to speak with Donna and then Patrick. It wasn't that she didn't believe her sister, but she had wanted to hear the fantastic news directly from the source. All those years of seeing her mother live as a hollow shell was over. Before hanging up the phone, she made the couple promise to come for a visit at Christmastime.

"I'm so happy for your mom. I can't wait to meet her and Poppa Patrick," Ava said, leaning over giving Karen a tight squeeze. For years, she and Summer sat by helpless as their best friend and her sister downplayed that not having their mom around hadn't affected them, as if it didn't matter. She didn't understand how they got by with seeing their mother on a once a year schedule. Whenever the sisters talked about Donna, the longing in their voices to have her around permanently was heartbreaking.

It did matter. Ava could attest that it did. Countless sleepless nights nagged her, reminding her how one's heart could literally ache when you couldn't have the one you loved.

Summer took a sip of her iced tea then set it down. "Are you guys still fighting over who they're staying with?"

Starr giggled. "We've decided it would only be fair if we shared them."

Summer lifted a perfectly arched brow. "Shared them?"

"Yup. Mommy is going to stay with me and the kids a couple of days—"

Finishing her sister's sentence, "And with me and Kevin a couple of days." Rolling her eyes she huffed, "You know my co-workers had a nerve to get mad at me because I wanted the week of Christmas off."

Starr didn't give a flying pig how mad they got. Over fourteen years had passed since her mother had come home and there was no way she was going to be at work when she did. Her supervisor *tried* to deny her the time off. However, Starr had to make the woman remember that she hadn't taken a vacation all summer. Having two nurses take time off to get married, another out on maternity leave and everyone else taking much deserved vacations, Starr had been a trooper and foregone her summer vacation. And now that she needed time off, the supervisor had a nerve to deny the request. The reason for the denial was some lame excuse about hospital policy and not taking time off during the holiday. Well, what about the policy that said every employee is entitled to have two fifteen-minute breaks and a thirty-minute lunch during a working shift? Plenty of nurses worked straight through eight-hour shifts without breaks. That policy sure wasn't being enforced.

The one evening Kevin managed to make it home at a decent

hour, she was in a foul mood, fussing up a storm. Snatching open cabinets taking down dishes slamming them on the table, she threatened to quit her job. That's how serious she was about spending time with her mom. Before she could slam the glasses down, Kevin gently removed them from her hands. "If you feel this strongly about getting time off, do what you gotta do, baby."

Giving him that, *Are you saying what I think you're saying* look, she asked to make sure she was reading him correctly, "You think I should quit?"

"Yup. Baby, you're a nurse, you can get a job anywhere. If they can't appreciate that you did them a favor last summer by not taking a vacation while everybody else did their thing, then I say the hell wit 'em." Filling the glasses with iced tea, he winked at her. "You know I got you."

Everything he said to her made perfect sense. Other institutions were always sending her literature in the mail about available nursing positions in the tri-state area. Starr was a team player when it came to her job. She couldn't count the times she's volunteered for overtime, came in on her day off because the unit was short staffed or was willing to be pulled to another floor that had a call out. Although she loved her job, cared about the patients she took care of, and got along with her coworkers, she would give it all up to be with her mom. It just didn't seem fair that she gave so much and when there had come a time she needed a favor, the boss lady had pulled some policy crap on her.

Picking up a plate from the table, she stopped to give him a quick peck on the lips before going over to the stove to fix his plate.

"Thanks honey, I just might do that."

The next morning, Starr waltzed in her supervisor's office with her letter of resignation in hand. Suddenly, the hospital's policy was no longer an issue. Starr watched over her supervisor's shoulder as she entered her vacation time into the computerized work schedule.

Sucking her teeth, Ava snipped out, "Doesn't surprise me one bit." She was all too glad to be out of the hospital away from all the politics. Certain policies only applied to certain people. Working as a school nurse gave her lots of autonomy, which she loved. When she had gone back to school to get her school nursing certificate, she tried to convince Starr to do the same. At the time, Starr was involved in several committees at work and felt she didn't have the time to dedicate towards getting her certification to become a school nurse. Not even the bribe of working nine months out of the year, having all major holidays, a week at Christmas and Easter, and all summer off, had convinced her to leave her job.

Starr opened her mouth to agree with her friend when a familiar face caught her attention. She couldn't believe it! What was she doing here? Oh, this was going to be too easy. She had hoped for this opportunity for weeks. No way was she going to let it slip through her fingers.

Taking the cloth napkin off her lap, Starr didn't say a word as she got up from the table. If she told them what she was about to do, they would have stopped her. Well, she didn't want to be stopped. She wouldn't be stopped. On a mission, she locked in on her target and followed.

Each of the women threw the other a curious look as they

wondered what had gotten into her. One second she was about to say something, and then the next she looked as if she wanted to kill someone.

Following Starr with their gazes, Summer was the first to recognize her target. Jumping up from her seated position, she frantically whispered as not to draw attention, "Oh no. Get her. Get her now. That's Trina she's going after."

Ava stood to her feet. Before either one of them could leave the table, Karen grab their wrists saying, "Wait a minute. I don't think we should go running up in there just yet. Starr can handle herself. If she's not back in a few minutes then we'll go." Pausing she looked at both woman, "Okay."

Karen knew Ava and Summer too well, especially Ava. There was no need for a group of sisters to be brawling in a nice restaurant. Having them sit and chill for a few minutes was for the best.

Both women took their seats. "All right, but if she's not out in five minutes, I'm going in," Ava coolly stated looking at the watch on her wrist and started the countdown.

"Five minutes," Summer reiterated holding up her hand spreading her fingers apart.

Each of them was livid when they found out about Trina and her trifling foolishness to get Kevin back. None of them gave Trina a second thought when it came to her coming between Kevin and Starr. Kevin loved his wife. Period.

However, what had peeved them all the most was Trina's harassment of Beverly Dawson. They couldn't believe she would stoop so low as to harass an elderly woman just to get at a man. It was all just so tacky.

As they sat and waited, idle chitchat occupied the space of

the five minutes.

"Five minutes up. Let's go," Summer said as she stood heading to the ladies' room with the others closely trailing behind.

Starr slowed her pace once Trina entered the ladies' room. She wanted to use the element of surprise to catch her off guard. Walking as quietly as possible, she surveyed the beautifully decorated room. Tiptoeing to keep her suede boot heels from clicking on the Italian tiled flooring, she stooped down to see which stall she had gone into. Standing, she slowly tiptoed over to marbled sink countertop and leaned against it. Studying her manicure, she counted backwards starting at a hundred. She wanted to kick the stall door in and bum-rush the ho. As soon as she heard the toilet flushing, Starr hurried into a stall leaving the door slightly ajar, giving her a good visual.

Trina hurried out of the stall as if she needed to be somewhere. Laying her purse on the countertop, she washed her hands with just as much urgency. Picking up a cloth hand towel from the wicker basket, she dried them. Reaching into her purse, she was startled by Hurricane Starr blowing out the stall in full force.

Her eyes widened in horror as she dropped her new tube of Mac lipstick on the floor. She immediately recognized Starr's reflection through the mirror. Swinging around she tried to back up, but had nowhere to go. Starr had closed in on her, and was now standing toe to toe with her. She was so close in her personal space, their noses nearly touched. Trina could feel the fire Starr was breathing from her flared nostrils.

If she hadn't been so angry, she would have laughed. So this was the infamous Trina up close and personal? She didn't seem so big and bad now as she swallowed and her eyes darted to the door contemplating how she was going to make her escape.

Now that she had her where she wanted her, she wanted to lash out at her for trying to come between her and Kevin. She wanted to tell her to keep her funky drawers to herself. And if she *thought* about dropping them on her doorstep again, she would wrap them around her neck and choke the life out of her. She was itching to threaten if she so much as walked on the same side of the street as her husband, she'd experience a wrath the likes of Hurricane Katrina.

No, she didn't have to go there. She was the one Kevin wanted and loved, not Trina. She was the one he wanted to keep his name and have his babies, not Trina. No way would she give this chick the satisfaction of thinking she was remotely a threat to her marriage.

Yeah, Starr's man didn't want Trina and that was cool. However, before leaving out of this ladies' room tonight, she would never again make the mistake of messing with Beverly Dawson.

Stepping back a bit Starr wanted to look Trina boldly in the eye. She wanted her to see how serious she was and meant every word she was about to say to her. But before she could get a word out, Trina straightened her spine and glared at Starr like she was about to jump bad.

Hearing heels clicking against the hardwood floors on the other side of the door, a cocky grin curved Trina's lips. Her cousin Keisha was in a hurry to get back home to go out to the movies with a group of her friends who were home from college for the holidays. She was certain the clicking heels belonged to her cousin coming to rush her out of the ladies' room. The show the girls wanted to see started in an hour.

As soon as Keisha saw Starr all up in her face, she would be ready to pounce. Trina wasn't a complete idiot. No way could she take Starr down on her own. But she and her cousin could take her with no problem.

"Look, Starr…that's your name right? I can get Kevin back anytime I want to." Looking Starr up and down, her lip curled in disgust as she taunted, "I didn't know he was into chunky now. Can you even *move* with all that weight?" Tossing her head back, she laughed. "But that's okay. When he gets ready for a slim goody again, I'll be waiting." Digging in even deeper she smirked, "I'm very *flexible*. Just ask him."

Trina knew Kevin would never be hers again. He had painfully made that plain the day she showed up at his office. However, that didn't mean she couldn't have some fun being spiteful. The hurt that briefly flashed in Starr's dark eyes fueled Trina's nastiness.

Hands balled in fists at her side, Starr wanted to punch Trina dead in the face. Heat crept up her neck as she goaded her about her weight. She had become extremely self-conscious of her recent rapid weight gain. However, she wasn't about to give this little tramp the satisfaction of knowing her words stung.

Shaking off the insults, Starr was back on her square and ready to attack.

"Yeah…well… whateva. I'm not going to even give you the satisfaction of responding to your babbling. You're downright pathetic."

"Look who's talkin'" Trina smirked sure Keisha would be coming through the door any second.. *What's taking her so long!*

Stepping back into Trina's personal space, Starr had had enough of this trick. Lifting her finger, she poked Trina so hard in the forehead her head snapped back. The deer-in-the- headlights look on Trina's face was priceless.

"That's right I'm talking and you better listen. First of all, just to let *you* know, my *husband* isn't going anywhere. He loves all of this, every ounce of this voluptuous size fourteen." *Okay, size sixteen but that ho don't need to know that.* Poking her head back again with her finger, "Second, you better keep your narrow behind away from my mother-in-law." Speaking through clinched teeth, she threatened, "I swear if you go anywhere near I will—"

Hearing the door to the ladies' room slowly creak open, Trina was relieved help had arrived. Swatting Starr's poking finger away from her face, she was ready to pounce on her the second Keisha crossed the threshold. As soon as she was about to tell Starr that she wasn't going to do a darn thing but get her behind kicked, in walked Karen, Ava and Summer. The first thing they saw was Trina hitting Starr's hand away appearing as if she had hit Starr in the face.

"Oh, hell no! She didn't just hit my sister!" Karen started taking off her gold hoop earrings ready to do battle. "Nobody put their hands on my baby sister! Nobody!"

Eying the three women closing in on her, Trina's cockiness went up in a puff of smoke. "I…I didn't hit her. I…I just smacked her hand from my face," Trina stuttered, explaining her actions. *Where the hell is Keisha?* Trina was shaking in her shoes as she envisioned the beat down she was about to get.

Easing up behind Karen taking the gold hoop earrings from her hand, Summer said, "Please tell me you didn't hit my friend."

"Our friend," Ava corrected gritting on Trina.

Shaking her head, Starr smirked, "She got better sense than that. I was just about to tell her before y'all came in that if she goes near Momma Beverly again I will beat her into next week."

Ava flicked off invisible lint from the sleeve of the baby blue cashmere sweater she wore. "Mmmm-hmmm." Lifting her gaze from her arm, she zeroed in on Trina who wasn't so tough anymore. "And I'll be right there with you."

"What's going on?" The young woman inquired looking from her cousin to the four women around her. They looked liked they were ready to do some serious damage, especially the two women who looked a like. *Oh snap! Trina done messed with somebody's man...again.* Any other time she would have had her cousin's back, but not this time. Keisha wasn't a fool. These sisters look like they could throw down. She wasn't about to get beat up when she had to look good tonight. *Shoot, I might meet somebody tonight while out with my girls. Trina, girl, you're on your own this time.*

None of the women acknowledged the younger woman's presence as the one standing closest to Trina hissed, "Remember what I said."

Not bothering to wait for a response, the posse turned leaving a shaken Trina with her cousin.

Once the coast was cleared, she snapped, "What took you so

damn long. They were about to jump me."

Rolling her eyes, Keisha thought, *you should leave people men alone then.* Besides, if they really wanted to do bodily harm to her they would have done so. From where Keisha was standing, they just wanted to send Trina a message. Waving her hand making light of the situation, "Girl, they weren't gonna do 'nuffin to you."

"Oh yes they were! That was Starr and her gang of witches coming up in here flying on their brooms!" Trina snapped again, stooping down to pick up her tube of lipstick.

Keisha's mouth formed into a slight circle. One of them was Starr and the other must have been her sister.

"Come on let's go!" Trina angrily gritted out, stomping out of the ladies' room.

On her heels, Keisha giggled, mumbling, "Serves you right."

Spinning around, Trina screeched, "What you say?"

Stopping abruptly to keep from plowing into Trina, the younger woman lied. "Nothing. I didn't say nothing."

"I didn't think so. I said come on!" Trina had never been so mad and frightened at the same time. Blowing out a breath of disgust, Kevin wasn't worth her getting beat down to the ground over. She was too pretty for all of that. Next to her scantily dressed body, her face drew men to her like a bee to honey.

Chapter 33

Needing to get away from the joyous crowd, Starr slipped off to her bedroom for a few moments of peace and quiet. She dearly loved her niece, nephew and godchildren, but all the squealing, ripping and running was bringing on a headache. If she got a good thirty-minute power nap, she'd be ready to go again.

Kicking off her shoes, she stretched out on the comfy California king-sized bed, closing her eyes. A smile touched her lips as she could still faintly hear her family and friends downstairs.

I am beat. Preparation for her Christmas Eve dinner had begun the night before. Wanting to do everything herself, she refused help from her mom and sister. She had stayed up all night, and then was up again at dawn to finish her preparations.

Letting out a deep breath, she was thrilled she made it through her first big production. Excitement fueled her all day as she floated around putting her special touch on everything. To her delight, all had turned out almost perfect; actually, better than expected. She beamed all day from the praises coming from everyone. She and Kevin had beautifully decorated their home for the festivities. The atmosphere created was cozy and welcoming to their guest.

Sheer happiness flowed through Starr as their guest began to arrive earlier this afternoon. Though she loved everyone in attendance, the icing on the cake was when Donna and Patrick showed up. Getting misty eyed, she still could not believe her mom was home for the holidays. She was so blessed to have such wonderful friends and an endearing mother-in-law who warmly embraced her mother and new stepfather.

Starr sensed Donna and Patrick were a little nervous about being introduced to everyone. She could only assumed her mother was worried about what her friends and new mother-in-law thought about her staying away for so many years. And then having the nerve to show up with a man she was shacking up with.

Starr wanted to hug Nick so hard until he was breathless when he came into the living room playing with the controls on his new remote control Hummer, a gift picked out by NJ and Autumn. Not paying attention, he maneuvered the toy vehicle into the leg of the coffee table. Lifting his attention from the controls, he gave Starr a boyish sheepish grin as if to say *ut-oh.* The boyish grin quickly faded to a brilliant smile of recognition, lighting up his face.

Nick's entry into the room had been the icebreaker from heaven, dissipating the couple's nervousness.

"Well, I'll be a son of gun! Patrick Wahl in the flesh!"

When Kevin mentioned to Nick Starr's mom was going to marrysome guy named Patrick Wahl, he hadn't given it much thought. What would be the chances it was the same Patrick he became acquainted with ten years earlier?

"I don't believe it! Nicholas Stiles!" Patrick boomed excitedly in his deep baritone, bringing the other adults into the room looking on as the two men greeted one another in a masculine embrace and friendly slaps on the back.

Turning his attention to Donna, Nick took her small hand in his. Leaning down he kissed her on the cheek. "You must be Donna, Starr and Karen's mother."

Proudly smiling, the tension easily rolling off her, she acknowledged, "Yes, those are my girls."

"I see where they get their beauty from."

All the women in the women rolled their eyes when Nick flashed his devastatingly, handsome trademark smile and then winked at Donna.

On Beverly's lead, Joan, Nita, Summer and Ava gathered around Donna. "Don't pay that big flirt any mind; he's been that way since he was boy. But if he gets out of hand with you, I got a strap for 'em."

Everyone in the room laughed as Nick ducked behind Patrick.

After introductions were made, the men migrated back to the den with the children in tow to finish watching the football game, while the women congregated in the kitchen getting acquainted with Donna. Donna was pleased that Beverly truly adored her child. Of the many tragedies in her marriage, a meddling mother-in-law who made it known she wasn't good enough for her only son had been one of them.

Not only was Beverly kind, but the other women also made her feel welcomed and part of their tight knit group. She enjoyed how the older women shared their wisdom. What she found even more impressive was how the younger women were attentive and respectful of what the older ladies had to say. They discussed everything from dating, to raising children, to marriage, and sex. Yes, sex! Donna wished she had brought her note pad. That

Joan and Beverly was a mess! They could recite a number of positions from the Kama Sutra! The easy going discussion and bantering between the generations was refreshing. Just knowing that her girls had wonderful friends and older women who'd become surrogate mothers to them made her heart happy. She thanked God for these beautiful women who had been there for her daughters at a time in her life when she couldn't.

Later over dinner, Patrick and Nick explained how they'd met years ago. Both their companies were trying to take over a small failing international cargo shipping company in New Orleans. Being from the area and coming from a family in the shipping industry since the early eighteen hundreds, Patrick had the advantage. Nick had been a formidable opponent. If Patrick's family business hadn't been stable and well versed in shipping and Nick had the resources back then that were at his fingertips now, Patrick didn't doubt he would have added the small, failing company to his growing empire. After all was said and done, the men parted amicably, each respecting the other's professional and business integrity.

Starr and Karen stared wide-eyed at Patrick upon hearing *who* he really was. They were stunned as they heard along with everyone else over dinner what he did for a living.

Out of curiosity Karen had asked, "What does he look like?" before she had gotten the opportunity to meet Patrick face to face.

Starr had seriously responded, "Like a card carrying Hell's Angel member. Girl, he scared the mess out of me when he opened mommy's front door. I thought he had her tied up somewhere."

Patrick openly shared with his new family how he had

been suffocated living his life in the shadows of his father and forefathers. Five years ago he semi-retired and turned the helms of the company over to his younger brother. His dream had been to ride his Harley cross-country and overseas. Living a life on the road had transformed him. For the first time in years, he felt free with his long hair and full beard. He was free, yet lonely. That rainstorm that dark, stormy night on the country road had been a blessing, an answer to his prayers.

Patrick racked up major cool points with the women. Smitten with Donna, he had uprooted himself to set out on a mission to capture her heart. It hadn't been difficult for him to leave everything behind in New Orleans setting up new roots in rural Virginia where he owned a vacation home. The beautiful lady with the sad eyes tormented him day and night. All he could think about was how he was going to love the sadness away.

Feeling a little refreshed, Starr sat up sliding her foot into her shoe. On second thought, she kicked the shoe off deciding to go barefoot. Crossing the room pulling open the door, Kevin stood on the other side.

Concern was etched across his features as his eyes washed over his wife. She had disappeared without saying anything to him or their guests. Lately she hadn't been feeling well, complaining of feeling run down. When he voiced his concern, she'd brush it off with, "Probably just caught that bug that's going around at work. I told you just about every day someone's calling out sick with it." Bug or no bug, if she didn't get any better he was taking her in for a check-up.

"You okay, baby?"

"Yeah, just a little tired. I had to lye down for a few minutes.

I was on my way back downstairs."

Crossing his arms over his chest, Kevin frowned.

Playfully hitting his arm, "You just stop it. You know I was up late last night and again at six this morning. A sista is tired."

Uncrossing his arms, he placed his hands on her shoulders. "You should have let your mom and Karen help you." His tone was firm, yet she heard the love and concern.

Looking up into his dark eyes, the butterflies fluttered in the pit of her stomach. She would never get use to nor tire of how much he loved her. Smiling she softly admitted, "I wanted to make our first big event special by doing everything myself."

Wrapping his arms around her, kissing the top of her head, he gently chastised, "Now your hard head is paying the price."

Covering her face with her hands, she leaned into his chest. "I know, I know. I should have accepted the help." Up until now, she hadn't thought about how much fun it would have been working in the kitchen with Donna and Karen. *Just like old times.*

Kevin automatically wrapped his arms around her. "Come on, little woman everyone's asking where you snuck off to."

Walking hand in hand, fingers intertwined, Starr saucily joked, "You could have joined me."

"Stop being a tease Mrs. Dawson."

Coming to the bottom of the stairs, Starr disengaged their fingers. Stepping in front of her husband, Starr made her way into the den with the rest of the family to let them know she was okay, just needing a little breather.

Certain his eyes were on her, for good measure she swayed her hips seductively, sending out the erotic pull she had over him. Glancing over her shoulder, she purred, "I'm no tease, Mr.

Dawson. You'll see…later tonight."

Heat rushed throughout his entire body, settling dead smack in his groin. He became hard as steel watching her strut her sexy self into the den. *Oh, dayum! I need some fresh air.*

Stepping out onto the front porch, he rubbed a large hand down his face. That wife of his had set his blood on fire. He prayed the cold December air would cool him off. He wanted her so bad until he ached. He was tempted to take her right back upstairs.

For goodness sake, he very well couldn't go barging into the den throwing his wife over his shoulder caveman style and carrying her off to his cave making wild passionate love to her. *Can I? Sure I can.* Kevin laughed at the absurd thought. Starr would have a fit if he embarrassed her like that.

Sitting his large frame down on the top porch step, Kevin inhaled the crisp air, willing his body to obey. It didn't help that visions of his beautiful wife, writhing beneath him were dancing in his head. Or how his hands were suddenly warm in the cold air as he imagined them roaming over the slopes of her breasts, down her belly, between her—

The loud barking dog broke into his reverie, capturing his attention. Coming to his feet, the hairs on the back of his neck bristled as his nostrils flared. He didn't like it one bit the way the man walking the dog was gritting on him or his house. Being raised on this block his entire life, he knew all his neighbors. This man was unfamiliar and Kevin didn't trust him.

"You lost?" Kevin asked, almost snarling as his body went into combat mode.

The man looked Kevin over, as if sizing him up. "Naw man,

just walking my dog."

Cutting the man another glance, he made his way back into the house. *This doesn't feel right.* He just couldn't shake the feeling that the man was doing more than walking his dog.

I'm going to have Frank Bass check this out. If this man was lurking around and up to no good, Frank was the best private investigator to have on the job. Frank was the guy all the big corporate cronies went to, to dig up vital information.

Gingerly sliding his hand from beneath his wife's hip, Kevin eased out of bed careful not to wake her. Looking down at her, a smile touched his lips as he watched her sleep. He softly chuckled remembering all of the sensual taunting she had done early and hadn't lived up to any of it. When her head hit the pillow, she was out cold. It reminded him of the night they married in Vegas. Except this time, she was out from working hard preparing a holiday feast for all those she loved and not from a drunken stupor. He was so proud of his baby. She had been the perfect hostess making sure everyone was well fed and having a good time. Leaning over he gently kissed her on the cheek. "I love you," he tenderly whispered.

Down in his office he dialed the private line of Frank Bass. The late hour of which he was calling wasn't an issue. Detective Bass was accustomed to getting calls at all hours of the day or night. The voice that came over the line was thick with sleep. "Bass. Talk to me."

"Hey, Bass, this is Dawson." Over the next twenty minutes,

Kevin informed the detective of the shady man who appeared out of nowhere and a little too interested in what was going on in his home.

After going back inside, Kevin noticed the man hadn't moved from his position. Primal instincts were pulling at him. Kevin's senses were heightened. Danger reeked all around him. Hissing a string of expletives under his breath between clenched teeth, his hand was on the doorknob when he felt a strong, firmness grip his shoulder.

Fury coiled through him as the strong hand stilled him. This predator was an imminent threat to his family. As a man, he vowed that nothing or no one would bring harm to his family. Not bothering to shrug the massive hand, he turned the doorknob.

Before he could fully open the door, the deep voice warned, "Son, think wise before you go out there."

On his way to the powder room, Patrick observed Kevin intently gazing out the window. When he came back out, Kevin had remained unmoved. Whatever or whomever was out there, had his tall frame so tense, it looked as if he would snap in two. Hearing the angry hissing, the older man knew there was a problem on the other side of the door.

Turning around Kevin glared into sky blue pleading eyes. At that moment his anger was somewhat quenched. Patrick was right. The last thing he wanted to do was ruin the day for his family and friends, especially Starr. He wouldn't disappoint her by acting a fool.

Kevin freely told Patrick his concerns when he encouraged, "Talk to me, son. Something obviously has you on edge." After telling Patrick of his suspicions, the older man offered to slip out the back door unnoticed to check things out. He reasoned with Kevin it would be better for him to go out there and feel the man out. "More than likely if he's up to something, he won't suspect we're kin."

Kevin curiously watched as Patrick approached the man engaging him in conversation. When Patrick leaned down and began to pet the dog, a smirk curved his lips. He had to give it to Poppa Patrick the man was smooth. He had gotten the lurker to let his guard down to the point where he went from petting to rough housing with the large dog. It was amazing to watch the older man literally rolling around on the ground with the dog. He was very agile for a man in his late fifties. The dog's excited barking could be heard up and down the street. Thank goodness everyone was engrossed in having such a good time no one seemed to notice the ruckus.

Ending the conversation, both men shook hands. Patrick slowly sauntered down the sidewalk paying close attention to the vehicle the man and the dog climbed into. What he also noted was that there was a woman in the passenger side. Unfortunately, he was unable to make out her features. However, all was not a lost cause. His astute mind, dealing with fluctuating economies for decades, had a knack for remembering figures.

Slipping back inside through the way he left, he stealthily made his way back to Kevin. A broad grin spread across his face as he tapped the side of his forehead. "I have a thing for numbers."

Kevin's visage considerably brightened as Patrick rambled off the license plate of the car the man got into. Giving him a pound with his fist, "Thanks, Patrick, you the man."

The older man chuckled. "Don't worry about it, we're family." Slapping Kevin on the back, he said, "Come on son, let's get back before the folks come looking for us."

Easing back in bed next to his sleeping wife, he gently snaked a muscled arm around her waist. Closing his eyes, he let out a deep sigh of relief. Detective Bass would get the investigation rolling tomorrow in the morning. Kevin questioned the detective about it being Christmas morning. The man let out a deep chuckle. "Man, holidays don't get in the way of an investigation."

Pulling the woman he loved closer to the fit of his body, he prayed Bass would soon have some answers for him.

Chapter 34

Christmas Night

Stretching, the female figure lying in bed smiled not so much from sexual satisfaction, she'd had better, but from the fact she hadn't spent Christmas evening alone. Her new lover was selfish. He only cared about taking care of his own needs, leaving her frustrated. Before her mind could wander to Kevin and how good *he* would have made her felt, her thoughts were interrupted.

"How are you coming along with our little project?" The masculine voice questioned next to her in the dark.

Glad she was in the dark, the young woman rolled her eyes. It took all her strength to keep from loudly sucking her teeth. *What the hell does he mean 'our little project?' I'm the one doing all the work, taking all the risks.* The showdown in the ladies' room with Starr last week came vividly rushing to her mind. Humph, he was nowhere around if Starr and her crew of witches had commenced to beating her and her cousin's tails, old fashioned North Philly style. The only thing he had done was laughed in her face when she told him about the incidence.

He *really* didn't want Starr, just her money. And now that he found out she was married to Kevin, he seemed even more pressed with getting his claws into her. Well, not her per se, but more like her bank accounts.

She wanted to tell him, "You can forget it. Starr ain't neva leaving that man for you." What? Was he crazy? Yeah, that had to be it. No woman in her right mind would leave a catch like Kevin Dawson. As much as she hated to admit it, Starr was one lucky woman.

Breaking into her thoughts again, he snapped, "Don't you hear me talking to you?"

Blowing out an angry breath, he could've reached over and choked her. He should've known she wouldn't deliver. All that talk about being able to come between Starr and her new man was a bunch of bull. The skank lied about having Kevin's nose wide open. A few months had gone by, and he was no closer to Starr than he was years ago when she had gotten fed up and kicked him to the curb.

He had had enough. He was doing things his way. He needed that money by New Year's Eve or else…No, he wasn't going to think about what could possibly happen to him. He didn't have time to dwell on that. He needed that money, at least a little bit of it. If he at least showed up with something, it might buy him some more time. His *creditors* were becoming impatient. New Year's Eve had been his last and final extended deadline.

With the impending deadline hanging like a boulder ready to come crashing down on his head, fear and anger seized his being. Bolting up out of the bed, he stormed over to the light switch on the wall. Flicking the light on, he bellowed, "Get the hell out!"

If you want anything done you gotta do it your damn self! And he knew exactly what he was going to do. At this point, he would do whatever was necessary to get out of the trouble he had gotten himself into. The irony of it all was that a woman had been his downfall.

For the first time in his life, he'd met his match; a woman just as cunning and wicked as he was. He fell in love with Lolita at first sight. And she knew it, too. Taking advantage of this knowledge, the beautiful, exotic woman with the almond shaped eyes and hourglass figure, drained every cent he had. He had even gone to the maddening point of getting not two, but three jobs, working like a dog to give her what she wanted.

This beauty had him trained like a circus seal. When working three jobs hadn't fed her appetite for wanting to dine in the best restaurants and shop in the most expensive boutiques. Where a simple cotton dress cost over two hundred dollars, the fool started gambling in hopes of hitting a big pot. The first few ventures in the illegal gambling house were profitable. With his winnings, he had lavished every dollar on the love of his life, giving her whatever her heart desired. Misery soon set in and his lover floated on to the next sucker as he dug himself deeper and deeper into a pit of subsequent losing streaks. Owing the Black mob thousands had brought him to this very hour of despair.

The young woman stared at him in disbelieve. What did he expect from her? Miracles? Every little scheme she tried hadn't worked. Starr and Kevin's relationship was solid. What was she supposed to do? Hand Starr over to him on a silver platter?

"Please, I tried everything. Isn't there another way you can get the money?" She questioned her lips trembling. So what he hadn't been the best lover she had. That didn't matter. All that had mattered was that she didn't have to spend Christmas alone wishing she was the one celebrating the holiday with the one man she would never have. So being with him, bad sex and all had been better than being alone.

Stalking over to her clothes on the floor, he snatched them up flinging them in her direction, not caring that every piece he flung hit her in the face.

Spending the day with her had been an absolute waste. Having burned all his bridges with family and friends, having her there with him hadn't seemed like a bad idea; at least he got a free meal and sex out of it. She had been so happy he invited her over to his studio apartment; she hadn't balked when he *told* her to bring groceries if they were going to celebrate their *first* holiday dinner together.

In her naïveté, she had prepared a spread for a king. After dinner, he had taken her to bed with the sole purpose of relieving his sexual needs and nothing more. He could care less if she'd gotten any pleasure out of their coupling. She wasn't worth the effort of pleasuring.

"I said get out of here. Don't you worry about how I'm gonna get *my* money," he growled at her through clenched teeth.

She hadn't moved quickly enough for him. Yanking her off the bed, he roared, "I'm not playing with you! Go! Get out!"

Scrambling to gather her clothes as he dragged her to the door, she cried, "Wait! Let me put my clothes."

"Hurry up!" He barked, as he stood naked with his arms crossed over his chest.

Not wasting any time, she put her clothes on and scurried as fast as her legs would carry her. Once outside she walked to her car in a daze as hot tears streamed down her face. She could not believe what started as somewhat of a decent evening had turned into a disaster. Again, her she was not wanted and thrown away like trash. Hate and fury consumed her as she plotted out her revenge. He would pay. Marcus Templeton would pay.

Who did he think he was? He sat back doing nothing, while expecting her to deliver Starr and her bank accounts to him on a silver platter. As much as she couldn't stand the woman, she could understand why she sent this loser on his way.

He was going down…Hard.

Chapter 35

December 26

Rolling over Starr reached out patting the space next to her. It was cold, which told her Kevin had left the bed sometime ago. Pulling herself up, she rubbed her eyes. Looking at the clock on the bedside table, she couldn't believe it was eleven-thirty. *I never sleep this late.* Yawning, throwing her legs over the side of the bed, she stumbled into the bathroom to empty her bladder. She couldn't believe how tired she was. True she hadn't gotten into bed until almost midnight. But still, shouldn't she feel well rested after sleeping so many hours?

Stripping out of her nightgown, she turned the shower on. Stepping under the spray, she hoped the water would rejuvenate her. Grabbing a thick, plush washcloth, she squeezed a generous portion of scented shower gel on it and began to lather her tired body.

The last few days had been full of endless activities. After hosting the Christmas Eve dinner, the next day she and Kevin spent their day going from house to house visiting. The first stop was to Beverly's. There they enjoyed a huge breakfast of French toast, scrambled eggs, sausage, turkey bacon, home fries, grits, fresh fruit, and a variety of juices along with a choice of coffee, tea or hot chocolate.

Although the food was superb, the best treat of the morning was Richard Jr. and his wife Audrey sauntering through the front door, faces beaming with smiles just as Kevin was about to say the blessing.

Rinsing her body and lathering it up again, Starr smiled as she remembered Beverly's surprised reaction. The sweet woman was beside herself. It had been quite some time since she'd seen her eldest son and his wife. Everyone laughed in good nature when she put her hand to her chest, excitedly exclaiming, "Oh my Lord, Richard Jr., Audrey, is that you? I didn't think you would make it!" Audrey's father was still on the mend after having a stroke. She hadn't expected the couple to travel to Philly for the holidays.

Not wasting any time the older woman turned her attention to Starr. "Richard, Jr., Audrey this here is your new sister." Starr was touched by her mother-in-law's enthusiasm at having her entire family together under one roof. She could appreciate how excited the older woman was as memories of her own family and friends from Christmas Eve flooded her thoughts.

Over breakfast, Starr became acquainted with her brother and sister-in-law. Richard Jr. and Audrey were wonderful people. She clicked with them instantly. Between the delicious food filling her belly to capacity and her laughing at Richard Jr.'s stories about Kevin and his crazy schemes as a little boy, she was about to burst. She almost lost it; literally, when he made fun of her husband because he thought he was Batman. As an adventurous seven year old, he'd tied a pillowcase around his neck believing he could fly. Jumping out of his second floor bedroom window, he landed in a thorny rosebush.

Starr thought she was going to embarrass herself and pee her pants when Kevin joined in on his big brother's ribbing. Standing, he stretched his long arms out to the side swaying his tall frame from left to right pretending to be an airplane. "This is how I was flying y'all until I had my crash landing."

Everyone hooted in laughter when he rubbed his butt and twisted up his face as if he could still feel the pain. "Man, that rosebush I landed in was no joke. I think I'm still pulling thorns out my butt."

Beverly wiped tears from her eyes. That boy was always getting into something or another as a child. It seemed like every other month she was taking him to the emergency room to get patched up. "Don't forget the broken arm. Starr, I hope your children aren't as adventurous as their daddy."

Holding her aching stomach from laughing so hard, she agreed with Beverly. "You and me both, Momma."

Next, they were off to Karen's. Everyone was having a good time engaging Kyle and Alicia in playing board games. At first, the kids sulked; they wanted to play with the new Nintendo Wii Grandma and Pop-Pop Patrick had brought them. They hadn't liked it at all Karen had put her foot down. "You guys already played with that Wii all morning. It's time to play something that's going to make you use some brain cells."

Of course being kids, Alicia and Kyle begged and pleaded to have their way. The little munchkins even attempted to sway the other adults on their side. "Auntie Starr, Uncle Kevin, Grandma, Pop-Pop pleeeeease tell Mommy we don't want to play that boring game. We're having fun playing Indiana Jones," Alicia pouted and whined all at the same time hoping one of the adults would come to her and Kyle's rescue.

"Yeah!" Kyle cosigned, crossing his toothpick arms over his chest.

Starr was about to jump to her niece and nephew's defense as she always did. That was until she noticed the expression on her sister's face.

All the begging and pleading ceased when Karen gave Alicia and Kyle the *Say another word and I'm sending you to your room,* look.

She appreciated the gift from her mom and Patrick, but she wasn't crazy about her kids turning into video zombies. She didn't mind if they played the game for an hour, but to sit in front of the television for hours was not about to happen. As far as she was concerned, they should've been happy she let them play the game as long as she had.

Initially the youngsters were disinterested, pouting and still refusing to play along with the adults. Ignoring the sulking children, the adults began to play a lively game of Monopoly.

Curiosity finally won out as they watched the older folks seemingly reverting to childhood. They looked on as everyone teased Pop-Pop Patrick as he landed in jail for the third time in a row. The women playfully accused the men of being cheaters. Patrick thought he was being slick and slid Kevin a couple of five hundred dollar bills in exchange for his get out of jail free card.

Wanting to be part of the fun, Kyle quietly eased up next to Donna. Peeping up at his grandmother through long thick lashes, he gave her a lopsided grin. Smiling down at the adorable little boy, she lifted him onto her lap. The small child grinned, bobbing his head up and down when Donna whispered in his ear, "You want to throw the dice for me when it's my turn again?"

Starr felt sorry for Alicia as she watched her brother now being part of the fun. Alicia tried to act as if it didn't bother her that she wasn't included in the fun. As lovable as she was, the pint size version of her mother had one heck of a stubborn streak. Her pride would not allow to her to ask the big people if she could play with them. After all, she didn't want to play *that stupid, boring board game anyway.*

Alicia's sullen expression tugged at Starr's heart. Before Starr could call to her niece to be her dice thrower, Patrick waved her over. "Come on over hear little darling and help Pop-Pop Patrick handle this money." Alicia's downcast expression brightened up as she skipped over to the table; thrilled she was the new banker.

The family was so engrossed, talking loud and laughing, having a wonderful time playing the classic board game, the chiming doorbell went unnoticed. It wasn't until the loud banging as if S.W.A.T. was trying to break the door down, that everyone stopped what they were doing. All the adults eyed each other as if to say *What the hell?*

As Karen got up to go to the door, the two men followed. No sooner than she opened the door, her father nearly fell as he staggered in.

Shaking her head, turning off the water and getting out the shower, Starr grabbed a towel and began to dry off as the events of yesterday continued to play in her head like a movie.

Starr and her mother told the children to stay put as they heard voices being raised. When they saw who the cause of the ruckus was, both women let out a frustrated sigh. Starr was about to light fire to the man who was partly responsible for her existence. She couldn't believe he had the nerve to show up drunk as a skunk, ranting and raving about his family being stolen from him. How nobody respected him as a man.

Karen had to take a step back when he staggered, angrily pointing at her and Starr. "Look at you all up in here treating this stranger like he's your daddy! I'm your daddy! Not him!"

Turning daggers on Donna, he yelled, "And you! You're still my wife! Living down there in them back woods shacking up with another man! You belong to me!" He slurred in his drunken stupor.

Kevin had to catch the drawn back fist that was about to connect with the drunken man's face. Everyone could see the fury raging through Patrick as he turned beet red.

"Come on, man, don't let him take you there. He's not thinking straight right now." Kevin reasoned with Patrick trying to diffuse the situation before it got any further out of control.

This only infuriated the drunk. Charging at Kevin he demanded to know, "Who the hell are you? You baldheaded bastard!"

"Daddy! You can't come in my house acting like this!" Karen hollered, embarrassed by her father's behavior.

That's it! Father or not I'm about to cuss him out! He don't be calling my man a baldheaded bastard!

Just as Starr was about to light fire to her father, Donna yelled, "That's enough! Everybody shut the hell up!"

All heads swung in her direction. Everyone stepped back making room for her as she approached the man she once loved and cared for. Standing before him, she looked him dead in the eye as she hissed through clenched teeth. "You have one hell of a nerve showing up here like this ruining our Christmas."

"But Donna, baby I want you back. I want us to—"

"To what? Be a family?" she snapped. "Negro pulleese! You should have thought about that before you kept walking out on your *children* and *me* time and time again! You should have thought about that every time I was stupid enough to take your sorry behind back! Believing all your sweet talk and lies!"

"I'm sorry, Donna! I swear this time I'll make it right!" He pleaded dramatically dropping to his knees grabbing Donna around her legs.

Rolling her eyes, sucking her teeth in disgust, she pushed him away from her. "Harold, get your drunk ass up off the floor and go home! It's over between us! It's been that way for years! That was *your* decision! Your daughters are grown with families of their own! And I've already told you that my life is with Patrick now."

All of Harold's begging and pleading went out the window at the mention of Patrick's name. Staggering to his feet, he attempted to lunge at the man that was solid as a tree trunk. The large man didn't even have to protect himself. All he did was step to the side, which sent Harold crashing to floor, banging his head on the coffee table knocking him out cold.

"Just stupid," Starr hissed under her breath as she wrapped the towel around her nakedness. Entering her bedroom, she went to the dresser and pulled out a pair of panties and a bra. If she didn't hurry, she would be late for her lunch date with Karen, Donna and Alicia.

Snatching the perfumed lotion from her vanity, she quickly moved over to the bed and flopped down. Smoothing the lotion all over she continued to grumble. "Showing up all drunk, messing up everybody's Christmas." Because of Harold's foolishness, she and Kevin hadn't made it over to Summer and Nick's. Although they'd just seen their godchildren the day before, they promised them a visit on Christmas day. Instead, Kevin ended up going with Harold to the emergency room, and Starr ended up going home alone. Too frustrated to sleep, she waited up for Kevin. Once he was home, she apologized profusely for her father's ignorant behavior and the fact he spent hours in the emergency room with him making sure he was fine.

"Baby, stop apologizing. I actually feel sorry for the guy." Starr just stared at her husband, momentarily speechless. Was he nuts? She couldn't believe what she was hearing and she told him so, too.

"How can you feel sorry for that man after he called you a baldheaded bastard? He didn't even know who you were before insulting you."

Kevin chortled. "I've been called worse. Besides he was so drunk he could hardly stand."

Letting out a un-lady like snort, "Yeah, I could see just how drunk he was. Reminded me of my childhood."

Blowing out a frustrated breath, she grumbled, "Should've let his drunk behind go by himself."

"Good morning sleeping beauty."

She smiled, a shiver running down her spine. She would never get tired of that deep, sexy as sin voice. Glancing over her shoulder at her husband, her stomach did a flip-flop. She nearly lost her footing and fell as she stepped into a pair of white lacey bikini panties.

Leaning against the doorjamb, arms crossed over his broad chest, the man looked good enough to eat. Worn, well fitting jeans and the new Gap sweater Alicia and Kyle had given him for Christmas dressed his well-chiseled form.

Starr desperately wanted to kick the undies off she just slid into. Her fingers were itching to snatch every stitch of his clothing off. Temptation was flirting with her, begging her to cancel her lunch date. *You know you want to.* Closing her eyes, she willed the pesky voice to *leave me alone.*

"Morning. How long have you been standing there?"

"Not long." Pushing himself away from his leaning post, he took the few steps required to stand directly in front of her as she was reaching for her bra and began putting it on.

"Not long. I just came upstairs to see if you were up." Gently moving her hands aside, with slow steady hands, he took his time fastening the front clasp of the white, lacy bra she was wearing. Letting his gaze glide over her from head to toe and then reverse, he wished he were removing the lacey scrap of fabric instead of putting it on her. Letting out a low whistle, he could feel his body betraying him. "Girl, you are too fine. I want you so bad."

Placing a delicate hand on his chest, Starr stood on her toes planting butterfly kisses on his full lips. "Thank you. And the feeling is mutual."

He couldn't resist pulling her in his arms giving her a long, deep kiss. The little butterfly kisses just weren't getting it. Kevin was going through some major withdrawal. It felt like weeks since he'd made love to his wife. He understood lately she'd been under the weather, not feeling well. So when she fell into bed at night totally exhausted, he'd just take a very long cold shower to calm his aching loins. This however, was only a temporary solution. The moment he slid between the sheets next to her warm, soft, curvaceous slumbering form he wanted her all over again. With great patience and restraint, he'd pull her close in his embrace until he drifted off to sleep only to wake up in the same condition as the night before.

Breaking the kiss, Starr took a step back. From the way he had kissed her, he wanted to take her right then and there. A wave of guilt washed over her. Kevin had been so patient with her. Honestly, she wanted her husband just as bad as he wanted her. But by the end of the day, she was just plain wiped out. "Baby, I'm sorry I've been so tired lately. I promise as soon as I finish getting dressed I'm going to see if Dr. White can fit me into her schedule tomorrow morning."

Kissing the tip of her nose, he smiled. "Good. I thought I was going to have to make the appointment myself."

When Starr hadn't come down stairs to join him for breakfast, he'd decided to let her sleep in. But when eleven forty-five rolled around and she still hadn't come down, he became concerned. Relief washed over him, she was up and getting dressed. If she had still been in bed, he had made up in his mind that he was taking her in for a doctor's appointment. She had been feeling bad for too long for his liking.

Wiggling into a pair of jeans, she told him, "Nope, I got this." Starr didn't want to admit it, but she was concerned as well. She couldn't remember ever feeling this tired and run down. No matter how much sleep she got it didn't seem to be enough. Pulling her sweater over her head she asked, "So what do you have planned for today?"

Kevin sat on the foot of the bed, enjoying the view. "Richard Jr. and I are going to hang-out at Dave & Buster's while Momma and Audrey do some shopping."

Finger combing her hair in the mirror, she met Kevin's gaze. "That's nice. Are we all still meeting up later for dinner?"

Standing, Kevin stretched his long limbs. "Yup. I'll meet you at Momma's tonight around six-thirty." Looking at his watch, he figured he had better get going if he didn't want to be late meeting his brother. Having been in the military for years the man was a stickler for being punctual. Going over to Starr he planted his hands on her waist, leaning in, he kissed her. "I'll see you later this evening."

"All right." Starr let out a groan as she watched Kevin leave the bedroom. Come hell or high water, she was getting her some tonight!

Sitting at the red light, Starr hummed the tune to the song on the radio. She couldn't wait to spend some time alone with her mother, sister and niece. Just as the light turned green, her cell phone rung. Grasping for the phone, she quickly glanced at the display. Smiling, she flipped the phone open. "Hi Momma."

"Starr, I need you to come over here now, sweetie."

Alarm coiled through her as she noted the shakiness of the older woman's voice. *Something's not right.* "Momma, are you okay?"

"Yes sweetie. I just need to see you. It's really important."

Starr didn't like the sound of her mother-in-law's voice. She could tell Beverly wasn't telling her the truth. "Okay. Do you want me to call Kevin? He and Richard Jr. are together."

Starr really became scared when Beverly urgently demanded, "No, don't bother them. I just need to see you."

"All right, I'm on my way."

Making a u-turn in the middle of the street, Starr didn't pay any attention to the honking horns and offensive hand gestures as she sped off to her mother-in-law's.

Chapter 36

Snatching the phone from Beverly's trembling hand, the man growled, "Is she coming?"

Even though she was scared out of her wits, Beverly tilted her chin and stared her captor dead in the eye. "Didn't you hear me tell her I needed to see her? She'll be here," she snapped, annoyed this sorry excuse for a man forced himself into her home.

When she heard the doorbell, she thought it was her neighbor Lucy coming for her daily early afternoon visit. Beverly was so excited to answer the door she hadn't thought to look through the peephole like she always did. Her mind had been on introducing Lucy to Audrey and inviting her out for a day of shopping and lunch.

Lucy hadn't had any children of her own, so when her husband of forty-nine years suddenly passed away last year from a heart attack, she felt all alone in this world. Although she had nieces and nephews that were kind to her and spent every holiday with her, it didn't seem to be enough at times. She understood they had careers and children of their own to raise; however, it would be nice to see them more often then at holidays.

When Lucy moved into the assistant living community a few months after losing her beloved husband, Beverly had been the first to reach out to her. Lucy had been so terribly lonely; she eagerly accepted Beverly's invitation to join her quilting club. Over the span of a few months, the two settled into a daily routine of spending time together.

If Lucy stuck to their regular routine, she should be coming over any minute. Every day she eagerly looked forward to her visit. She and Lucy always had a wonderful time together as they reminisced about days of old. For once, she prayed her friend, for whatever reason, would be held up. The last thing she wanted was to have another person involved in whatever this madman had planned.

Audrey patted Beverly's hand to calm her. "Mother, please don't get yourself all worked up." The younger woman didn't want to further rile up the man holding a gun on them. One second they were in the kitchen having tea waiting on Lucy, and the next they were being shoved over to the sofa with this maniac waving a weapon demanding to see Starr.

"That's right you better shut that old woman up." The man growled as he paced back to the front window. Neither woman said a word as they kept a cautious eye on the disturbed stranger.

Pulling back the curtain, he spied an elderly woman hobbling up the walkway using the assistance of a cane. Letting out a string of expletives, he threw an evil glance at Beverly. This was not supposed to be going down like this. Last night, when he cased the place, the man and the woman had left around nine. He was caught off guard when the couple showed up again later this morning. He hadn't count on the old woman having company today. Frustration began to swarm all around him in the confines of his beat up 1989 Honda Civic. His plans were not going as smoothly as he would like. He had counted on the old woman being alone.

Some of his frustration was alleviated as Richard Jr. hopped back in his car and drove off. He didn't care about Audrey being left behind. If he had to, he would do whatever necessary to keep her quiet and out of his way. So far, he hadn't seen a need to get rid of her. If anything, she was keeping the old woman in check.

He hated old people, especially old women. They reminded him of his evil grandmother who would beat him every chance she got. If he had his way he'd put them all on an island to starve to death. Just like his drunken granny had practically done him every summer, he was forced to stay with her. It wasn't bad enough she would take the money his mother would send weekly to help pay for his food and recreation spending it on liquor. The old hag treated him like a slave. She would make him work from sun up to sun down cleaning her junky, filthy house that only seemed to get any attention once a year during his visits.

His lip curled into a snarl as Lucy rang the doorbell. Wrapping his hand around the doorknob, he yanked the door open. An evil grin slid across his face from the startled expression on the elderly woman's face as he held the gun tightly in his hand. His grandmother had that same expression on her face the night he pushed her down the steps causing her to break her hip.

Just as Lucy was about to turn around, he reached out tightly grabbing her by her fragile wrist. "And where do you think you're going Granny?" Lucy shuddered from the cold, deathlike tone of the young man's voice.

"Get over their with your smart mouth friend," he demanded, waving the gun at her.

A wicked laugh erupted from his lips as Lucy hobbled on her cane taking a seat next to Beverly. His laughter wasn't so much because of the elderly woman nearly falling in the process of trying to put some distance between them. That was funny, but not as funny as what he thought was a failed plan, turning out to be the perfect plan. No doubt, he would definitely get the money he needed, maybe even a little extra cash to get as far away as possible. He went from having two to four hostages. If this Kevin punk was the man everyone claimed he was, he will pay the ransom. A sinister smirk curled his lips. *I'm a freakin' genius. Four lives are worth more than two.*

Anger rose up in Beverly. How dare he have the gall to, not only intimidate them, but to poke fun at them as well! Pulling away from Audrey's hold, she stood to her full height of five feet four inches. No longer caring he held a gun, Beverly refused to go another second longer being terrorized in her home. "Who do you think you are? You little black nappy-headed bastard! This is my home and I want you out of here, now!"

"Oh dear, oh dear," Lucy cried as the menacing man stalked toward her friend balling his large hand into a fist.

"Mother," Audrey nervously pleaded as she stood wrapping an arm around her thin shoulders and bringing her back down to a seated position on the sofa.

The frantic ringing of the doorbell stopped him in his tracks.

Starr gasped as the door opened and she felt herself being roughly yanked inside the house.

Chapter 37

"Man talk to me." Richard Jr. yelled at his younger brother as he darted in and out of traffic. The brothers weren't in D & B's but two minutes before Kevin's cell phone went off. Richard Jr. knew something was horribly wrong when all of the color drained from Kevin's face.

"I'm gonna kill her." Kevin gritted out through clenched teeth. Bass had called confirming the license plate of the vehicle belonged to a Trina Jones. However, he still hadn't uncovered the identity of the man driving the vehicle. Kevin immediately lost his cool. Trina was still interfering in his life. The detective pleaded with Kevin to sit tight while he did some more digging.

"I can't do that," had been Kevin's abrupt response as he rushed over to his ex's house. He couldn't explain it, but his instincts were telling him that something really bad was about to go down.

"Kill who? Baby brother you're not making any sense."

Gripping one hand on the steering wheel, the other he ran quickly down his face. Blowing through a stop sign, he began telling his brother all of the drama that had been going on for the past several months.

His brother hissed a curse under his breath. He wanted to ask Kevin why he hadn't told him any of this until now, especially the part about Momma being harassed by this woman. He kept his tongue in check. Kevin would never allow a single hair on their mother's head to be harmed if he could help it.

Bringing the car to a screeching halt, both men jumped out the vehicle. The two women with shopping bags in each of their hands looked like deer caught in headlights as they watched the twins of thunder come barreling up the walkway.

"Trina, didn't I tell you to stay the hell away from my family?" Kevin barked, charging in her direction.

"Leave me alone, Kevin! I don't know what you're talking about!" Trina cried as she frantically dug into her coat pocket searching for her keys. Nervous jitters made her drop them to the ground. Dropping her shopping bags, she quickly attempted to retrieve them.

She hadn't been quick enough, though. Richard Jr. deftly swung his foot, sending the ring of keys flying into the withered, dead grass.

"Isn't that your car right there?" Kevin yelled, pointing to the dark vehicle that sat on his block two evenings ago.

"Yes, that's my car! But I still don't know what you're talking about!" Again, she attempted to get her keys, but Richard Jr. blocked her path, stopping her efforts.

"You better tell me something and you better tell me now, because some man was watching my house and driving your car Christmas Eve night."

A sick feeling overcame Trina as she slightly swayed. She hadn't gone out Christmas Eve night. She stayed in all night thinking about her life and admitting for once how miserable she really was. Crying and drinking wine all night, she promised when the New Year came in she would be making some changes.

Waking up the next morning, she was sick as a dog from drinking the cheap wine on an empty stomach. She felt so horrible she couldn't manage to drive herself to her mother's out in West Philly to spend Christmas day with her family.

Turning her gaze to Keisha, her knees slightly buckled. Even though Kevin was angry with her, he was gracious enough to catch her from falling to the ground. "Keisha, girl, what did you do?" she whispered, too afraid of hearing the answer. When Keisha had asked to borrow the car, Trina assumed she was going out with her girlfriends.

Keisha eyes darted from her cousin to the two angry men. All day she had tried to tell Trina what she had gotten herself involved in over the last few months. But every time she tried, the words were caught in her throat. Yes, she had sworn revenge, but if she told on him that meant her cousin Latif would be going back to prison.

Latif was a good kid and only got in trouble because he followed down behind her. She was the reason he'd done a brief stint in a juvenile prison in the first place. The weed he was caught buying was for her. Instead of snitching on her, he took the fall. So she owed him. She couldn't let him go back to prison.

"Keisha?" Trina repeated. The girl was holding something back. The fear etched across her face spoke volumes.

Shaking her head from side to side, Keisha's voice trembled as she spoke. "I can't."

She desperately wanted to tell them what was going on. But how could she? How could she tell her cousin that she had played her all because she wanted Kevin? She was the one responsible for the red thong in the newspaper and slashing Starr's tires. How could she tell Trina that she and Latif had given his dogs the command to destroy that beautiful garden?

Furthermore, would her cousin ever be able to forgive her for goading her own, encouraging her to do the little silly pranks like calling Kevin's home and showing up at his job? Of all people, she understood how much Trina wanted Kevin back and how determined she was to get him back. Her sole purpose had been to fuel Trina's actions on hoping and praying she'd drive a wedge between Starr and Kevin.

All she had to do was lay back while Trina did all the dirty work and wait for the right opportunity to seduce him into her bed. She was young and pretty. Why wouldn't he want her too?

Kevin and Richard Jr. glance at each other. The young woman standing before them held the key to the mystery. It was clearly apparent Trina was just as clueless as they were as to what was going on. Taking a few steps to stand in front of her, Kevin gently, yet firmly placed his hands on Keisha's shoulders. "Please, if you know anything, tell us."

"You're gonna be mad at me," she whispered like a frightened child.

"Keisha, I have a feeling this man is going to do something really bad to my wife or my mother. Right now, I have a private investigator trying to find out who he is. If you are in any way involved, it's best for you to speak up now before it's too late."

Now was the time to get revenge; now was the time to tell everything she knew. Why should she continue to protect him when all he had done was used her and she in return used her cousins?

Taking a deep breath, she gazed up into Kevin's eyes. As the first tear fell, she began to tell her story.

After Keisha told them of Marcus' blackmail, they were stunned. They couldn't believe that a grown man would go through such lengths to do something so diabolical. And to use someone who was practically still a child was inexcusable.

Keisha felt awful as her cousin looked on in horror as she told her story. She wanted to run and hide when Kevin's facial features became stormy as she disclosed she had taken Marcus to Beverly's home.

Richard Jr. had to reach out and catch Trina from falling as she became lightheaded again. Realization dawned on her that Keisha was able to give this information to this madman because she had taken Keisha with her over to Beverly's on numerous occasions while hunting Kevin down.

As tears welled up Keisha's eyes, Kevin felt sorry for. She was so young and had been used by a man who preyed on women. The hard expression he wore melted.

Giving Keisha a tight hug, Kevin thanked her. Turning to Trina, "Please call the police for me and send them to my mom's."

Nodding her head, she pulled her cell phone from her purse. As Kevin and his brother ran to the car, Trina yelled, "Kevin!" before she dialed 911.

As he turned, their eyes locked and held. "Tell Starr and your mom I'm so sorry."

Chapter 38

Stumbling, Starr wasn't able to catch her fall as she was yanked and then pushed to the floor.

"Starr, sweetheart, are you all right?" Beverly cried, attempting to go to her side, but was stopped by Audrey firmly holding her in place.

Before she could answer, the man reached down and roughly grabbed Starr by the collar of her coat to her feet. "Get up!" He hissed through clenched teeth.

"Marcus, what are you doing here?" she snapped pulling away from his hold. What had she done to deserve this good-for- nothing bum, popping back up in her life? Wasn't dealing with her father's drama last night enough?

Marcus threw back his head and laughed as if her were a lunatic. Shoving her towards the sofa he said, "Sit your ass down and stop asking me questions!"

Briefly taken aback by his bark, she stumbled again and then froze, clued to the spot where she stood. It only took a second for her to realize he had shoved her again. Letting out a low growl, she gathered all the strength her tired body could muster and shoved him back. "Don't you put your hands on me again!"

Quickly recovering, he raised the gun and pointed it at Starr. "Are you going to sit down on your own or am I going to have to sit you down?"

Defiantly, Starr stood her ground. This could not be happening. No way was her ex-lover waving a gun around threatening her and holding her mother-in-law, her neighbor and sister-in-law hostage. Why was he here? What did want?

"Did you hear what I said?" Marcus gritted out between clenched teeth as he advanced towards Starr.

"Yeah, I heard you," she snapped, removing her coat before taking a seat next to Lucy. The three women collectively let out a terrified sigh of relief.

"Are you all all right?" Starr questioned the women, a sense of guilt settling over her. It was her fault Marcus was here. But for the life of her, she couldn't figure out why.

Nodding, all the women agreed they were okay. "He hasn't hurt us yet." Audrey mumbled under her breath.

"Did I say you could talk?" Marcus questioned, glaring directly at Starr. She was going to be a problem. He could feel it. What if she didn't cooperate and do what he wanted? Marcus was a desperate man who had gone to the length of holding hostages and now was about to add demanding a ransom to the offense.

Rolling her eyes, Starr ignored his question. *Really, what did I ever see in you?*

Snatching the cordless phone from the end table, he stalked over to Starr and dropped it on her lap. "Call your husband."

Starr looked at him as if to say *you must be crazy out of your mind.* "Why?"

"He's got something I want." An evil grin split his face as he looked at her with a lustful glare. "And I got something he wants." Initially Starr's defiant attitude had annoyed the hell out of him. But now seeing her sitting there seething was turning him on. Boldly, he adjusted his growing manhood. It didn't bother him the elderly women gasped in disgust. His thoughts were on how he was going to get Starr alone so he could have his way with her. Yeah, he would get him a little taste before calling lover man for the fifty thousand dollar ransom.

His lustful, leering gaze made Starr feel dirty and molested. Repulsed by the thought she had ever let this man touch her; her stomach suddenly began churning. Covering her mouth with her hand, she gagged. "I'm going to be sick."

Quickly coming to her feet, Starr ran to the powder room with Marcus on her heels yelling, "Get back here. I didn't tell you, you could move!"

Feeling like he was losing control, Marcus reached out to grab Starr's arm as she made it just steps from the toilet. As he roughly turned her to face him, he wished he hadn't. She let loose the contents of her stomach all down his pant legs and on his shoes. Jumping back, he flung his arms behind his body. The force of his hand hitting the marble sink knocked the gun out of his hand, sending it flying into the hallway.

Marcus attempted to leap for the gun, but tripped over Starr's outstretched foot as she kneeled in front of the toilet dry heaving.

Barging through the door, Kevin, Richard Jr. along with several police officers, rushed down the tiny hallway. Coming to an abrupt stop the men couldn't believe their eyes.

Marcus was balled up in a fetal position covering his head and face as Audrey stood over him, her shaking hands pointing his gun at him. Lucy and Beverly were putting a terrible whipping on him. Lucy was whacking Marcus with her cane as Beverly was thrashing him with her leather strap. Starr was in the background hugging the toilet and dry heaving.

The entire ride over Richard Jr. and Kevin silently prayed they'd get to their mother's before the police. The brothers were geared up to do a citizens arrest with excessive force. However, Momma and Ms. Lucy had literally beaten them to it.

One of the officers pried the gun from Audrey's hands as another calmly requested around a chuckle, "Ladies, please step back so we can arrest this man." Both of the elderly women reluctantly backed off as the officer moved in pulling Marcus to his feet, handcuffing him and leading him out to the squad car.

"Go check on your wife. I'll see to Audrey, Momma and Ms. Lucy." Richard Jr. said gently nudging Kevin into the small powder room.

Taking a washcloth from the towel holder, Kevin saturated it with lukewarm water, then rung it out. Kneeling down beside his wife, he gently rubbed her back with one hand as he offered her the washcloth with the other. "You okay, baby?"

Putting the cloth to her bowed down face, Starr patted away the sweat. Lifting her head, she stared at the man she loved. Her bottom lip trembled as she saw the tender love and concern in his eyes. How could he still love her after putting his mother and others in danger?

"I'm sorry," she cried as she let her head fall. She couldn't stand to have him look at her. How could she face Momma, his brother and sister-in-law or Ms. Lucy again? All of their lives were put in danger by someone from her past. If Marcus had hurt any one of them, she would have never forgiven herself.

Kevin lifted her chin to meet his gaze. He knew she blamed herself for Marcus holding them at gunpoint. "Hey, baby it's not your fault that jackass did what he did. No one's going to hold you responsible."

Standing, he pulled her to her feet. Starr winced from the pain shooting up her leg from her right ankle.

"What's wrong?" Kevin anxiously inquired, concerning lacing his deep voice.

"I think I hurt my ankle when I fell."

"You mean when he pushed you." Beverly corrected as she came in the powder room to check on Starr.

Kevin's body went stiff as his eyes did a sweep over her from head to toe. "He put his hands on you?" he asked through clenched teeth, his caramel complexion turning crimson.

Before Starr could get a word out to calm him, Beverly blurted, "That nasty, low-life dog yanked my sweetie through the door and threw her to the ground! Then he snatched her up by the collar and put that gun in her face." The elderly woman's petite frame trembled with fury as she spoke. She wished that police officer hadn't stopped her and Lucy from whipping that nasty thing's tail!

Although Beverly had just replayed the most terrifying time in her life, Starr smiled. Momma still loved her and hadn't blamed her for anything. This good feeling was short-lived as Kevin stormed out of the tiny bathroom.

"Kevin! Kevin!"

By the time Starr hobbled outside on her ankle that was now swollen double its size, three officers were blocking the back passenger side of the squad car. Why hadn't they driven off yet?

Kevin was desperately trying to get around the human barricade to get to Marcus.

As she approached, she could hear the one officer say, "Mr. Dawson, we understand how you feel, but we need you to take a step back. We really don't want to have to arrest you."

Arrest him? Panic overtook Starr. Gingerly touching Kevin's back she pleaded, "Come on back in the house, baby. He's not worth it."

Feeling his wife's touch and hearing her voice, Kevin swung around. Gazing down at her, his expression softened. Panic and fear gazed back him. He wondered if she had worn that same expression when Marcus shoved the gun in her face. *My God, what would I have done if anything had happened to you?*

Kevin wrapped his arms around his wife and hugged her with every ounce of love he had in his soul for her. It was that love that checked his anger, because right at that moment he didn't care about going to jail. He wanted to beat Marcus to a bloody pulp for putting his hands on his wife and terrorizing his family, and worry about the consequences later. However, feeling Starr's trembling frame further quenched his anger.

Easing back a bit, he lifted her chin to meet his gaze. Gently kissing her lips, he whispered, "What are you doing out here?"

"Trying to keep you from going to jail," she answered softly, a quiver in her voice.

Although she had been terrified as Marcus held them against their will, it had not frightened her nearly as much as Kevin had. His entire countenance had transformed from love and concern to pure murderous hatred as Beverly told him how Marcus played a roll in her injury.

Taking his thumb, he wiped away the tear that slid from the corner of her eye. "I'm not going to jail."

Kevin gave one last lethal glare in Marcus' direction. *Bastard, you better be glad I love my wife.* The coward had scooted over to the other side of the squad car and turned away from Kevin's stare. Everything male in him wanted to rip Marcus' heart out. However, as he looked again into his wife's pleading eyes, he was grateful that she'd only suffered a minor injury.

Looking over his shoulder at the police officers, he nodded his head. "Thanks for everything."

The officers returned the nod, "No problem."

Lifting Starr up into his arms, he noted the size of her ankle. "You know I'm taking you to the emergency room to get that checked out." It was more of a statement than a question. Frowning he said, "It doesn't look too good."

Starr winced as she felt another shooting pain radiate up her leg. "I know. And it doesn't feel too good, either."

Chapter 39

Three hours later in the emergency room

Starr sat on the hospital gurney waiting for the doctor to come back with the x-ray results of her ankle. Shaking her head in disbelief, she asked, "Why did Marcus think he could get away with such a crazy scheme?"

True, at one time she had been a fool for him. She had even allowed him to nearly financially ruin her. But did he really think if he had been successful with his ridiculous plot to break her and Kevin up she'd go running back into his arms? He had to know that after everything he done to her he didn't have a snowball's chance in hell of getting back with her.

Pacing back and forth, Kevin was getting antsy wondering what was taking the doctor so long. Starr had gotten sick every time they gave her something to eat. She didn't, however, have a problem with keeping small amounts of liquids down, which he was really glad about. The doctor had informed them if she couldn't keep the liquids down, she would have to stay over night for observation, which meant he would be staying, too. After everything she'd been through tonight, he wasn't letting her out of his sight any time soon.

Shrugging his broad shoulders, he figured he better answer her before she noticed how worried he was. "The man was desperate for money to pay off illegal gambling debts."

Just as he was about to tell her he didn't want to talk about Marcus right now because he was sure they'd be retelling the story again for the rest of their family and friends soon enough, the doctor walked in.

From the moment they had arrived at the emergency room, both their cell phones were blowing up. He had to talk Starr's mother, sister, Ava and Summer out of storming into the ER. "I promise I will call you as soon as I get her home. Y'all can check on her then."

"So do you want the good news or the bad news?"

Going to Starr's side, Kevin took her trembling hand in his. "Just tell us wants wrong." Kevin's voice came out agitated. He didn't have time for the good news, bad news game.

"Well, your ankle isn't broken, just severally sprained. You'll have to stay off of it for the next two weeks or so. No heavy weight bearing or lifting."

Flipping through the chart, the doctor scanned the results of her lab work. "And you don't have a virus."

Kevin frowned as he looked at the doctor. What did he mean she didn't have a virus? She'd been feeling sick for weeks now. If it wasn't a virus, the bug that everyone had at work, what was it?

Starr voiced Kevin's concerns. "I've been feeling tired and run down for over two weeks now."

The doctor smiled as he eyed the anxious couple. "That's because you're expecting a little visitor in about" the young man shifted his eyes to the ceiling as he did a quick calculation in his head, "seven months from now."

"What?" Starr asked not believing she heard the doctor correctly the first time.

Smiling, he reconfirmed, "Your lab work came back positive for the HCG hormone. You're definitely having a baby."

Kevin let out a loud shout "Yeah!" as he pumped his fist in the air. "My baby's having a baby!"

Excitement overtook him as he picked Starr up spinning her around.

Laughing, she cried, "Stop, Kevin before you make me get sick again."

Settling her back down on the gurney, he apologized. "Sweetheart, I'm sorry. I'm not thinking straight."

Tenderly, a large hand possessively cradler her belly. Leaning in he rested his forehead against hers, kissing her lips. "We're having a baby. You're having my baby."

Starr gently touched Kevin's jaw letting her fingers softly stroke the day old stubble. "Yup, I'm having your baby. A little girl that's gonna put ribbons and barrettes all over your head."

Leaning back, she tilted her head to the side. An impish grin danced at her lips. "Oops, my bad. You don't have any hair.

Kevin threw back his head and laughed as he remembered how she had teased him months ago. *God, I love this woman.*

Eight weeks later

Starr held Kevin's hand as the technician glided the ultrasound probe over her round belly. She didn't understand why she was getting huge so fast. Instead of four months pregnant, she appeared to be more like six months. Everyone assumed she was having twins, even Dr. Neil, that's why he wanted to have an ultrasound done today.

"What's wrong?" Starr nervously inquired as the technician's eyes bulged.

"Um, nothing. Let me call your doctor."

The young woman quickly exited the room to contact Starr's obstetrician.

"Kevin, I'm scared." Was something wrong with their baby? Had she waited too late in life to have a baby? No, that was nonsense. Women older than her were having healthy babies all the time. Her mother-in-law had been in her early forties when she had Kevin. And he came into this world healthy as an ox.

"Come on baby, don't do this. Everything's going to be all right." Kevin lovely assured his wife attempting to calm her fears as well as his own. He couldn't let her see that he was just as afraid that something was wrong as she was.

"But what if—"

Cutting her off, he placed a finger to her lips. "Hey, our baby is going to be fine."

Twenty minutes later, Dr. Neil came bouncing in the room his usual animated self. "How's it going?"

"All right," Kevin answered speaking for the both of them. Starr was a bundle of nerves. The twenty-minute wait for the doctor to come had felt like twenty hours.

Sitting on the stool, Dr. Neil squeezed another glob of gel on her belly. Taking the probe, he firmly glided it over her belly. "Well, what do we have here?" His eyes twinkled as he concentrated on the monitor.

The couple was drawn to the tiny screen the doctor seemed so fascinated by.

Grinning at Starr, he asked, “You here that?”

Nodding her head, “That’s the baby’s heartbeat.”

“That’s right.” Dr. Neil said smiling. “How about this?” He asked slowly sliding the probe to another area. “You hear that?” This time he glanced at Kevin, a huge grin on his face.

“Uh-huh. Sounds like another heartbeat.”

“That’s right. And what about this?”

Wide-eyed, Starr stared at Kevin. “Another heartbeat?” They said in unison.

Chuckling, the doctor confirmed. “Yup. Now look at the screen right here.” Kevin and Starr followed Dr. Neil’s finger as he pointed out each precious beating heart on the screen.

Little fish everywhere. Momma Joan’s dream came rushing back to her. Kevin and Dr. Neil hunched their shoulders as Starr laughed and cried uncontrollably with joy. “My little fish. They were my little fish.”

Smiling through her tears, Starr pulled Kevin’s hand to her lips and kissed it. “I thank God for you. I love you so much.” *I’m going to be a mommy and I have a man who loves me. He loves me.*

Kevin leaned over and gently placed a kiss on her forehead. “I thank God for you, too. And I thank you for trusting me with your heart. Baby, I love you so much.”

Epilogue

"Oh Lawd, look at our grandbabies." Beverly said to Donna, laughter in her words.

Donna linked her arm through Beverly's. "They are just too adorable, if I say so myself."

Beverly chuckled. "You won't get any argument out of me."

The grandmothers stood off to the side as they watched the photographer try to get the one year olds to cooperate. However, the Dawson triplets weren't in the cooperating mood this afternoon. Uh-uh, they weren't having it.

As soon as the photographer had the little ones settled in the perfect pose with Kalvin in the center, Sydney to his left and Shayla to his right, Miss Sydney decided it was time to get up and go. Standing up balancing herself on chubby legs, the oldest of the crew, teetered off taking Frankenstein like steps towards the toy chest in corner of the den. The bright orange, stuffed lion lounging on top caught her attention. Kalvin decided to give Shayla, the baby of the bunch, a big wet, drolly kiss in the eye. When her little mouth turned into a frown and she began to do that little pant babies do right before they cry, her big brother tried consoling her by kissing her again. Leaning in, he put his tiny hands on her chest as he landed another soaking kiss on her pudgy cheek. Trying to right himself up, he lost his balance sending them toppling over on the plush, carpeted floor.

The photographer didn't become frustrated with the babies who obviously had minds of their own. Instead, he used this as an opportunity to snap some really cool, candid shots. He loved taking pictures of the Dawson triplets. From the time they'd come home from the hospital, Starr had a standing date every three months to capture them in various stages. With each visit, he marveled at how their personalities blossomed. And today on their first birthday, he could see just how different they were.

Sydney, the oldest, was the leader of the pack. The other two didn't make a move until she did. Kalvin was the affectionate one, he always wanted to kiss and hug everyone whether a friend or stranger. Shayla had a tendency to be cautious, the no nonsense one. Whereas her sister and brother happily went to any friendly smiling face, Shayla scrutinized strangers and would scream bloody murder if they dare tried picking her up.

Her arm around Kevin's waist, Starr rested her head on his shoulder. She softly giggled. "Look at *your* children."

It was still so very hard to believe that they were here. And that she and Kevin had conceived three babies without the aid of fertility drugs. Every time she held them in her arms or sat in the nursery watching them sleep, she realized just how much of a true miracle they were.

Being sleep deprived from taking care of three, sometimes-cranky babies had been trying. Many a day she became overwhelmed, doubting her ability to be a good mother, wondering if she had gotten in way over her head. Kevin had been there loving her every step of the way. Each time that she panicked, worried she wasn't doing something right, he was right there assuring her she was doing a wonderful job of raising their children.

Although there had been some rough days and nights in the beginning, she loved her gifts, her blessings, and wouldn't change one minute of those trying days or nights. Now that they were in her life, she couldn't imagine ever being without them.

Smiling, looking up into his handsome face, she teased, "They're acting like *you* again."

Kevin chuckled as he watched his children. It seemed like every day they were becoming more and more independent. He desperately wished time would become suspended so his family would remain as is, for eternity. There was something about the love of a good woman and the innocence of babies that made his world a better place. Nothing could compare to what his heart felt when he came through his front door every evening to a woman who loved him and three happy, smiling cherub faces trying to get to him at once. *Yeah, this is the life. Now I know what Nick was talking about.*

"So, they only act like me when they're out of control."

Standing on her tiptoes, she brushed her lips across his mouth. "Yup. When they're good, they take after me."

"Whatever, Starr, everybody knows you're the hell raiser between the two of us. And right now, our babies are showing your DNA."

Sucking her teeth, she playfully nudged him in the ribs. Being silly, Kevin doubled over as if he she had hurt him.

The two women switched their attention from the grandbabies to their children. Each woman had her own reason to be filled with joy on this day. Beverly Dawson had waited so long to be a grandmother. At eighty-four years old, she wasn't as young as most grandmothers of one year old triplets. Her age, however, didn't bother her one bit. She enjoyed spending time and helping to raise her grandbabies.

Looking over at Starr, Beverly's heart swelled with love. *I knew she would be the one to make an old lady happy.* Starr was the kind of young woman every mother wanted for her son. From the first day she had met Starr, the younger woman had done nothing but showed her love and respect. Even after the babies came, she continued to spend time with her. At least twice a week Beverly got a call announcing, "Be at the door waiting, we're on our way over." Within twenty minutes, she was pulling up in her new minivan with her little crew in tow.

Beverly loved and appreciated Starr for being so generous and allowing her to help raise her grandchildren. She understood Beverly wanted to cherish every moment as long as possible while she still had good health.

Donna never imagined she'd be back in a city that held so many painful memories, but here she was. She had regretfully missed seeing Karen's children growing from infants to small children. She refused to do the same with Starr babies. This had been the fifth time she and Patrick had been back to visit since their births. And each time they came, they stayed for weeks. She wanted to give as much support as possible to Starr and Kevin.

It had taken the young couple some time to get adjusted to having three infants at once. One morning, a few months after Starr had given birth; she called to check on her. Sensing the weariness in her child's voice from the screaming babies in the background, Donna didn't hesitate to jump into action. "I'm on my way, baby. You hang in there until Mommy gets there." Sure enough, later that night Donna and Patrick were on Starr and Kevin's doorstep.

Donna admired Kevin for how well he treated and loved her daughter. It didn't matter that he worked a fulltime job. When he came home in the evening, he rolled his sleeves up, and helped his wife to feed, change dirty diapers, bathe and put their babies to bed.

One evening Donna praised Kevin for being such a good dad. "That's so nice of you to help out with the babies after working all day." Smiling at her, he lovingly corrected his mother-in-law. "I'm only doing what a father is supposed to do. I don't deserve any recognition for doing what I do." He went on to make it clear that Sydney, Kalvin and Shayla were just as much his responsibility as Starr's. That he loved his wife and children and would do anything in the world to ensure that they were taken care of and happy.

"Okay, come on everybody let's get a group photo. Starr, Kevin, grab your little people." Chuckling, the photographer mused, "It was so much easier to get these guys in a group photo three months ago."

Kevin lifted Shayla from the floor throwing her up in the air. "How's my baby girl number two?" His reward was drool and squeals of delight. Before he could get to Kalvin, the baby had crawled over to his dad's leg and pulled himself up. Smiling down at his son, he adjusted Shayla on his right hip. Squatting down, "Come on up here, Tiger." Kalvin excitedly bounced and clapped his hands the second his daddy lifted him into his arms.

"Come on here Miss Sydney," Starr cooed as she lifted her daughter from the toy chest. Kissing her chubby cheek, Starr sat next to Kevin.

"All right, let's get this picture taken. I think your guest is getting a little restless." Kyle had come into the den for the third time, complaining, "Aunt Starr, Uncle Kevin we're ready to sing happy birthday so we can cut the cake." And for the third time, Donna chased him out the house. "Child, have some patience. As soon as the photographer's done we'll be out." With his head hung low, the young boy moped back outside with the rest of the guests.

"Kevin and Starr, I want you sitting hip to hip." The photographer said motioning with his hands for them to come closer.

Both did as they were instructed. "Now, set little man between the two of you. Now put Shayla on your right leg Kevin and Sydney on your left leg Starr."

After the triplets were positioned, the photographer held up a yellow rubber ducky, the kind that made a squeaking noise when squeezed. Peering through the digital camera, the photographer waved the ducky in the air and sang, "Over here babies," as he squeezed the plastic toy.

On cue, the Dawson family smiled as the photographer snapped the perfect picture.

From the Author

Dear Readers,

I'd like to take this opportunity to thank you for reaching out to me letting me know how much you enjoyed *A Special Summer*. As a debut author I truly appreciate and do not take for granted your support. I realize there are numerous, wonderful established African American romance authors for you to choose from, so thank you!

Your expressed interest in Starr and Kevin's story was beyond overwhelming for me. At the end of *A Special Summer* you got a sneak peak of Starr and Kevin in *When Love Comes Around*. Well, I hope you're not disappointed, but Starr and Kevin would not cooperate with *me* while writing *their* story. I had no choice but to tell *their* story of love they way they wanted it told.

Please feel free to reach out to me at: author@victoria-wells.com with your comments.

Again, thank you for support!

Peace and Blessings,

Victoria

About the Author

VICTORIA WELLS is a Philadelphia native. In 1991 she graduated from Community College of Philadelphia under her legal name Gaye Riddick-Burden with an Associates Degree in Applied Sciences majoring in Nursing. She furthered her education and went on to earn a Bachelor's and Master's Degrees in Nursing from LaSalle University.

Wells (Riddick-Burden) is employed as an adult nurse practitioner at a center city hospital. She has dedicated her fifteen year career as a nurse to taking care of patients with sickle cell disease.

In 2005, Wells was nominated for the Nursing Spectrum's Nursing Excellence Award in the category of Clinical Care for her work with sickle cell patients. On May 10, 2005 Wells became the regional winner of the 2005 Nursing Excellence

Award in Clinical Care. On October 24, 2005, Wells was awarded the Nursing Spectrum's National title, "Nurse of the Year" in Clinical Care at the Chicago Ritz-Carlton. Nursing Spectrum wrote, "Riddick-Burden is a strong advocate for patients with sickle cell disease. She was instrumental in designing and implementing the outpatient Sickle Cell Day Treatment Unit for these often underserved patients. The program is driven by Riddick-Burden's desire to provide timely and effective care to patients with sickle cell crisis, decreasing long waits in the ED and avoiding inpatient stays that separates patients from their families."

On March 19, 2006, Wells was awarded the Movers and Shakers Award presented by the American Women's Heritage Society, National Association of University Women, National Association of Phi Delta Kappa, Top Ladies of Distinction and Two Thousand African American Women. This recognition was bestowed upon Wells because of her dedication to the nursing profession and community outreach.

Wells has been a lover of books since childhood. As a child she would spend hours reading. To this day reading remains a favorite pastime. Wells' favorite genre is African American romance.

While taking a creative writing course in college, Wells became interested in writing. The final assignment for the course was to rewrite the last chapter of The Color Purple. Wells received not only an A for the assignment, but for the course as well. Professionally, Wells has written and lectured extensively on sickle cell disease. However, in 2005 after being encouraged by family and friends, she decided to pick up her pen and write her first romance novel.

A *Special Summer* is Wells' first novel which she self-published and was re-released by Xpress Yourself Publishing in 2008.

Wells is married with three children. She and her family live in the Philadelphia area.

Visit Victoria Wells online at www.victoria-wells.com.

Xpress Yourself Publishing

A Publisher of Fine Books

and

2008 AALAS Independent Publishing House of the Year

Visit us online:
www.xpressyourselfpublishing.org

Printed in the United States
209985BV00004B/4-12/P

9 780981 80947